CLARE LITTLEMORE

Break

First published by Clare Littlemore in 2017

Copyright © Clare Littlemore, 2017

ISBN: 978-1-9998381-2-6

*This book was professionally typeset on Reedsy.
Find out more at reedsy.com*

Contents

Dedication

For Mum and Dad, who instilled a love of books in me from birth, and who never fail to support their children in whatever they do.

Brit Alert!

If you are reading this book and not from the UK, a brief warning that I am a British author and use British spellings throughout. In The Beck, there is a 'harbour' instead of a 'harbor', characters wear overalls of different 'colours' (not 'colors') and may, on occasion, have to apologise (rather than apologize). Happy reading!

Chapter One

Screams echoed upwards through the valley. I struggled to keep my head above the water, feeling the heavy weight of the harness pulling me under. Gasping for breath before I became completely submerged, I fought to keep control of my limbs, to swim, to break through the mirrored surface above me. It seemed smooth, like glass, though I knew that from above, the water was always moving: rippling gently or whipping back and forth, spray shooting out at angles, splashing over the shale on the narrow beach.

There were others around me, but I couldn't feel their movements. I knew they were struggling just like me, striving to reach the surface, no matter how weak their wasted limbs became. I remembered being told during a climbing lesson once that legs are always stronger than arms, and I kicked with all the force I could muster. The top of my head broke the surface and for a second I could see above the water. The beach was lined with Shadow Patrol officers, a line of them staring out to sea, vacant expressions on their faces. I wondered for a second why they didn't have their faces covered.

Tilting my head skywards, I gasped another desperate breath. The heavens were an inky blue, a few stars visible here and there, tiny pinpricks of light which were further away than I could possibly fathom. As my head sank into the depths again, I watched. They blurred, the sharp daggers of light becoming indistinct as the sheer volume of dim, shadowy water grew above my head. I was sinking. With no strength left to fight it, I could do nothing but fall gently down into the depths of the bay.

I jerked awake, sweat pouring off my body in the narrow cot. Glancing to my left, I was relieved to see the other members of my pod were not awake yet, and instead lay in various poses of sleep, some shifting restlessly, some snoring gently, and others not seeming to breathe at all.

Closing my eyes again, I forced myself to take a deep breath. I was powerless to ward off the recurring nightmare. It did not visit me every night, but often enough that I was quite used to waking up suddenly, the faint light of dawn creeping into the pod around me, with the distinct need to calm myself before anyone else awoke. The only saving grace was the fact that my dreams were silent. I had yet to cry out in my sleep. Screaming at night could only lead to other citizens speculating about my state of mind, which would in turn cause real issues for me during the next Psych Test. I could only imagine the conversation.

"So Quin, how well do you sleep at night?"

"Well, I often wake up silently screaming after a terrifying nightmare."

"I see. Do you have this nightmare often?"

"All the time."

"And what's the nightmare about?"

"I dream that I'm drowning. Being drowned. By the people in charge of The Beck. And there's nothing I can do about it."

"And why do you think you have this dream?"

"Because I witnessed it happening! Not to me, obviously, but to others I know."

I watch as a frown comes across the assessor's face. She takes a large rubber stamp from the drawer underneath the table and punches it down on my assessment form. When her hand withdraws, large, red wording is inked on the bottom of the page: CLEARANCE.

In reality this would not happen. But I know that if those in charge were to discover the regularity of my disturbing dream, I would not pass the assessment. I would no longer get to live here in the Patrol Compound. I would be banished to Clearance like so many others before me, and there the nightmare would eventually become a reality.

I rubbed my eyes fiercely with my fists clenched, trying to regain control. There were no tears. Only a white-hot ball of lead in my stomach. I had cried. Night after night, unable to prevent the tears from staining my cheeks, under my scratchy blanket on this very cot. But weeks had gone by and I knew that my very survival rested on me hiding my heartbreak from the people around me and maintaining an iron mask of control while I adapted to life as an ordinary Patrol citizen.

So I had buried the memories of Clearance citizens floundering in the waters of the bay at the foot of the mountain which hid them from the rest of The Beck. Erected a mountain in my head, which mostly managed to hide these thoughts from view and allowed me to continue with life as though I had never seen such horrors in the first place.

Shifting into a sitting position, I leaned over to the cot next to me and gently tapped the arm of the girl who still lay sleeping. She moaned in protest as she felt me wake her, and rolled on to her side, her face turned away.

"Jackson!"

My voice was no more than a hissed whisper, born of years spent in the Lower Beck where free speech was not permitted. I was still unused to the differing rules in Patrol, where citizens could, within reason, speak to one another without fear of reprisal. One of the many privileges allowed up here, and which I found difficult not to feel guilty about.

I turned my attention once more to the sleeping form in the next cot. Determined to wake her, I prodded her more ruthlessly now. Eventually she shifted back to face me, sleep clouding her eyes.

"What?"

"It's morning."

"So you say."

"Well almost. Want to go for a run?"

She made a face. "Not really."

In Agric, my previous sector, our freedom had been very limited. Here in Patrol, citizens were permitted to engage in certain pursuits during their off-duty hours, as long as it didn't interfere with their work assignments and duties. Patrol was extremely physical, so keeping fit was positively encouraged. On the plus side for us, it allowed conversations to take place out of the earshot of other pod members we did not necessarily trust. We didn't have a lot of free time, and early morning was used by most Patrol Officers to get some very necessary rest, but my days in Agric had showed me how I was capable of functioning on far less sleep than others, and dawn was a perfect time to run in private.

Jackson on the other hand, valued her sleep, and it was often more difficult to persuade her to give up those precious moments of rest. But today I wanted to speak to her.

"Please, Jac?"

She sighed, glancing around at the rest of the pod, who were all still sleeping. Shaking her head, she hauled herself into a sitting position and shuffled to the edge of the bed.

Minutes later we were running along the side of the field which led up into the hills that flanked the Upper Beck area. We jogged uphill, towards the Solar Fields, the steep incline preventing us from speaking at all. It was hard work, but I revelled in it, all my focus being driven into catching my breath, making it up the punishing slope, reaching the top. Together, we raced through the woods, coming out on the other side and working our way up into the meadows which housed the large panels, their shiny surfaces catching the light and glinting in the rising sun. Unusually, it looked as though it would be a fine day today.

At the edge of the fields we slowed, and nodded at the two officers guarding the panels. Neither of them were very familiar to us, and, united in our desire to avoid conversations with those we didn't trust, we circled the fields and began our descent, the density of the trees hiding the Patrol Compound from view for now.

"Nightmare again?"

I nodded, not trusting myself to answer.

"We all have them you know."

Entering the canopy of trees, she glanced around and slowed to a walk before bending down to rest, her hands on her knees. At this hour of the morning the woods were usually deserted. I leaned heavily against a tree, marvelling at how my muscles had developed in the short time I had lived in Patrol, how better rations and more regular training had hardened and shaped my body.

"There's no way we could see what we saw and not be affected by it Quin," she paused, dropping her voice to a whisper, "It's about not letting it show."

"I know. I don't. But it doesn't mean I can stop it from happening."

She placed a comforting hand on my arm, "No it doesn't. But you're dealing with it. I'm dealing with it. We're learning to manage."

I sighed, "Ok, let's stop feeling sorry for ourselves. Big day today."

She nodded.

"How many new recruits are they planning to bring up here do you think?"

"Who knows? From what Cam told me, they have a large-scale plan of how all the training is going to work. There will be far bigger groups than when we were recruits, and they're going to train them much faster."

My heart lurched, "You saw Cam? When?"

"A few days ago. I had a shift on the wall and he passed by." I could feel Jackson's curious gaze on mine, "You haven't seen him?"

"Hardly at all. He's managing the defence project and spends most of his hours in the Lower Beck. I think he even sleeps down there sometimes."

She grimaced, "And eats down there too. He looked exhausted."

I looked away. We didn't have much longer, and I didn't want to waste time talking about Cameron.

"How's Mason?"

"He's ok. Still angry as ever, and I haven't spent a lot of time with him, but, he's coping." She smiled sadly, "Sometimes I wish he didn't hate so much. It takes up so much of his energy."

"But I think that's what keeps him sane."

"You're probably right. I'm hoping we get assigned a shift together at some point soon. It would be nice to see him," she blushed slightly, "you know, alone."

I smiled at her. She and Mason had been together for a while now, but didn't always get to spend a lot of time with one another. Governance tended to ignore such couplings in Patrol, as long as they were conducted fairly discreetly and didn't interfere with our day-to-day tasks. Work always came first. Private meetings were often difficult to arrange around the shift patterns that different citizens worked. But we all knew to avoid going too deep into the woods at night, for fear of disturbing any citizens seeking privacy. In the last three months, Jackson and Mason had managed a few hours of time together, but it never seemed to be enough for either of them.

I couldn't resist pushing for some more information. "How's it going between you then?"

She looked up. "When I see him alone, it's great. When he's kissing me, he seems to forget his anger for a while. I hate coming back to reality when we have to return to the compound."

"I'm glad things are still good between you."

"They are!" She grabbed hold of my hand and squeezed. "Quin, I can hardly keep my hands off him. Of course, we don't let things go too far, but... I don't know, it's like the fact that I don't see him alone too often makes it more special when we are alone together, you know?"

Now it was my turn to blush. I did know, but my own relationship with our Patrol Super, Cameron, was even more difficult than Jackson and Mason's. If you could call it a relationship. I had hardly seen him since our one proper embrace, and it was driving me crazy. But I didn't want to admit as much to my friend.

I straightened up, changing the subject. "Better get going."

"Ok. If I see Cameron, do you want me to pass on a message?" she paused, as though judging how much she should say, "I'll probably have a few more shifts on the wall this week and I know you've been stuck up here in the Solar Fields all the time."

"Message?"

"Yeah, you know, do you want me to tell him anything?" Clearly my nonchalant act had not fooled her. "From you?"

I shook my head fiercely, "Don't be ridiculous."

I plunged past her into the woods, running with ease now that I was travelling downhill, pushing my body to move faster. Even as I felt the strain in my muscles and struggled to catch my breath, memories of a shared kiss refused to stay buried. The wall which kept images of the drowning figures in Clearance hidden from view did not seem to work on Cameron. The man who had single-handedly rescued me more times than I could remember, who in equal turns infuriated and enthralled me, seemed to be seared into my brain. At night when I lay down to sleep, in the mornings when I woke free from the nightmare, during long, dull shifts at the power plant, my thoughts returned to his lips on mine and my body responding to his in ways which were completely new to me.

In the months which had passed since that kiss, he had been put in charge of a group of citizens from the Lower Beck. Together, they were creating a large barbed wire structure which would make accessing the wall that protected our community from outsiders far more challenging. His time appeared to be divided between the Dev compound, which I had never entered, and the wall, where I had frustratingly few shifts. On the few occasions I had seen him, he had been distant and avoided my gaze. I had resolved to forget about him, and the kiss, but so far my attempts to do this had been utterly useless.

Pounding footsteps from behind told me that Jackson had caught up. She thundered past, grinning back at me over her shoulder, understanding that I didn't want to discuss my feelings at the moment and the best thing she could do for now was to distract me. I raced to catch up with her, the physical exertion for now driving all thoughts of the nightmare, the reassignments, training new recruits, and Cameron out of my head.

Chapter Two

An hour later we sat in the Patrol canteen eating breakfast when Director Reed and Governor Adams appeared on the raised stage. The room, previously filled with a muted chatter, silenced immediately. The two men did not visit us together often, so their presence marked an important announcement.

"This morning we will be recruiting more citizens to come up here and train to be Patrol officers," Adams began, his voice soft and rich. "But we will not be conducting our usual assessments, as they aren't due for another three months. The need to recruit more officers is part of our plan of action to deal with the perceived threat of invasion we've been experiencing over the past year or so. Groups of people from a community over the water have been attempting to invade The Beck and it is imperative that we prevent this from happening. We have taken several courses of action: better wall defences, the development of more effective weaponry, and additional training of Patrol citizens. Today's recruitment is a large part of that." He paused and nodded to his right. "I will let Director Reed explain more about the logistics of the day."

Reed stepped forward to the microphone. More used to giving orders than discussing policy, his voice was much deeper and less charismatic than Adams'. "Over the past few weeks we have been appealing to any Lower Beck citizens who feel they might be suited to a Patrol assignment. They have been made aware of the strength and fitness levels necessary to survive, and asked to volunteer for today's trials if they wish to be considered. We have also," he paused and glanced at Adams before continuing, "made sure that citizens understand that the trials today will in no way reflect the usual pattern followed by the assessments. Citizens are volunteering, and either will be accepted to or rejected from Patrol with no other consequences. Those who fail to be accepted will simply return to their usual Sector with no questions asked."

I was seated next to Mason, and felt him fight against a shudder as he listened to Reed's words. He was no doubt remembering the harsh reprisal he had been dealt by Reed when he was caught in an attempt to visit his old Sector during our own training period. The whipping he had received had almost rendered him incapable of continuing with the training programme, and only through the understanding actions of Cam and our trainer Tyler had he managed to survive the assault. I knew from Jackson that he still bore the scars of the whip's brand on his back.

"Many of you," Reed continued, "will be required this morning to assist with the trials. Usually the bulk of the assessments are completed by Governance and Development citizens, but the challenges today will purely be physical, and as Patrol citizens you are perfectly placed to model and judge the appropriate Patrol attributes. Please check the list of assignments which has been posted on the work boards in the Jefferson Building to see whether you have been reassigned to work in the Trials area this morning. We require a large number of new recruits, but they need to be the right type of citizen. I trust that you understand this and will act accordingly to help us make informed judgements on those citizens who attend the Trials. Thank you. That will be all."

Reed and Adams left the podium together, deep in conversation. I wondered where Adams' Superintendent, Carter, was today. Perhaps already supervising the set-up of the Trials area, putting her vicious nature to good use while she observed the height of the rope climbs, the quantity of mud underfoot, the potentially hazardous conditions the assault course might provide for any citizen trying to prove their worth.

My heart sank as I thought about my close friend Cassidy from the Agric Sector. I hadn't seen her for three months, ever since I had taken the Patrol pledge, but my last conversation with her had been about her intention to make the move to Patrol if she could. I knew her well enough to understand that she would try out for Patrol the first chance she got. How would she fare? I knew she was determined. She was also in good physical shape, an excellent climber, and pretty strong. She stood a great chance of being selected, but part of me wanted her to fail. Although I knew she would do well up here in Patrol, I also wanted to protect her. The Beck was not what it claimed to be, and once she was up here in Patrol there would be no shielding her from the truth.

I had once longed to find out more about the inner workings of The Beck. A promotion to Patrol had given me that insight, but at a cost. Now that I had witnessed the terrible fate of the Clearance transfers, directly ordered by The Beck Governance, I could never return to the more pleasant ignorance of the Lower Beck citizens. Cass still held on to that innocence. Life in the Lower Beck wasn't easy, but the belief that everyone had it just as bad and that we were all working together towards a better future was some comfort. Once you knew the truth, that comfort was gone.

I also doubted the word of Governance. Yes, they claimed that those citizens who failed to make it into Patrol would be allowed back to their original Sectors to resume their old lives, but could we trust them? I had seen Clearance, the Sector citizens no longer useful to Beck society were sent to, and it was a terrible place. Harper, another old friend from Agric, still resided there, and I had worried myself sick over what would happen to her after the next assessment. If Cass was sent there too, I wasn't sure I could cope.

There had been rumours that several hundred people were going to attempt the Trials today. If that was the case, they could not all pass, but neither could the workforce of the Lower Beck exist if all those who failed to make Patrol were simply reassigned to Clearance. No, we had to trust that, for practical reasons, Governance meant what they said. If Cass failed the Trials, she would simply return to her position as Super in Agric. A position she excelled at.

And I would remain here. In Patrol, growing more frustrated by the day. Cam had promised that he was trying to form the Resistance, a group of citizens who were just as frustrated as we were about the way things were in The Beck. The idea was to gather enough people to put up some sort of fight against the system, but we couldn't do that until there was a significant number. In The Beck, citizens were treated extremely harshly if they showed any signs of rebellion, and a small group of people attempting to buck the system would simply fail. So Cameron had said we would wait. Wait, gather intel, and recruit.

But it was easier said than done. Many citizens were unhappy, but all citizens were scared. So scared, they didn't dare to risk trouble of any kind. And Cam had been so busy lately I had no idea how far he had managed to get with the Resistance. In the meantime, those of us who had promised to support him were stuck here in The Beck, having to go about our day-to-day lives attempting to keep ourselves out of trouble. Miserable. Many of us with friends in Clearance, knowing every day how much closer they came to being given the harshest assignment of all. Because my nightmares were not fiction. I had witnessed the last group of unwanted Clearance citizens being disposed of. Dumped in the sea, weighed down by harnesses which gave them no chance of survival. Drowned.

I shook myself, noticing that the canteen was beginning to clear now that most citizens had finished breakfast. Across the table from me, Jackson and Davis were rising and Mason gave me a sharp nudge as he too stood up. Cramming the last mouthful of bread roll into my mouth, I followed suit quickly, disposing of my tray as I hurried from the canteen. Once outside, I joined the ever-increasing queue to access the notice boards in the Jefferson Building which would indicate who was supervising the Trials today. Part of me wanted to be there, to help mentally cheer on Cass. But the rest of me acknowledged that I would welcome the usual boring shift guarding the Solar Fields or Hydro Plant.

As I reached the door to the Jefferson Building, the line in front of me shuffling forwards inch by inch, a figure was exiting. The citizens in front of me backed away to let the Super through. It was Tyler. She nodded as she passed our little group. Since she had ceased to be our trainer she had been generally pleasant to us. She and Cam were quite close. I knew that he would have shared the information with her about our illegal trip to Clearance where we had witnessed the drownings, as well as our desire to join them in their fight.

Tyler too was a member of Cam's Resistance, and had helped Jackson and myself in particular to adjust to life in Patrol. If you wanted to survive in this Sector, it was vital to maintain a low profile and complete the shifts doled out to you without attracting too much attention to yourself. The only citizens who stood a chance of fighting the system in the future were those who were prepared to watch and wait before taking action. Open rebellion was a sure path to Clearance or worse. I envied the iron hold Tyler had on her feelings. She seemed to be able to hide even the strongest anger or sadness behind a wall of calm.

As she passed me, the last one of our group in the line, she tripped slightly and tumbled towards me. Instinctively I reached out a hand to catch her, and prevented her from hitting the ground. I wondered if she was ill. It was not like Tyler at all to be clumsy; she was as lithe as a cat most of the time, another reason I admired her. When she straightened up she met my gaze intensely.

"Annexe. Ten minutes."

Her voice was barely a hiss in my ear, and anyone watching would have assumed she was thanking me for steadying her. She was several paces past me before I managed to react. Mason and Jackson were both behind me. As I turned towards them I knew they had realised there was something more to Tyler's trip than met the eye. Nodding slowly, I leaned forward and whispered into Mason's ear.

"Annexe. After assignments."

He nodded in reply, then stepped through the door and into the Jefferson Building without another word. Moments later we were all staring at the work assignments board. Davis and Jackson remained on their usual shifts, but Mason and I had been transferred from our Hydro Plant shifts to the Trials. I saw Jackson and Mason exchange a disappointed look and I knew they wished they had been reassigned together. They got to spend little enough time together as it was.

We had less than an hour before the shift began, and it took more than half that to jog down to the Lower Beck where the Trials were taking place. Wasting no time, the four of us walked briskly over to the Annexe, the small bunk house we had all been assigned to when we were training for Patrol. Since our allocation to the central pods, the Annexe had been left empty, and we were sometimes able to sneak over there under the pretence of moving equipment around or cleaning duties. It usually guaranteed us a private five minutes as long as someone kept a lookout.

As the canteen had just emptied, there were few citizens around. Most people were gathering equipment and grabbing five minutes rest before their long day began. They would be either in the Jefferson Building or close to their pods. The Annexe was completely deserted as we slipped inside. Mason closed the door quietly behind us and Davis pulled out some of the blanket stock which was kept in here, to use as an excuse if anyone arrived.

We waited nervously, knowing we didn't have long. Tyler was also aware of this, and ducked through the doorway a few moments later.

"Sorry for the subterfuge." She sounded a little breathless. "Just wanted to let you know about a meeting. The Resistance. Tonight in the woods – the clearing beside the cliff? Remember it?"

Jackson glanced at me sharply. We were unlikely to forget it.

Tyler continued, seemingly oblivious to any tension. "At midnight, or as soon after as you can manage. We shouldn't keep you long."

"Do you think tonight is a good idea though?" Jackson was ever the voice of reason. "Won't there be people everywhere because of the recruitment Trials?

"Maybe," Mason peered into the courtyard through a crack in the doorway as he spoke, "but at least it means taking some action at last." He glanced at Tyler before continuing. "Sorry, but we've been desperate to do something since our little trip to Clearance."

"I know. We've all been frustrated." Tyler's voice was calm as always. "But there just hasn't been the time or the opportunity. I promise things have been happening behind the scenes. We just haven't had the chance to report back yet."

Mason looked slightly appeased.

"So, I'll see you all later? Got to go. Don't hang around too long, will you?" Tyler nodded before slipping soundlessly out of the door.

Mason closed it behind her, a sigh escaping his lips. "Finally. Some sign of progress. We might actually be able to do something at last."

Jackson butted in. "I'm still not sure that tonight's a good idea. Too many citizens out of their usual compounds."

"Maybe that's their plan. So much chaos no one will notice we're missing."

"Let's hope not."

Mason shifted in position at the door, "We should go. Jackson, Davis, you first. Quin and I can follow in a minute. Safer that way. There's no one out there."

Davis cast a slightly forlorn look my way, and I smiled weakly as he turned to go. Seeming to make a sudden decision, he turned abruptly and marched out of the door. Jackson went to follow him only to be stopped by Mason's hand on her arm. Pushing the door closed slightly in front of her, he bent and touched his lips to hers for a moment. Shoving him away gently, she smiled before ducking round him and following Davis across the courtyard.

I glanced away, fighting the stab of jealousy I couldn't help. When I looked up, Mason was looking at me curiously.

"Do you mind?"

I stared at him, "Mind?"

"About me and Jac?"

"Oh. No." I stumbled over my words, feeling a blush spread over my cheeks when I thought of late-night conversations I'd had with Jackson about her relationship with Mason. In reality, I was simply wishing myself and Cam were in a similar position, but I didn't want Mason to know that. "No. I just – I'm glad for you both…" I heard my voice trailing off and knew I sounded unconvincing.

Mason chuckled, as though he could read my mind. I stared at the ground, feeling increasingly uncomfortable with the direction of the conversation. Seeing my discomfort, his face softened slightly, "I know you and Jac are close friends. I just didn't want to come between you… that is, you looked a little angry just then."

I shook my head, desperate to steer the subject away from something which felt so private. "I'm not." He looked doubtful.

18

"Honestly Mason."

Letting it drop, he shifted his gaze to the courtyard outside again. "They're gone. You ready?"

Replacing the blankets Davis had removed, I nodded. We slipped out of the door together. As we crossed the yard towards the fields which would lead us to the Lower Beck and the forthcoming Trials, I attempted to stem the growing feeling of dread I had in my stomach.

Chapter Three

When Mason and I reached the Assessment Compound we had to make our way past a large crowd of citizens waiting outside the gates. There must have been at least a hundred people standing there, all looking nervous but eager. I felt for them. They assumed that a promotion to Patrol could only be a good thing, but had no idea how the knowledge they would learn might well poison their minds for years to come.

I spotted Cass among the group, looking impatient. It was a shock to see her after so long. It was hard to imagine now that we had spent the best part of every day together when we worked side by side in Agric. I knew she had seen me too, and her familiar eyes flashed with recognition, but she looked quickly away without speaking. This, at least, she had learned. Three months ago she would have been calling out my name and attempting to approach me, but now she understood at least part of the danger linked to associating with me, a former member of the same Sector.

I knew that her trying out for Patrol was at least partly an attempt to resolve this issue. When I had been reassigned and Harper sent to Clearance, she had really felt our loss. The three of us had been almost inseparable since we started in Agric and we all felt somewhat ripped apart by the move. But Cass also felt left behind. She was as strong, as fast, and as agile as I was, and very well suited to a role in Patrol, if only she could control her temper. I was far calmer than she was, and that was an important part of existing in Patrol. If life here made me angry, I could only imagine what it would do to her.

Mason and I had passed through the gates now and were met by a slightly harassed looking woman in a white Dev uniform. She took our names and directed us to the assault course, where Mason was assigned to man the starting line. The idea was for me to divide the large crowd of citizens into smaller groups and give them instructions about the course before they began. Then Mason had to check off each participant on a clipboard and number them so they could be observed by the Patrol and Governance Supers on duty around the course. It was essential to keep a steady flow of recruits on the course at all times to minimise the amount of time it took to get all the participants through the Trials. Governance didn't want this number of citizens away from their usual posts for too long.

Around ten minutes later the citizens were allowed into the compound and I instructed them to line up. It was the same assault course as usual, but instead of running the whole thing in one go, participants were being asked to repeat an obstacle more than once to demonstrate their tenacity and perseverance. They would be ranked throughout the morning by the Patrol Supers assigned to each station and at the close of the day the top citizens would make it through to Patrol. The Supers hadn't told us how many of them would be allowed through, and I wasn't sure they had even been told themselves.

My job turned out to be more interesting than I had anticipated. I got to greet each citizen upon their arrival to the arena and learn their name as I grouped them. I tried to encourage each one with a slight smile, though it was easy to see how desperate they all were for promotion to Patrol, as though they understood that it would secure them a better way of life. I had never seen so many citizens from different Sectors gathered together in one place before. It was strange. Although they were not communicating with one another, there were many shared glances between citizens who had clearly not associated with one another before now.

The Beck kept the majority of its citizens under control by a careful process of separation and a number of strict rules. One of these was the ban on having conversations with one another, unless it was work-related. This meant that citizens were unable to have any kind of in-depth discussion, and therefore did not know much more than they were told by Governance about the rest of their community. It was easy to tell from the glances they shot at one another how new this was to them.

I liked it. I wasn't sure if Governance would.

As the morning passed by, it was clear that the majority of the citizens who had opted to try out for Patrol were among the strongest and most able of the Lower Beck. Very few of the weaker ones were among those running around the assault course. Those who were clearly unsuited were quickly dispatched by the Supers and, looking a little disappointed, made their way back to their previous Sectors. This at least set my mind at rest about the fate of the citizens prepared to risk their position for a chance at promotion. No one was being reassigned to Clearance at this stage.

Most of the recruits did well. There were no dramatic collapses and no one appeared to be failing miserably. Although

Mason and I couldn't see every obstacle up close from our position, we had a good view of most of them. Aside from some taking longer than others to complete a section of the course, and some of them slowing down after attempting an obstacle more than once, they all seemed fairly fit and healthy. Cass's turn came halfway through the morning. When I had grouped her earlier, we had only exchanged a slight nod of acknowledgement. I heard Mason ask her name and when she answered, he looked up at her inquisitively.

"Are you…" his voice trailed off as he nodded at me, "Yes you are – I recognise you from the night of the storm."

Cass glanced at me for confirmation. I wandered across casually, as though I needed to speak to Mason.

"He was in the barn with us that night." I answered quietly.

She leaned in close to my ear, attempting to make sure that only I heard her. "Do you trust him?"

I laughed softly, "Yes."

She backed away slightly, still looking unsure.

"It's fine Cass. He was a recruit alongside me. He was whipped for returning to the Livestock Sector one night. He only wanted a quick visit to his old LS friends. That's when we got the warning about fraternising with our old Sectors." Cass glanced at him, a look of respect crossing her features as I continued. "Believe me, he understands and we can trust him."

"Ok. I just didn't want–" she paused momentarily, "I was trying to do it better this time. Make sure I didn't get you into any kind of trouble."

"Well don't worry, you didn't." I smiled at her. "This is Mason. Mason, this is Cass."

"Hey." He jerked his head towards the running track in front of us where the previous recruit was just finishing. "We need to get you set up to go or there'll be trouble."

Cass nodded and straightened up. To anyone else she would have seemed completely unfazed by the challenge ahead, but I could see the slight tension in her eyes which meant she couldn't meet my gaze for longer than a few seconds and that she was indeed nervous about the physical.

Mason continued, knowing that we had to get Cass started before any kind of attention was drawn to the length of time she was taking to set off. "So, Cassidy. An Agric citizen. Promoted to Super three months ago at the last Assessment. Female. Seventeen years of age. Correct?"

She nodded.

"Well you need to proceed to the track to begin. Quin has already explained the course to you. You'll be expected to complete each obstacle a number of times. Keep an eye on the Supers. They'll give you any further instructions. After you finish, return to Agric as normal. The results will be posted outside the canteen tonight." He smiled, which he didn't do often, before continuing. "Best of luck. And… nice to meet you Cass."

I added my own smile as she turned to go, knowing that I couldn't have spoken myself without betraying the fear I felt over her performance today. I knew she would have trained, and trained hard. She would be ready. But anyone could slip up, fall, get a cramp at the least appropriate moment. I still couldn't decide whether or not I wanted her to get through to Patrol or not, but I certainly didn't want her to be noticed for the wrong reasons. She smiled at me as she left and I was certain she understood my feelings. We had known each other too long for her not to.

Glancing at Mason, I noticed that he was watching Cass leave with admiration in his eyes. After a moment he met my gaze and then shifted it away quickly, looking to see if the next volunteer was approaching.

"Seems brave, that friend of yours."

"She is."

"We could use someone like her. Would she-" he paused to double check that no one was close enough to overhear us. "Would she join us?"

I knew he meant Cam's group of recruits as well as Patrol in general. "Yes. Yes she would join us like a shot. That's part of what worries me."

He looked confused.

"Well she's a lot like you are. Determined. Reckless to the point of-" I broke off, not wanting to anger him.

He chuckled softly, "Reckless to the point of losing control, you mean?"

"Well, I didn't want to say it, but now that you mention it..."

"Sometimes I think we need more people who are like that. Less measured, less cautious. Maybe we'd make more progress. Actually achieve something."

I nodded and looked back at the course where Cass had begun her second lap of the track. Her running was effortless. She barely looked out of breath. And they hadn't seen her climbing yet. There was no question she was as good as, if not better than, many of the others we had seen. And that worried me more than anything.

I was about to return to my post when I heard footsteps approaching from behind. Readying my smile for another recruit, I found that instead of a nervous figure in green or brown overalls, a grey suited figure stood before me.

Superintendent Carter.

So far I had not seen her, my assumptions about her supervising the set-up of the assault course seemed to have been incorrect. But here she was now, and she was looking directly at me.

"How are things?" Her steely gaze bored into my own for a few seconds before she turned her attention to the participants in front of us.

"Um…ok? Seems to be running smoothly at the moment." I was just about managing to breathe.

Carter had a fearsome reputation and I had witnessed first-hand how she enjoyed the power her position afforded her. She was twisted, seeming to enjoy catching citizens doing the wrong thing and administering the appropriate punishment.

"Plenty of suitable candidates in your opinion?"

I wondered why she was asking us, ordinary Patrol Guards, rather than the Supers in charge of the obstacles themselves. Mason took over.

"Yes Ma'am. Most of them seem to be fit and healthy and are performing well." He hesitated before continuing, "How many of them will we take in Patrol?"

She returned her glance to him sharply for a second, "That's not your concern, is it?"

"I suppose not." Mason didn't seem fazed by her tone of reprimand. I dug him in the ribs quickly as she turned back to the assault course.

"I'm satisfied that we will… have enough for our purpose," Carter continued, "What's your name officer?"

I groaned inwardly at her seemingly simple request. Any senior officer from Governance knowing your name was dangerous.

"Mason."

"Well Mason, I suggest you keep your mouth shut and your questions to yourself in the future." Carter was smiling as she spoke, but her expression was not a kindly one. She and Mason stared at one another intently for a moment, neither one breaking the gaze, until the sound of radio static stuttered from Carter's belt. She walked out of earshot, speaking quietly into the radio and listening to the reply.

"What are you doing?" I hissed at Mason.

He shrugged, "Nothing. I'm just so sick of sitting around waiting for something to happen. I hate her. I hate them all. I want them to know that."

"But you said you'd wait! You agreed that we'd get nowhere without some planning, some concrete idea of how we would escape from all this."

"I know. But I'm tired of waiting for something else horrendous to happen. We're like sitting ducks here. I want to get out of here. For good. Still think we stand a good chance if we plan it properly."

I sighed. When we had witnessed the drownings taking place in Clearance we had all been horrified, but it had affected us in different ways. Mason had always wanted to escape. Since hearing that there were other people in other communities over the water, he had been convinced that if we could reach them, we could find a better life. Cameron had convinced him that the idea was, for now, madness, and he had agreed to wait, but I wasn't sure how much longer he would be prepared to sit around doing nothing.

Even I had to admit that I'd believed Cameron would have a better idea of what he was doing by now. Three months had gone by and we seemed to have stayed still, achieving nothing, while Governance was only becoming stronger, more powerful, capable of manipulating citizens more than ever before. We all hated it. But so far, there was no sign of any progress against those in charge.

"We have to wait." I ignored the furious look he shot me, "We said we would. It doesn't make sense to rush into anything. At least not until there are more of us."

"But will there ever be more of us? And if not, shouldn't we just take our chances? I don't want Jackson hurt. Don't think I could stand it. If your man Cam doesn't start to make some plans soon, I'm not sure I can wait around for much longer, that's all."

I was taken aback by his use of the term 'your man.' I couldn't see how he could have got the idea that Cam in any way belonged to me. As I opened my mouth to argue, he shot me a sharp look. I swallowed my words, turning to see Carter approaching again, radio in hand, a far more determined look in her eye this time.

Chapter Four

Carter didn't waste any more time on idle questions as she approached us. She was all business.

"I need someone to deliver an item to the teams working on the wall." She paused, taking a long look at us both. "You." Her gaze settled on Mason. "Can you handle both jobs for now?"

He nodded slowly, a concerned look crossing his face the moment she turned to me.

"You. Your name?"

My heart sank. At least she wouldn't associate it with anything negative. I hoped. "Quin," I managed to get out quietly.

"Quin. Go to the Dev compound. Ask the gate guard to let you see Montgomery. You will be given a package to deliver to the wall. You need to go to Ladder 18. That's closest to the Hydro Plant, understand?"

I nodded. I knew very well where Ladder 18 was.

"Take the package to the officers at the top of the ladder. A Super called Cameron. Do you know him?"

Panic washed over me at the question. I had no idea whether it was safer to admit I did or to deny ever having met Cam. Realising that he had been involved in my training and it made no sense to lie, as I could legitimately demonstrate how

29

I knew him, I eventually managed to nod my assent.

"Good. Give the package to him. It's imperative that he receives it in the next hour. Got it?"

"Yes."

"Well get going then!"

I wished I had been given a moment to discuss the situation with Mason. I knew a second opinion on the strange quest would have made me feel a little more secure as I set off to complete Carter's task, but she was staring at me, clearly waiting for me to go. With a sideways glance at Mason, I gave one last nod before taking off across the course, making sure I avoided any of the key obstacles as I went.

My last view of the course took in Cass as she moved from the initial track-running to a crawl under the heavy cargo nets. I took comfort in the fact that she didn't look in the least bit tired so far, and hoped that she wouldn't notice me leaving and let it affect her progress.

Turning left out of the assessment area, I set off towards the Dev Sector. Development was the most mysterious of all the Sectors. All I really knew was that the citizens there were responsible for the creation of the technology used in The Beck. I felt strangely excited. I had never been inside the compound before. Not that there was any guarantee I would be allowed inside today, but even to be sent on an errand which involved accessing the Dev Compound gate was quite an adventure. I had always wondered what really went on there, and perhaps now I would be given the chance to find out.

It took me less than fifteen minutes to reach Dev, which was situated on the very edge of the Lower Beck. I could now run as fast as most of the other citizens in Patrol, and enjoyed any exercise which helped to block out unwanted thoughts. Soon, the Dev Compound gates loomed in front of me. Dev was so unlike the Sectors I was used to. Agric and LS were sprawling, open compounds where the fields of crops and barns filled with animals made the work taking place inside obvious. Dev simply had a small number of pods and two or three large, low buildings which presumably housed their work areas.

No wide fields where the workers picking crops could be observed. No barns with huge swinging entrance doors propped open while the animals were herded in and out at the various different times of day. Just small-windowed buildings which the white uniformed citizens of Dev scuttled into to complete their allotted tasks that day. Whatever those tasks were. While the Agric compound gates were permanently propped open, day and night, and the LS gates only closed when the livestock were on the move, the Dev gate remained closed unless citizens were entering or leaving. It was also accessed only by speaking to a Dev Super at the gate which I now stood in front of.

The Compound usually had a sentry waiting to speak to anyone wanting access, but there was no one there today. I rang the bell at the side of the gate and waited. Dev was one of the only places in The Beck which was not guarded by Patrol. They were so secretive that they preferred to use their own citizens to guard, although I suspected that the Dev guards had been transferred from original positions in Patrol or been trained by Patrol Supers.

As I waited, I noticed how quiet it was down here. In Agric, despite the no talking rule, there was always some kind of noise: digging or watering, or footsteps stamping back and forth. The animals in LS were never silent. In the canteen, the Sustenance staff clattered the plates and cutlery around. And wherever the Rep staff went there was the sound of hammers and saws at work as they mended buildings and rebuilt sections of the wall. But here, all seemed still and calm.

A door in the side of the building ahead of me swung open slowly and a man in white stepped outside. Observing me carefully with little reaction, he walked slowly towards the gate until he stood facing me, an almost blank expression on his face.

"Yes?"

"I've been sent by Superintendent Carter. To see Montgomery?"

His expression didn't alter. "For what reason?"

"I'm here to collect a package and transfer it to the wall."

He nodded slowly and pulled a radio from his belt. "Name?"

I stared at him.

"Your name?" he repeated, a slight note of annoyance entering his voice.

"Oh. Quin. My name is Quin."

Turning away, he pressed a finger on the radio's communication button and wandered away from me to speak to someone. Despite the distance, I could still hear some of what was said.

"Quin... Dev gate. Yes. Package for Montgomery... from Montgomery... allow entrance? To the wall. Right."

Nodding his head at me, he returned to the entry and swiped his hand across a metal box close to the wall. A low bleeping followed by a click signified that the gate was unlocked. He backed away and swung it open, waving an impatient hand to let me pass.

"Montgomery has the package in Zone Three. Carter has allowed you access. I'll take you."

Not waiting to see my reaction, he moved off purposefully, making his way towards the building at the rear of the compound. I hurried after him, not believing that he would wait for me if I dawdled. I was surprised they were letting me inside, and a little nervous. Who knew what went on in Dev and what new information I might discover?

Passing the first two buildings, presumably Zones One and Two, I learned nothing more than I already knew about Dev. The windows were small and reflective, meaning that it was impossible to see inside. I found myself wondering if that was a purposeful choice on the part of those in charge of Dev, and decided that it probably was. There were so many secrets in The Beck, and Dev surely hid many of them.

At the final building, the man halted and again swiped his wrist across a metal plate on the door. I noticed a flat metallic band fastened around his wrist which appeared to give him access to secure or unlock various doors. Thinking about the openness of the greenhouses and the barns and fields of Agric, the closed off air of Dev created a very intimidating environment, and one I was fairly certain I did not want to experience very often.

Stepping back, the man ushered me in front of him through the door. Inside, it was quite dark and I had to allow my eyes to adjust after the brightness of the day outside. When they did, I was disappointed to see a long hallway running almost the length of the building, with a number of doors leading off it.

"Fourth door on your right," the man said, nodding down

the corridor, "Off you go then."

He stayed where he was as I set off down the hallway, slightly concerned that I was alone and didn't have any kind of wrist-wear which would allow me access to the rooms around me. Reaching the fourth door, I paused for a second before knocking hesitantly on the wood in front of me. The sound was dull and did not echo down the hallway as I thought it might. It crossed my mind that perhaps the building had some kind of soundproofing which rendered the noises coming from inside unnoticeable to the outsider.

Looking back down the hallway, I noticed that the man was still standing there. He was definitely checking to ensure that I got where I was supposed to, and did not stray into places I was not permitted. His face remained expressionless as he observed me waiting for the door to open. When it did, it moved smoothly and noiselessly. Behind it stood a tall, slim woman dressed in the usual Dev uniform, with the addition of a small white mask fastened across her face. It hid the majority of her features from view. Above the mask, her intensely blue eyes observed me coolly.

"Quin?" The voice was slightly muffled through the mask.

"Um, yes. That's me."

I felt awkward next to her, clumsy even, as she moved back and waved me inside. Turning her back to me, she strode across the room, swiftly side-stepping the table in the centre. It was a space like I'd never seen before, small, but packed with shelves containing all manner of jars and bottles. Some were filled with liquids, others empty. In the centre of the room, the large wooden table held a number of beakers and other equipment I didn't recognise. A second, smaller table stood empty at the side of the room, except for three large metal pots.

From behind the table, the woman resumed what she had obviously been doing before my entrance. Without looking at me, she measured out different amounts of the substances contained within the beakers in front of her, mixing them thoughtfully with a long glass rod. I was standing awkwardly, wondering what I was expected to do, when she finally spoke again. Her voice seemed somewhat disembodied behind the mask.

"So you're from Patrol?" Her tone was not friendly.

"Yes."

"How long have you worked there?" She didn't glance up from her work, but I could feel her waiting for my response.

"Around three months now. I'm a recent transfer."

"I see." She looked up suddenly, startling me, "Do you like it there?"

I thought of the psych test I had taken on Assessment Day, feeling very much like I was being scrutinised as part of some experiment. Montgomery's question felt intrusive, as though she was watching me for a reaction and mentally recording my performance under pressure. The Dev staff I had come across were often like this: curious, questioning, detached. I wasn't sure what the appropriate answer to the question was, so for a moment I simply regarded the figure in white, meeting her gaze in a way which felt almost rebellious. There was certainly some kind of challenge in her eyes, although I wasn't sure why.

She raised a soft, delicate hand to her face, making me want to hide my own work-worn fingers. Sliding the mask down to reveal a hawk-like nose and a pair of thin, pale lips, she did nothing to conceal her impatience.

"Well?"

"Yes. I like it. I'm getting used to it now."

She turned away, again dismissing me and continuing with her work. Despite my nerves, I was fascinated. No matter how she was treating me, there was no denying the expertise in her fingers as she tilted the beaker and mixed the different substances together. I wondered where she had learned how to combine the different ingredients to create the desired effect. Certainly my own Minors education had not involved anything so complex. One of the liquids had an oily sheen on the top which caught the light as she swirled it around inside the beaker. Another was blue and thick. They had a strange kind of beauty about them and I found it difficult to tear my eyes away.

Eventually she spoke again. I couldn't shake the thought that she was enjoying keeping me waiting. "You came to collect the package, yes?"

I nodded.

"There-" she waved a hand without looking at me, "on the table. See the three pots? Take one of them."

I moved towards the table, making to pick one of them up. Before I could reach them, she was standing next to me, her hand slicing in front of my body. I froze, confused.

"Take these." She pulled something from the pocket of her overalls. "Gloves." She smiled the twisted smile again. "You'll need them."

"Why?"

"It's nasty stuff this. Contains dangerous chemicals. You have to be careful."

The packet she gave me was surprisingly heavy and the gloves inside were made from a dense material I had never seen before. As I pulled them on, I wondered why they were so necessary. I ensured that both hands were completely covered, before looking again towards the pots. Hesitating for a moment, I turned to her.

"Is it safe to touch?"

She smirked, her eyes glittering dangerously. "Why yes, as long as you're wearing the gloves, you'll be just fine."

I couldn't help but think that she had purposefully allowed me close to the dangerous substance before providing the safety equipment. Another demonstration of her power over a lowly Patrol recruit. I took hold of one of the pots and lifted it. It took quite a bit of effort and I wondered why they hadn't sent Mason, who would have had far less trouble moving the heavy pot.

"Just one of them? Or do you need me to take all three?"

"Just one for now." She turned to look at me, sizing me up again. "You Patrol girls are so strong."

I stared, unable to work her out. She was so very different from anyone I had ever come across in The Beck. But then perhaps all Dev citizens were a little like this. I didn't know many of them, only Anders, who I had trained with when I first transferred to Patrol. He was an intensely private person, keeping to himself, but had never been unpleasant. Montgomery seemed far more calculating and judgemental. Turning to go, I wondered if she would insist on me having an escort.

"Wait." She turned and hooked her finger around a radio beneath her work station. "I'll call someone to take you out."

I waited while she spoke into the radio, presumably calling the same guard who had brought me in.

"He'll be here in a second." She turned back to her work.

"Oh – and take some more gloves with you for Cam. Tell him Montgomery sent them. *He'll* understand the necessity." Her sneer told me she knew Cameron and respected him in a way she did not respect me. As I backed away, I realised that my hands were clutching the pot far more tightly than necessary.

There was a light knock on the door, followed by the return of the guard from earlier. Turning to leave, I glanced at Montgomery again, determined to look her in the eye, convince her that she didn't intimidate me. Seemingly lost in her work once more, she never raised her head to give me the satisfaction.

Chapter Five

Within minutes I was standing alone again outside the Dev gate, feeling more than a little frustrated. I couldn't work out why Montgomery had annoyed me so much, and was angry that I had let her get under my skin. Recently, I had begun to feel like I was changing since the move to Patrol, and the reason I believed I had been initially selected to work in the Sector, my calm, unruffled attitude to most things, seemed to be disintegrating. It worried me that my old self was gradually being replaced by someone with the same short fuse as Cass.

Laden down with the mysterious pot and the gloves, I moved far more slowly. There was no way I wanted to drop the container and spill its dangerous contents. I found the reduced pace allowed me to clear my head and gave me time to prepare a little for the impending meeting with Cameron. I steeled myself, no longer knowing how to act around him. My mind drifted back to the kisses we had shared. I had just returned from Clearance, having witnessed the drowning of a large number of completely innocent citizens whose only crime was to become ill or old or weak. I was devastated. Cameron had finally tried to explain the true situation in The Beck, revealing facts he had previously kept hidden from me.

But he had also given me hope. Hope that there might, someday, be a way to fight the system. And that hope had been what had sustained me ever since. And then there had been the kisses. Kisses which he had told me he wanted, but had resisted, fearing my reaction. In the end, it had been me who had kissed him, despite having no idea what I was doing. But he had responded, I was certain of it. I had gone to bed that early morning with my head spinning. And that had been the first time I had the nightmare.

I had seen him the next day at the Pledge Ceremony, but not spoken to him. And then the whirlwind of Patrol truly began: we were assigned to permanent pods, given more in-depth training, and put on guard-duty rotas as we started to serve in Patrol properly. Governance did not waste any time putting us to work. They were worried about invasion from across the water, and determined to prevent it from happening. This had led to a number of projects in development being accelerated, their aim to make it all the more difficult for anyone to access The Beck from the exterior.

One of these projects was the extension to the defensive wall which surrounded the Lower Beck. Cam was in charge of it. He made an excellent Super. He was organised, fair, got along with others, and could somehow give orders without seeming overbearing. This made him the perfect candidate for a position where he had to liaise with several different Sectors, as well as manage the large team of citizens responsible for implementing the new wall defences. He had since spent much of his time actually sleeping down in the Lower Beck in order to ensure that his work on the project was interrupted as little as possible.

I knew that he was probably throwing himself into the work to make sure that no one suspected him of any kind of rebellion, but he was almost too believable. I had no qualms about what Governance thought of him. He did an excellent job of appearing to be the perfect Patrol citizen: his passion for the project spoke volumes about how dedicated he was to protecting Beck society and this looked good to those in charge. But sometimes I felt like he went too far.

We had literally spent no time alone together since the night of our first kiss. Any time in each other's company had involved a group of other people: a work situation, a training session, other Supers or Governance officials surrounding us. But even when we were in the same room, he had barely even looked at me. I had begun to wonder if he regretted what had happened between us.

I had no prior experience of this kind of thing. My only point of reference was Mason and Jackson, whose relationship, although challenging as they were kept apart a lot of the time, was very simple. When they were together, they were together, and anyone could see how much they cared for each other. I envied their easy closeness as I lay awake at night, trying unsuccessfully to put Cam out of my mind.

Approaching Ladder 18, I took a deep breath, knowing that I was returning to the place where I had first met Cam. I smiled, remembering how he had saved us after we had sneaked up onto the wall on our last night in Agric and he had been on Patrol duty. That night, he had been a good guy. He had risked a lot for three strangers, demonstrating his compassion and desire for fair treatment. That was the Cam I liked. But I hadn't seen much of him lately. Sighing, I decided that today I would simply remain detached. Give him the package, the message that came with it, and leave. If he wanted anything else, he could do the talking.

Feeling better for making the resolution, I paused at the bottom of the ladder, unsure of the best way to transport the pot to the top. Glancing at the wall top, I could see no one, although I could clearly hear the sound of citizens working up there. I wondered if I could somehow secure the pot to my belt. As I was considering climbing to the top to request a rope, I heard footsteps on the ladder above and saw a male figure in blue beginning the climb down. My heart began to race as I waited for the Patrol Officer to get to me, but slowed when I realised that the figure was not Cameron, but Donnelly. He reached the base of the ladder and jumped down.

"Hey Quin." His voice was a slow drawl, and it always felt like he was appraising me whenever I spoke to him.

"Hi. I'm here to deliver this," I waved my hand towards the pot on the ground.

"I can take it."

He leaned down to pick it up and I lunged towards him at the last moment, remembering Montgomery's warning.

"No!"

In my haste to stop Donnelly touching the pot, I lost my balance. Shooting a hand out, he steadied me with ease. We ended up standing far too close to one another for my liking, both a little out of breath. He smiled lazily, not letting go of me.

"Um. Thanks." I tried to step back but he kept hold, if anything edging a little closer to me. I could feel his breath on my face and refused to look at him.

"Careful clumsy. What's your rush? You don't have to fling yourself at me."

The tone of his voice made me even more uncomfortable and I longed to move away, but his hands were still firmly clasping my own.

"I wasn't."

"What?"

"I wasn't. Throwing myself at you."

"Could've fooled me."

"You can't touch the pot without gloves. It's from Montgomery over in Dev. She... she warned me that we needed to be careful."

His expression changed and he instantly let go of me. Stepping back, he regarded the pot again, this time with a look of unmistakable annoyance on his face.

"Well you need to be more careful. Don't just leave it lying around for anyone to pick up!"

"I wasn't. I was going to take it up to the top but I needed a rope. I was coming up to find one."

He looked back at me, narrowing his eyes. "Who's it for?"

"Cameron."

He nodded, another dark expression crossing his face.

"Leave it here. I'll get it up to him."

"No." I hesitated, not wanting to make the situation worse, "Thank you, but I was supposed to deliver it to him myself. Carter sent me. I need to follow her exact instructions, or..."

"I'm a Super too. Same rank. It's as good as giving it to him."

"Sorry, but it's not. I need to hand it directly to Cameron."

His eyes flashed with fury for a second but then they cleared and he took another step back. Seeming to make a decision, he drew the radio from his belt and barked some instructions into it. There was a rattling sound and some kind of pulley was lowered over the side of the wall. With it came a basket of sorts, bumping against the concrete as it descended.

"Is it secure?"

He nodded. "We've tested it with a lot of heavy stuff recently. It's been strengthened. You'll be fine. Just make sure you fasten the catch before you send it back up."

Backing away, he managed a smile which didn't reach his eyes. "See ya Quin. Next time try to stay on your feet."

He took off across the field towards the Hydro Plant, not looking back. I was glad to see him go. Turning my attention to the pulley, I saw that the basket had almost reached ground level. I stretched up and brought it within reach before opening the lid and placing the pot and the gloves inside. Fastening it again, I realised that there was a chance that whoever was at the top would open it and take out the pot without using the gloves. Realising there was little I could do to prevent the basket being pulled up from above, I decided that my best course of action was to reach the top of the wall before it did and intercept it.

With that in mind, I thrust my own gloves into my overall pockets and took hold of the first rungs of the ladder, beginning to hoist myself up the wall. I was a strong climber, not as agile as Cass, but far better at ascending than I used to be. I reached the top with a little while to spare, having raced the basket up and won easily. The Patrol Guard raising the pulley, one I only vaguely recognised, was still hauling it up when I reached him, and smiled at my approach.

"This yours?" He nodded at the upcoming basket.

"Yes. Don't touch it please." I raised my hands in the gloves to demonstrate the reason.

"Ah, I see. No worries. It's all yours."

He finished raising the pulley, secured it to a metal rod anchored in the side of the wall and stepped back.

"There you are. I'll get back to work."

He sauntered away along the wall towards a small group of Agric citizens who were struggling with a large roll of vicious-looking barbed wire.

"Do you know where Cameron is?" I called after him.

He turned and pointed further down the wall top in the opposite direction, "That way. Think he's checking the strength of the sections of wire we've already installed."

Glancing along the wall I could see that the work on the wire defence system was already well underway. In the distance I could see a couple of figures working with large sections of the thick silvery threads which were fixed to the existing wall top and rose around a metre into the air. They looked forbidding even from this distance. Nodding my thanks, I turned back to the basket and pulled my glove back on. The latch on the basket was stiff and it took me a few minutes to work it loose. Once I had, I hauled out the pot, thinking how glad I would be to get rid of it.

Walking along the wall in the direction the guard had pointed, I looked out over the water. It stretched for miles, and only on a clear day was it possible to see the mountains in the distance. Today the sky was unusually cloudless, although the water was as grey as ever. I wondered about the people living out there. Until fairly recently, I had been completely unaware of the existence of others outside The Beck. Now I knew of them, no matter how much Governance claimed they were dangerous to us, I couldn't help but wonder. Did they live the same way as we did? Or were their lives better, happier?

I didn't understand why they would want to come over to The Beck unless their lives were more difficult than ours, but come they did, so we must have things that they desired.

But they couldn't all be monsters, surely? I knew The Beck contained such creatures: people who were willing to sacrifice the very people who had worked hard to feed and clothe them, while they lived in relative luxury. But it also contained people like Cameron, Jackson, and myself. People who wanted to find a better way to live than simply existing, and obeying. Surely there would be some people across the water who were similar?

Reaching them was a different matter altogether. I sighed and looked back in the direction I was walking. The figures were closer now, and I could see that they were both dressed in Patrol uniform. As I watched, one of them backed away and began to make their way back towards me. The officer was female, and as I got closer I recognised Tyler. She smiled a greeting when she got close enough.

"Hi. What are you doing up here? I thought you were manning the Trials?"

"I was. Carter sent me on an errand." I gestured to the pot in my hand.

She looked puzzled for a moment, "Where'd that come from?"

"Dev. Woman called Montgomery."

She frowned, "Oh. I see. Well Cam's been waiting for that, whatever it is. You'd better get it to him."

She bent slightly closer to me before she turned to go, "See you tonight at the meeting."

I nodded, feeling slightly apprehensive despite knowing that there was no one close enough to listen. Tyler moved off towards the other group of workers on the wall and I turned back to walk towards Cam, who was now a lone figure in the near distance. My heart rate picked up again as I realised that

I would be seeing him alone for the first time in a while. I had no idea how he would react.

Chapter Six

Cam seemed completely immersed in the task of repairing a section of the barbed wire which was fixed along the top of the wall. He had no idea that I was approaching, even as I got within ten metres of him. Not wanting to startle him, I cleared my throat as I drew near. He spun round at the noise and his face went through a myriad of emotions as he spotted me.

"Quin," he eventually managed.

"Hey."

"What are you–?" He stopped when he saw the pot in my hand, "Is that–?"

"Montgomery sent it. She said to give you these too."

I held out the gloves for him. At first, he didn't move, but eventually a reluctant hand was offered. He took the gloves from me with the tips of his fingers, seeming to want to avoid touching me at all costs.

"You met her?"

"Montgomery? Yes."

He looked troubled. "How did you end up in Dev?"

I shrugged. "Carter sent me. I was manning the trials with Mason. She needed someone. She picked me."

Sliding the gloves on with practised ease, he leaned towards me and took the pot. As he came closer, I caught the scent of his body, both familiar and exotic to me. For a second, I was transported back to those moments together in the forest. I closed my eyes to hide the feelings which flooded over me. When I opened them again, he was standing a few feet away, gazing up at the wire, as though he hadn't noticed at all.

Biting my lip, I tried to pick up the conversation, "What is it?"

He glanced at me quickly, "In the pot?"

"Yes of course."

"Part of our new defence system." His tone was sarcastic, but I didn't think his anger was directed at me.

"What kind of defence?"

He sighed, "Don't worry about it Quin. You don't want to know."

I fought back the urge to scream at him. He had to understand that I needed to know. He knew me better than that. Yet here we were, back to him attempting to protect me from the horrible truth. I was determined not to let him get to me though.

"Ok. Well make sure you use the gloves." He didn't react. "There was no other message."

I turned to leave, attempting to maintain the detached air that I had promised myself I would. I made it three steps before he called to me, his voice strained.

"Quin."

I stopped walking but refused to turn around.

"I'm sorry. I know you want to know. I know I promised that–" his voice caught on the words and for a moment he seemed unable to continue.

I waited where I was, sure there would be more but determined not to give him the satisfaction of knowing how hurt I was.

"Quin," His voice was low and urgent. "I know that I should tell you everything. I know that you think I didn't mean what I said in the woods. I do, but there's so much at stake. So much that could go wrong…"

I spun round to face him, unable to stop myself, "You don't think I know that?"

He took a small step towards me, his hands shaking a little, "I know you do. I can't really explain it, at least, not up here in plain view…"

"But you haven't even tried to see me alone since–" I faltered slightly, "since you know when. How am I supposed to know what you're thinking?"

"You're not." His face hardened. "You can't."

"Half the time you look like you're on their side!" A pained expression crossed his face and I pressed on, almost glad that I had hurt him. "It doesn't seem at all like you want to start that rebellion you promised us." I hesitated. "Was it all talk?"

"No. It's more complicated than that. I can't let them see– I can't let anything get in the way now. That's just how it is."

I sighed and turned away again, feeling worse than I had to begin with. I wished he had just let me walk away the first time and not even attempted to explain himself. I was only more confused now.

"Did you get the message from Tyler?"

I nodded sadly, feeling very much like I would dread the meeting now, rather than looking forward to it.

"You'll be there?"

The hope in his voice was unmistakeable. Of course. He needed foot soldiers to be a part of his Resistance, and couldn't afford to risk angering a potential recruit. That was all I was to him. But he was the only hope I had of ever getting out of The Beck. I nodded slightly, so he would be sure of my answer, before walking away. I didn't look back until I reached Ladder 18, and then he was only a speck in the distance, reaching up again to test or fix the wire on the top of the wall.

By the time I got back to the Trials they were almost over. Mason was sitting at the starting point looking bored. He nodded as I approached, looking relieved to have some distraction.

"Hey, how was it?"

"Strange." There were too many people around to warrant having a conversation about the mysterious pot I had transported to Cameron and I didn't want them to overhear.

Mason looked as though he was going to protest and I held up a hand to prevent him.

"Later."

He settled back again, looking a little disgruntled but accepting the wisdom of my words, for now at least.

"How's it been here?"

"Ok. Boring. Citizens came, most of them managed the course well. The Supers have been watching them and taking notes. That's it really."

"And you've still no idea what they want? How many they need?"

He shook his head. "Not a clue. They're not saying anything."

I looked across the assault course. There were only four or five citizens still competing. None of them looked particularly spectacular, nor did they seem in danger of collapse. I wondered when we would be given permission to return to Patrol.

"Carter stayed a while." Mason looked thoughtful. "She kept asking questions, wanting to know what I thought of each recruit. Didn't know what to tell her."

"I know what you mean. Honesty's not always the best policy with her."

"I usually work hard to make sure I don't have to say anything to her at all, but with you gone and all the direct questions, well... it was a challenge."

I chuckled slightly, "I'm sure you managed." I scrutinised him more closely, "Or did you? You didn't get angry with her, did you?"

He sighed, "No. I mean I did... inside I was furious. But I promised... I promised Jackson that I'd try to make myself less of a target. Draw less attention to myself, you know?"

I nodded. This was the proof of how much he cared for Jackson. She appeared to be the only one of us with any kind of influence to calm him or change his mind.

"Did you see Cam?"

I flushed at the question, turning away so Mason couldn't see my face.

"Yes. Had to pass the package to him."

"Did he say anything?"

I stared at Mason silently, not sure what he was asking.

"Did he mention the meeting?"

Visibly relaxing, I managed a slight smile this time before I replied. "Yes. He wants us all there."

"Good. Perhaps he's finally ready to do something."

"Perhaps he is."

A whistle blew from the far side of the assault course, signifying that the Trials were finished. The last few stragglers completing the course were wandering out of the gates and returning to their usual Sectors where they still had a day's work ahead of them. The Supers who had been watching the citizens compete made their way back towards us, clipboards in hand. I was surprised to see Donnelly among them.

"When did he arrive?" I nodded at him, certain that he hadn't been there at the start.

Mason followed my gaze, "Around half an hour ago he came and replaced another Super. Not sure where he came from. Why?"

"He was at the wall when I delivered the package."

"And that's bad because...?"

I shrugged. "Not bad, just... I don't like him. He makes me nervous."

"He's another kind of officer altogether."

I remembered back to the night that Mason had received his punishment for attempting to sneak back to see friends from his old Sector while we were training for Patrol. Donnelly had been the one who had caught him and reported him, which had led to his whipping.

"Way I see it, there are two types of citizen in our Sector. Those who are suited to Shadow Patrol and those who aren't. He's Shadow Patrol all the way."

I repressed a shudder, thinking of the masked faces of the officers responsible for drowning the unwanted citizens in Clearance. It required a certain inbuilt cruelty to be someone who could willingly, knowingly put an end to another person's life simply because they were surplus to requirements. I knew that I would rather die before being a part of it. I also knew there were plenty of Patrol citizens who would accept a Shadow Patrol position, as I suspected it carried with it more advantages than other positions in The Beck. Add to that the

53

sort of personality which enjoyed exerting power and control over others, and you had a dream job.

The Supers were drawing nearer and I had no wish for them to overhear our conversation. I could feel Mason's arm shaking with suppressed anger next to me at Donnelly's approach and wished that I hadn't brought the situation up. Here he was trying his best to keep his feelings under control for Jackson, and I was only making it worse. Glancing at the other Supers in the group, I was relieved to see Tyler among them. She made a beeline directly for us.

"You two, walk around the perimeter of the course and check that all the other officers know we're finished. If you can secure the course and get back up to Patrol in the next hour that would be great. You'll be reassigned for the afternoon, since we've finished earlier than anticipated."

I nodded, glad of the excuse to leave and occupy ourselves before we were faced with Donnelly again. Nudging Mason, who was still glowering in Donnelly's general direction, I pointed at the obstacles in front of us.

"Huh?"

"Hey, we have another job to do." I gave him another gentle shove. He nodded, trusting that I knew what we were supposed to be doing, because I was certain that he hadn't listened to Tyler's instructions.

"Here," Tyler held something out to me as I turned to leave, "for the gate."

I looked down at what she was handing me to find a metal key in the palm of my hand. She leaned closer and lowered her voice, "I think I can trust you with it."

I had never been left in charge of a key before. It meant we would be the last to leave the course, to secure it. I didn't know whether or not Tyler had permission to leave it with us, but the other Supers didn't seem to be paying that much attention and were mostly comparing notes with one another. I wondered briefly how Cass had fared, before feeling a slight sense of pride that Tyler had put so much trust in me. It had been a while since I had felt appreciated in my job, back in Agric probably. Getting to grips with a new Sector had been more of a challenge than I could have anticipated.

Mason and I walked to the first of the climbing walls to begin securing the ropes safely, as the course would not be in use for a while. I looked over at Donnelly, concerned that he might have noticed Mason's dark glare. He wasn't one to let a grudge go, and I knew he could potentially cause a lot of trouble for someone if he wanted to. But he wasn't looking at Mason. Instead of relief, I felt an intense discomfort flood over me as I realised that Donnelly's eyes were firmly fixed on me, and his face wore the same predatory smile I had noticed earlier.

Chapter Seven

It took Mason and I far less than an hour to secure all of the Assault Course equipment until it would be required again. Sending the other Patrol officers ahead of us, we locked the gate and began the journey back through the Lower Beck. Knowing we had a little extra time, Mason and I walked at a comfortable pace past the Agric fields, the Hydro Plant and the LS barns. I glanced up at Ladder 18 as we passed but there was no sign of life from above. I wondered if Cam was still up there.

Once we were in the woods which led to the Patrol Compound, we relaxed a little and slowed our pace even further.

"So... Donnelly. Why does he bother you as much as he bothers me?"

Mason's question unnerved me a little. I was not used to him being so perceptive.

I considered my answer, not wanting to make more of my fears than was necessary, "It's silly really. It's the way he looks at me."

Mason didn't look at me, but waited patiently for me to go on.

"I saw him coming off the wall this morning. Presumably he was heading for the Trials to take a shift over from another Super."

Mason nodded.

"I had the package for Cam. It was heavy. I wasn't sure how I was going to get it up onto the wall top. He wanted to take it for me." I paused, thinking about what I had said. "That sounds ridiculous, doesn't it? He was just trying to help me. But it was the way he did it. He was... too close, you know? Tried to take it from me, and when I stopped him, he had hold of my hands... he wouldn't let go."

Mason didn't hide his grimace. "That sounds just like him. You didn't want him to take over. But he tried to anyway. He's a creep. You had specific instructions to deliver to Cam didn't you?"

"Yes. I told him that, and he radioed someone to send down a basket on a pulley."

"So he was helpful in the end."

"I suppose, but... but it was the way he reacted when I told him no. His face..." I stopped, a little afraid to go on.

"His face?"

"It seemed like he was really angry. But then he hid it with a sort of twisted smile. I felt like he was covering something up. Like he wanted to say something– or do something else, but he stopped himself."

"I know what you mean," Mason's voice was strained, "he seems to really get off on the power, like he wants to... lord something over you – take over... or something."

"I agree." I stifled a shudder, "Did you mean what you said about Shadow Patrol?"

"Oh yes. He is the perfect candidate. Can you imagine the satisfaction he would get from handing out those harnesses?"

"No!" My response was instant. I didn't want to think that anyone could get pleasure from forcing innocent people to their ultimate deaths, but my horror stemmed not from my disbelief at Mason's statement, but the frightening feeling that I agreed with him.

We were silent for a few minutes, the path through the woods fairly steep now, and I was glad of the lull in the conversation, which felt slightly uncomfortable. The Patrol field was not far away now, and I wondered when Mason would ask about Cameron and the package again. There was no way he would let it go altogether.

As the field came into view, Mason slowed to a stop and gestured to me to join him in some trees which would hide us from view slightly. I moved past him and leaned heavily against a large oak tree, dreading the conversation.

"Ok I know we don't have long, but when are you going to fill me in on this mysterious package?"

"I don't know much really. I had to go into Dev–"

"Really?"

I nodded, unsurprised that he found this fact unusual.

"You went inside?"

"Yes. It wasn't as eye-opening as I thought it might be though— a single building, a hallway with doors leading off it. I went into one room, a kind of laboratory maybe. A woman called Montgomery was working with substances, making some kind of mixture."

"Mixture?"

"You know, a liquid – maybe some kind of medicine, or maybe a fertiliser for Agric?"

He was silent for a moment, looking puzzled.

"She gave me a pot of something," I held up a hand to stop his question before he began, "no idea what it was, but she made me wear protective gloves to touch it."

"Like it might have hurt you?"

"Yes. I had to carry it to the wall and take it up to Cameron. That's it."

"So you didn't go anywhere else in Dev?"

I shook my head.

"And when you got to the wall?"

"I told you – I saw Donnelly, then the pot was hauled up to the top. I found Cam, delivered it, and left."

Mason's scrutiny left me with no hope that he would leave it at that. He pressed me with no regard for the discomfort talking about Cam clearly gave me.

"What did Cam say about it? The pot I mean?"

I was grateful that Mason's attention was fully focused on the package rather than Cam's reaction to me. "He was pretty evasive actually. He didn't seem to want to tell me what it was all about. Something to do with the new wall defence was all he would commit to."

"Did he seem happy to get it?"

"No. He seemed angry if anything. And he wasn't happy that I'd been sent into Dev and met Montgomery."

"Wonder why?"

Mason looked like he wanted to ask more, but I didn't feel like I could cope with much else. Pushing myself into a standing position, I moved back towards the path.

"Shall we get back? They'll miss us if we aren't there soon."

Reluctantly he joined me and we continued on through the woods. Thankfully, he had stopped his incessant questioning for the time being, and we arrived at the Patrol entrance before too long. Crossing directly to the Jefferson Building, he strode past the guard on the door and headed directly to the rear of the building to look at the work boards again.

I headed up to the equipment store and handed the gate key to the citizen on duty, concerned that she might question why it was not being returned by a Super. She barely paid me any attention and I wondered what I had been worried about. When I caught up with Mason there were already several citizens scanning the boards, checking how the schedules had altered since the morning. Davis was among them. He cast a sideways glance at Mason and myself and nodded a greeting.

"I just finished a shift in the Canteen. Preparing the stew for tonight. If I see another fish today..." He made a face. None of us enjoyed the shifts we worked there. We hadn't joined Patrol to become Sustenance workers, but the secrecy of Patrol's operations required that we run our own food service. "Jackson isn't back yet."

Mason's face fell slightly. "Where was she today?"

I put a comforting hand on his arm, "Hydro. I'm surprised we didn't see her heading through the woods."

"She won't be back yet," Davis added, "Some of Dev were doing an inspection there this morning. She'll have been busier than usual."

Mason nodded begrudgingly and shuffled towards the boards as some other citizens moved away.

"Nothing surprising here."

I peered over his shoulder, "Nope."

Mason, Davis, and Jackson had all been assigned wall guard duties, and I was up at the Solar Fields. I hadn't been given a wall assignment for weeks now, and after Cameron's reaction this morning, I wondered if he had something to do with the scheduling. Perhaps he didn't want to see me. I tried not to take it to heart.

Often the Solar Fields was a boring shift, but Tyler was

assigned with me and I enjoyed her company far more these days. Now that she was not in charge of implementing our gruelling training schedule, she was usually friendly. She was also an expert in most areas of Patrol and very easy to learn from. The Solar Fields were generally quiet and peaceful, which I had thought dull when I first came here, but after the turmoil of the morning, I knew a few hours up on the fields would be a pleasant change.

An hour later, after grabbing some fruit, a bread roll and a little much needed rest, I headed off to my shift. It was fairly warm, and my overalls were sticking to me uncomfortably by the time the glinting panels came into view. The two guards already on duty looked grateful for my approach. I knew them vaguely, though they were both more experienced than I was. The one closest to me smiled at my approach.

"Hey. Glad to see you. Who else is on?"

"Tyler." I nodded back down the hill, "I don't think she'll be long."

He looked at the other officer, a woman with dark eyes who I vaguely recognised from my early days in Agric. "Mind if I head back first?"

She shook her head. He smiled at her before taking off down the hill at quite a pace.

I watched him go, amused. "Was he hungry?"

"Think so. All the men I know are moved to dramatic gestures by their stomachs!" She laughed heartily and I realised it had been a long while since I had heard such a relaxed, good humoured sound.

"Are you from Agric originally?"

She turned her attention to me, smiling, "Yes. Do you recognise me?"

"I do."

"I remember you. I'm older, obviously, but when you first transferred from Minors I was on duty with you a couple of times. I remember you and your friend who was so good with the soil – Harper was it?"

I swallowed a sob, managing to nod.

"She was such a natural in Agric! I'd never seen someone take to it so well."

"She was."

"But you – you were never that suited down there. I always knew you'd end up somewhere else."

"Really? How?"

She regarded me seriously, "You were decent at the work, don't get me wrong. But you always had a look on your face like it wasn't enough for you. Like you wanted to do more. And you were tall and strong. I wasn't a bit surprised when you turned up here."

"When did you transfer?"

"Oh, a long time before you. We were only in Agric together for six months before I transferred. Tried for it for years before that. Then finally they let me up here." She grimaced, the first sign of any negative expression on her face.

"What?"

"Sometimes I wish they hadn't."

I nodded my agreement. "I know how that feels."

"I cope, you know… but I lost some friends in the transfer and I just–" she trailed off, "I just miss them, you know?"

"Are any of them maybe thinking of trying for a transfer themselves? Maybe you could get to work with them again in the future?"

She shook her head sadly, "When I say lost, I don't just mean left behind…"

"You mean…?"

"Yes. They're gone for good."

"I'm sorry."

"So now I keep my head down, paste on a smile, and try to forget that I ever knew them."

I wanted to say that it was a sad way to live, to forget old friends, but knowing the pain my own friendships with Cass and Harper were currently causing me, I had to question whether or not hers was a better approach. At least her laughter had suggested she managed to bury the hurt and found a way to be happy sometimes.

I was disappointed to see Tyler approaching in the distance, finding that I wanted to speak to this woman for longer. "What's your name?"

She was already standing ready to go, but turned and smiled. "Williams. Call me Will."

"See you later Will."

She nodded at me before heading down the hillside at a more relaxed pace than the previous guard. Passing Tyler, she called out a greeting, and continued on towards the compound and some much-needed rest.

Tyler reached me minutes later. She didn't speak, but smiled her greeting and we went about completing the checks required at the start of every shift up at the Solar Fields. These didn't take very long, and involved us making a circuit of the field. She travelled the length of the south side, and I took the north. When we met up in the middle we took a seat together on the ground, facing in opposite directions to keep a clear watch. We were silent for a long time. Tyler generally didn't speak unless there was a good reason to do so, and I respected that.

The clearing around the field was buzzing with insects and the hum wove a mood of tranquillity around the field as we sat in companionable silence. Tyler was a respected Patrol Super, but I sometimes found her success and control to be intimidating. It was a while before I found the courage to speak.

"Thank you."

She didn't turn, but I felt her body straighten at my words. "For what?"

"For trusting me with the key before. It's a while since I've felt valued like that."

She stayed silent and for a moment I wondered if I should have kept quiet.

"It's no problem. You're turning into a great Patrol citizen Quin. I knew you could, if you could manage to gain more control of your feelings. You're really starting to do that now."

I smiled despite myself. Though I hated so much about The Beck and Patrol, there were aspects of it I felt proud to be a part of: defending the other citizens from attack, protecting them from the various threats which were a part of daily life here. I just wished that I was able to protect them from the ultimate threat they didn't know about: Governance itself.

I thought that the conversation was over, but a moment later Tyler spoke again. This time her voice had a far less relaxed tone, and I was glad we were facing away from each other so she couldn't see my face.

"How did you find Cameron today?"

Surprised at the question, I found myself unable to reply for a second. Not one to harass people, Tyler waited. I remembered the time I had witnessed a kiss between Tyler and Cam, just after my transfer to Patrol. It had been initiated by Tyler, and although not immediately rejected by Cam, was not returned. He had told me since that they were close friends, and there was nothing more between them, on his side at least. I believed him.

But Tyler's feelings seemed as strong as ever by the sound of her voice. I tried to decide whether or not she was simply seeking my opinion on how he looked, or trying to discover if there was more to my relationship with Cam than she knew. I dismissed the thought immediately. How could she think there was anything between us when I had barely seen him for three months? Only Jackson, Mason and possibly Davis knew about the kiss between us.

Finding my voice, I finally managed to reply. "What?"

"You saw him… at the wall, after I left."

"Oh. Yes, I did."

"How did you think he looked?"

That settled it. She was simply concerned about him, maybe as she hadn't seen him herself lately. She was worried he was working too hard, missing his company, wanting to reassure herself that he was ok.

"Um… he looked fine? A little harassed maybe, busy, but… um… healthy, I suppose. You saw him yourself."

She sighed audibly. "I know. I thought he looked tired. Stressed. He's been so busy with the defence project at the wall."

I stayed silent, waiting for her to continue, not really knowing what kind of response she wanted.

"I'm worried about what he's got himself involved with. Hopefully he can tell us more tonight."

"Hopefully."

"It's just he's been so distant. Working closely with a Super from Dev. A woman who is creating something for the defences. I'm not sure what."

"Montgomery?"

I felt her spin around to face me, "Yes. How do you know her name?"

"I was sent up to the wall today with a package from Dev. Montgomery gave it to me."

"What did you think of her?"

"I've never met anyone like her."

Tyler snorted, "No. Me neither." She sighed again. "I'm sorry. I shouldn't be talking to you about this. It's just– he used to tell me everything. We were quite a team... but now..."

She trailed off and I let the silence continue, not knowing how to comfort her. After a moment, she pushed herself to her feet.

"I'll patrol the field for a bit I think. Stretch my legs and make sure there's nothing amiss. Back soon."

I turned to reply, trying to offer some support, but her slim figure was already retreating into the distance.

Chapter Eight

The rest of my shift with Tyler passed uneventfully. She continued to divide her time between restless circuits of the field and sitting staring into the far distance with a serious expression on her face. I didn't attempt any more conversation, knowing that I couldn't offer her any relief from her torment. I didn't think that admitting I had the same concerns as her would be helpful. She didn't need to know how I felt about Cameron. Perhaps she would never have to, I thought gloomily. Not if he never came near me again.

I made my way back down to the Patrol Compound once my replacement arrived. The canteen was busy and it was easy to get lost in the conversations going on around me and remain mostly unnoticed. I shared the same table as Mason and Jackson, eating the fish stew Davis had been preparing, but no one seemed to feel much like talking. We were all hoping for some kind of revelation tonight from Cam, some hope for the future of our tiny revolution. At the same time, I could feel the silent tension. We knew what was at stake if we were caught out at night discussing the downfall of Beck Governance.

After the meal, we split up. Jackson and I returned to our pod together. We had a small amount of Rec Time, but rather than use it to read or catch up with one another, the two of us used the time to grab an hour of extra sleep, knowing that we would be up and awake later on. I had never had any trouble falling asleep. Beck work shifts were long and physical, whether in Agric or in Patrol, and I got to sleep quickly, missing the rest of the pod returning from their own Rec Time.

Jackson shook me awake well before midnight. Silently, we pulled on thicker overalls and headed out of the pod into the night. We were lucky that the rest of our pod were heavy sleepers, although we had only tested this theory on a couple of occasions. Most Patrol citizens disliked The Beck Governance, but were too afraid to challenge it. My hope was that if anyone did wake up, they would be respectful enough not to report any unusual occurrences. Or put it down to a late-night meeting between couples. Jackson had gone out a few times at night to meet Mason, and so far, no one had questioned it.

We made it across the pod field without issue and were soon skirting the edge of the field which led past the Jefferson Building to the woods. This was the riskiest part. Whilst the guard on the Jefferson door was quite far away, there was always the chance that he or she would spot us, but we hugged the edges of the path in the shadows and there were no shouts of alarm as we passed.

I found myself lagging behind, allowing Jackson to go ahead of me as we approached the woods. I had been looking forward to the meeting earlier, but after the conversation with Cameron I dreaded coming face to face with him again. At the gate which led into the woods, she seemed to realise what I was doing and slowed down.

"What is it?"

I shook my head, not wanting to give her an answer.

"Quin!"

Her voice hissed through the darkness and I automatically glanced back towards the Jefferson Building to check that no one had heard. Knowing from her tone that she wouldn't let the matter drop, I leaned a little closer so that my own whisper would not be heard.

"Cam."

"Ah." She smiled sympathetically, "maybe it will be good to see him?"

"Not likely."

A frown crossed her freckled features. "Have you seen him?"

"Today. On the wall."

I purposely hadn't told her, not wanting to discuss the feelings I was trying to fight. Although Jackson knew how I felt about Cameron, she still seemed to believe that there was a chance that something could happen between us, while my own hopes only grew dimmer. I wasn't sure I could stand any of her optimistic sentiments today.

"Was it bad?"

I nodded.

She paused as though she wanted to say something, but then changed her mind. Now was not the time.

"Well there isn't much of an option now is there? Let's get it over with."

Grateful for her understanding, I took a deep breath and forced myself to keep in step with her as we left the field and headed into the cover of the trees. I felt grateful that the night was fairly cloudy and would hide my expressions as long as I wasn't too close to Cameron.

Once in the woods it was easier to relax. A few paces into the trees we were joined by two shadows which melted out of the darkness. At first I was startled, but as one of the shapes sidled closer to Jackson, taking her hand in his, I realised it was only Mason and Davis. Clearly they had been waiting for us, presumably prearranged by Jackson. I was, for once, glad of Davis' company, knowing he would stick as close to me as I would let him.

Always unswervingly on my side, Davis was a good friend on whom I had grown to rely. He was a fellow recruit who had come, like Mason, from the LS Sector and had trained alongside me. I had managed to help him out of a difficult situation once and protected him from taking actions which would have landed him in Clearance. Ever since that day, he had been a faithful devotee who, if I was honest, I knew had stronger feelings for me than I had for him. Since we spent so much time with Jackson and Mason, he seemed to be forever hopeful that he and I would end up being as close as they were, despite me rebuffing him regularly.

He was nice, and it was good to know that he was always on my side. But I knew that I didn't feel the way about him that Jackson felt about Mason. And, if I was honest, the way I felt about Cam. I just wished that Cameron would make his feelings for me as clear as Davis did. Things would be a lot easier if I knew where I stood with him. For a while, things between Davis and I had been strained, as he tried to get closer to me and I resisted, as gently as I could. Tonight, however, as we walked side by side through the woods he seemed to understand my need for peace and was simply happy to remain with me, offering silent support.

As we moved through the woods, I marvelled at how quickly

we had become used to the different paths through the trees, considering how foreign they had been only three months ago. We followed the path which led to the cliff we had been made to climb on our first ever training day. It brought back bad memories. Fin, a fellow recruit, had slipped off the cliff face and seriously injured her ankle here, which had resulted in her assignment to Clearance and, ultimately, her drowning. I knew that Jackson hated the place. But its advantage outweighed the bad memories associated with it.

The cliff formed a barrier across the clearing, creating a kind of funnel with a single path being the only way in or out, unless you were prepared to climb. No one could approach from behind and sneak up on us, and the area was rarely used aside from honing citizens' climbing skills. I knew couples wanting privacy sometimes used the clearing, but presumably Cam or Tyler had made sure that there would be no one here for that reason tonight. Mason and Jackson slowed down ahead of us as the trees began to thin out. We approached with caution and were surprised to hear a number of voices in hushed conversation.

Leaving the shelter of the last few trees, we walked forwards warily. I looked up at the cliff from which Fin had fallen and took a deep breath. Jackson's eyes were firmly fixed on the ground and she seemed unwilling even to look at the place where her friend had been abandoned. We turned our attention instead to the citizens sitting in the clearing. There seemed to be around thirty people seated on the ground in the shelter of the cliff. At our approach, there was a low whistle and we glanced up to see a single sentry posted in the trees above our head. The group fell silent immediately and turned to watch our approach.

71

At first I recognised only Tyler and Cameron, but as the moments passed I started to make out other, vaguely familiar faces, Patrol guards I had perhaps worked a shift with yet did not know particularly well. I noticed Will, the ex-Agric citizen I had met earlier in the day, and I was surprised to see a couple of citizens in Governance uniforms sitting to one side.

As we settled on the ground at the rear of the group, Cam stood up and held up a hand to silence the muffled whispers which had started up again. Immediately everyone fell silent. I marvelled, as I always did, at the respect people held for him.

"We don't have long," he began in hushed tones, "but I wanted to gather us together tonight, because I don't know when we will get another chance. It's been too long since we last met–" he shook his head to stop the murmurs which sprang up at his words, "too long. But we have not had sufficient chance or reason to get together recently."

One or two Patrol Officers looked like they were going to argue, until Tyler stood up.

"Cam and I told you last time that there was no point meeting until we had either a firm plan or greater numbers." Her voice was firm and clear. "We have a few more recruits now, as you can see," she gestured towards us, "and Cameron also has news to share."

Cam smiled briefly at Tyler before continuing, "Yes. We now have a few more members to swell our ranks, but it still isn't enough. We have, in the past, discussed our options. These are limited: fight, which we simply cannot do without huge numbers of citizens and better weapons, or flight, which means risking considerable danger, and probably leaving friends behind."

"Most of you know that we have experimented with escaping The Beck in the past with no success. Our ranks were decimated when those who tried to leave by boat died in the attempt."

Mason raised a hand. I was surprised at his respectful gesture, but supposed that he felt just as intimidated as I did in the presence of these rebels who had been a part of the cause for so much longer than us.

Cam looked vaguely annoyed, but nodded, "Go ahead Mason."

"Haven't you considered trying again? An escape across the water?"

"We've made two attempts now. Both failed."

"Are you certain? When you spoke to us, just after we saw the drownings in Clearance, you said the second group that was sent just disappeared. They could have made it elsewhere, but not returned."

Cam looked exasperated, "Yes, they could. But how does that help us here?"

"Plus the whole idea of finding an escape lay in us being able to work out how to do it more than once, so that others could follow," Tyler added.

"But what if they never came back because they succeeded? They're over there, in some other mountain range, happily waiting for you to go and join them?"

Cam's sigh was audible even from the back of the group. "Look, Mason. We have come at this from all angles. We've been a part of this Resistance far longer than you have. Those who left made a promise that if they could return, they would. I don't believe that they would all go back on it. And even if they did make it, and others follow, and more after that, we need to consider the long-term implications."

"What do you mean?"

"Think about it." Tyler's voice was calm, reasonable, but had an undertone of concern. "We discover a way out. A place where we can escape to and live, who knows how, but putting that aside for now, live elsewhere. And others follow. How long before Governance notices that large numbers of citizens are leaving?"

"And how long before they come after us?" Cam's voice was quiet, but the challenge was clear.

Mason didn't reply, clearly mulling over the idea.

"If Governance is so concerned about those over the water, they are not going to stand for their own citizens, who they have reared, fed, trained, who sustain Beck society exactly as they want it, going over the water and joining the ranks of those who are already their enemy. Making them stronger."

Mason seemed to finally understand, "And presumably feeding them information about the way things are run over here. Dangerous information which would put The Beck at even more risk of attack."

Cam nodded grimly. "Exactly."

"So any other ideas about escaping from here over the water are to be considered very carefully," Tyler qualified. "And not tonight."

We all turned our attention back to Cam, who was unfolding a document he had drawn from an overall pocket.

"No. Not tonight. Tonight we have other things to discuss."

Chapter Nine

The group was silent as Cameron unfolded the paper. The Beck was generally a place of practical tools: knives, hammers, spades, saws, and ladles, depending on your Sector of origin. Paper was rarely used by ordinary citizens, and remained mostly in the hands of Governance and Dev, aside from the work schedules displayed in the various Beck Sectors. And a schedule would not have been worthy of bringing us together tonight. No. The paper in Cam's hand, whatever it was, was more significant.

He took a breath before speaking again.

"Some of you might know that we have been trying to subtly recruit others to join our cause who are from compounds other than Patrol. We have known for a long time now that the organisation of our society prevents citizens from communicating with people from other areas. The separation of the Lower and Upper Beck, the near-silence which reigns in the areas at the bottom of the hill, the fact that citizens from different Sectors rarely work together… it all means that Governance can carefully control the information they feed to each of us. Different groups know different things. There's little trust. The sanctions for sharing information with others are harsh and put people off any kind of rebellion."

Tyler took over, "But things are slowly changing. Governance is so concerned about the threat from across the water now, that they've been forced to take action. That has meant changing things here in The Beck, trusting some citizens more than they used to."

Again Cam took over, and I wondered at how synchronised they were. Tyler's earlier fears about Cam's health seemed a distant memory, almost as though I had made them up. "The wall defence project that I've been working on has meant I've been able to spend far more time in the company of citizens from other Sectors. I have been in charge of a team of Lower Beck workers, taken mostly from LS and Rep, but also had to collaborate with Supers from Dev and, occasionally, Governance. This has led to many conversations which demonstrate just how dissatisfied citizens from those compounds are. In truth, they're as unhappy as we are in Patrol."

Cam paused and motioned to one of the citizens in grey. It was a man, a little older than I was used to seeing, dressed in the grey suit of Governance. He pulled himself to his feet and approached the front of the group with some caution.

"I'm Harris. Originally a Rep citizen. Recruited to Governance eight years ago now. I'm a Super. Have been for five years. They trust me."

I wondered what it would take for us to trust Harris. He seemed genuine enough, but many citizens were so afraid they found it difficult to trust other citizens in their own Sector, so trusting someone in Governance, the very place where Adams and Carter lived, where the rules were made and sanctions issued, would take a lot.

He seemed to understand this, and nodded reassuringly as he continued. "I know what you're thinking. I know you believe I could be a spy, someone sent by Governor Adams to root out those who are thinking of rebellion, but I assure you I am not. Cameron trusts me." He paused and glanced at Cam for confirmation. "And you trust Cameron. So you have to believe that he wouldn't have brought me here without first making completely sure that I was genuine."

Cam stepped forward, "I have known Harris for several months now. The things he has shared with me have clearly demonstrated that he's on the same side as we are. He's risking a lot just by being here tonight, so I am asking you to put your trust in him and believe that he's just as angry as you about the way things are."

Harris continued, "My role in Governance is simple: I complete all the administrative tasks required by Governor Adams. I know, admin hardly seems like a significant role. But Adams is paranoid. He would no more allow an untested Gov citizen access to his personal documentation than he would strap himself into a harness and board a Clearance boat. I had to work hard to be trusted. Prove myself. The citizen I took over from was dispatched to Clearance for sharing the most insignificant piece of information with a fellow Gov citizen and drowned almost immediately. It took years for Adams to leave me in charge of all the documents I now have access to. But he did eventually trust me, and now I am able to see documents about every aspect of life here in The Beck."

"Which is where," Cam said, cutting in, "the document here comes in."

Harris nodded. "For a while now Governance has been paranoid about outsiders making attacks on The Beck during times when we are left vulnerable, such as storms. After the last storm, several bodies were found at different locations throughout The Beck. Gov believed that these people were sent here to investigate the layout of our community, and report back with their findings. As far as we know, these spies all died in the storm, but Adams was extremely concerned about the situation. Concerned enough to mount a secret mission to gather more information, in case some of these spies survived and escaped with insider knowledge about our society. And to make the announcement to Upper Beck citizens about the need to improve our defence systems rapidly."

He paused for a moment, watching the faces of his listeners closely, seeming reassured enough by our silence to continue. "This document details the mission, but I'll sum it up for you as simply as possible: Gov sent a number of Shadow Patrol officers over the water in a couple of the smaller Clearance boats. Firstly, they were tasked with looking for a community close enough to be able to access The Beck, who might want to invade. They reported a number of other settlements within reach of The Beck, but only one seemed large enough to pose a potential threat to us."

"A second mission sent only two Shadow Patrol officers to the settlement in question. This time they were asked to go ashore for a period of time and attempt to discover more about the other community's plans. They managed to successfully infiltrate the settlement for a two-day period, and in that time discovered some extremely worrying facts. This other community lives in an area far less appealing than The Beck. Its soil is not as fertile and they are grossly overpopulated considering the size of their land. They are the ones who sent citizens to spy on The Beck during the recent storms. They have been watching us for longer than we thought. They have appraised our style and standard of living, and wish to take over our society in its entirety."

He stopped, watching the severity of his words sink in before continuing. "Gov is obviously extremely worried about the future of Beck society. They anticipate an invasion is being planned as we speak."

Cam took over again now, "Most of you are aware that I've been working on a project to strengthen the protection the wall gives us from outside attack. I won't go into detail now, there isn't enough time, but these defences have involved me working with a brilliant scientist in Dev called Montgomery, who is developing chemical weapons with devastating consequences for those unfortunate enough to come into contact with them."

I thought of the protective gloves with a shudder.

"Throughout the project I have also worked with a number of citizens from Governance, Harris included. Over a period of time we've developed a rapport and, now that he's shown me some of the documentation he has access to, I trust him. This particular document goes on to detail the Governance plans for developing our defences, as well as acting swiftly to repel these attackers and secure The Beck against invasion."

Harris took over again, "We don't have time to go into much detail at this point, but, for obvious reasons, Governance is keen to take action against these interlopers. The new wall defences, the extra Patrol recruits, they're just the start of the plans. Gov has Montgomery and others in Dev developing new weaponry all the time, a plan to construct a second wall around the harbour in Clearance, and," he paused and lowered his voice for the next revelation, "the new Patrol citizens will not be just like you. They will be highly trained in combat skills, and not just the defensive stuff you're usually trained for. Governance wants to build an army capable of fighting off these dangerous invaders."

Tyler cut in with the final, chilling remark, "Put simply, Governance is preparing for war."

Whispered conversations erupted all around us, the words 'war' and 'army' clearly dividing opinion within the group. Some seemed excited, others frightened, more still seemed simply to be in shock. Cam and Harris stood at the front, observing the hushed conversations, allowing the news to sink in. Next to me I heard Davis and Mason arguing furiously, and watched Jackson's face drain of colour as she realised this was exactly what Mason wanted to hear. He had been frustrated ever since he found out the truth about The Beck, and desperate to take action.

He had been looking for some way to fight, and a war might just give him that chance. Because if he was a trained soldier, even one trained by Governance to fight against the outsiders, he would finally have the skills he desired. Skills which would allow him to turn Governance's own weapons against them and stand a chance of winning. And despite sharing his anger and frustration over the way we were treated here in the Beck, I knew that Jackson was desperately afraid that Mason's hot temper would get him into trouble. She was terrified of losing him.

Finally, Cam held up his hand for silence again. It took longer this time, but eventually the citizens around me quieted.

"So this means a few different things for us. One, we stand a chance of perhaps being better trained in a range of new defensive measures if they allow us to opt into the training for the new Patrol soldiers. As yet, we have no idea if this is a possibility. Two, and perhaps more importantly, we have a chance to significantly swell our ranks from the large numbers of recruits being brought up here."

Tyler stepped forward to address the group. "We have seen from the behaviour of previous recruits that we are more able to convince citizens to join our Resistance if we get to them while they are in the early stages of transferring to the Upper Beck way of life. Those first few weeks when they begin to discover the differences between our community and theirs, the way they've been treated in comparison to the lives of the citizens up here, the fact that those left behind are still suffering the same unjust treatment... they're vital. Usually there are between ten and fifteen recruits moved up at one time. On this occasion, there will be significantly more. If we can speak to them while they are still adjusting, before they get used to the privileges afforded them here, and forget those they left behind, we can often bring them onside."

I thought about the group sitting around me. How that, out of ten recruits, four of us were here tonight, dedicated to Cam and Tyler's cause. It made sense now, that they were both involved in the training of new recruits. They wanted the position, had perhaps angled for it, so that they could get close to each new batch of recruits and work out which ones might be right for them. They were then in a perfect position to convince the transfers that their cause was just, and give them hope that, if they joined, they could make a difference to the lives of everyone in The Beck.

I wondered how Tyler evaluated the suitability of each new citizen before bringing up the subject of the Resistance. Surely it was dangerous to recruit those who would never be that way inclined? If they shared information about the Resistance with the wrong people, we would be shut down immediately, the second the citizen had the chance to run to Reed and tell tales. Yet Tyler had always been a good judge of character, and understood what made people tick. Presumably she watched us throughout training and made decisions about those of us who were worth taking the risk with.

And Cam, although he didn't oversee the new recruits, was involved in some of the training sessions, and clearly participated in the evaluation of the newest members of Patrol. He watched us just as carefully as we learned to throw a knife and trained to become fitter and stronger. Had conversations with us about the way things were different in Patrol, clearly taking in everything we said and deciding whether or not we could be trusted, could become useful allies. I imagined private conversations taking place between Tyler and Cameron about each of us. Suddenly I felt used, part of a system which had been honed over years. Perhaps Cameron's interest in me was feigned only to have the desired effect of persuading me to join. It would certainly explain his lack of contact since I had agreed.

The point at which the information about the Resistance was shared with us also seemed significant: when the visit to Clearance was over and the new recruits had seen the worst The Beck had to offer. This was an excellent time to hit recruits with the hope of change. Even without knowing about the drownings, seeing Clearance was shocking, and angered or frightened most people. This left us in exactly the right state of mind: reeling from the shock, disappointed and furious as we were faced by the truth of what The Beck did to previously faithful citizens. Afraid that one day we would end up there. At that point, the idea of fighting for a better future certainly did seem appealing.

Tyler was still speaking, but my angry thoughts had temporarily deafened me. Despite my feelings about the way we were recruited, I knew that I still agreed with the arguments behind the Resistance. Forcing myself to tune back into the speech, I tried to convince myself that I could participate in this rebellion without getting overly emotional about the way I was recruited.

"...these new recruits will almost be fodder for Governance to send into war. Potentially just as bad as being sent straight to Clearance, depending on the size and strength of the opposing force. We have to convince as many of them as possible to join us. Then we can work together as a larger group. Finally do something meaningful which will make a difference to our lives here."

I had to admit she was a convincing speaker. Both she and Cam were easy to believe in, and I knew that despite their recruitment methods, they shared a desperate need to alter things for the better. I wanted to be a part of that, no matter what my feelings for the two of them were. I knew I would fight alongside them to try and make those changes actually happen.

I wondered how many new recruits there would be in the coming days, and how many of them we could convince to join our cause. For a moment I felt excited about the real possibility of taking action against Adams and Carter, with the assistance of the new recruits. And then I remembered Tyler's comment about the new Patrol citizens being recruited as cannon fodder, branded as dead before they even began their training. And I thought of Cass, running so hard around the track today, determined to convince them she deserved a role in Patrol, to be near me again, and I wondered whether she would ever get that chance.

Chapter Ten

The meeting didn't last much longer, and concluded with the promise of more information at a later date. Tyler and Cam asked us to keep an eye out for the new recruits, and explained that once decisions were made about the way their training would work, we would be given further instructions. They were planning on assigning a few recruits to each of us to work on, in terms of sussing out whether or not they might be right for the Resistance. It made sense, but I felt a little like I was participating in the same sort of manipulation I had felt so aggrieved at myself.

We were instructed to leave the clearing a few at a time and, once back in the main body of the woods, to separate and use a couple of different routes back to Patrol. There were too many of us to head back all at once, despite how practised we were at moving around the Compound in near silence. We were asked to wait until the end and sat close together, not talking much. Davis seemed to be lost in his thoughts, frustration at his earlier exchange with Mason clear from his loud sighs.

Mason and Jackson simply leaned against one another, their eyes closed, looking for all the world as though they were simply asleep. They couldn't have been, but Mason's face was the calmest I had seen it in a while, and Jackson's earlier concern was, for now at least, erased from her face. They had this effect on each other, seeming to settle and balance each other out without even trying. I envied their easy rapport.

Eventually the clearing emptied and there were only a few citizens left behind. Harris had stayed back, and Cam still seemed deep in conversation with him. The evening had not been as difficult as I had anticipated. Cam had simply ignored me. As long as I could do the same, perhaps things between us would improve. Yet as I watched the two men talking, I found my eyes straying to Cam's face every few seconds, despite me trying to focus on Harris too. Cam was so serious, conversing so intently, determination etched into his face as he discussed plans for the future. After a while I stopped fighting it and simply allowed myself to watch him, marvelling at the focus he gave to anyone he conversed with. I had felt that focus, those eyes fixed on my face alone. I missed it.

Tyler approached us and indicated that it was time for us to leave. I tapped Jackson gently on the shoulder. She and Mason hauled themselves to their feet, clearly sad at the realisation that they would soon have to part. Davis was already up and waiting to go, his eyes reflecting his exhaustion. As the four of us set off for the woods, I looked back at Cam and Harris, expecting them to be as intent on their discussion as they had been previously. Instead I was met by the serious gaze which only moments ago I had been admiring. This time, the eyes were focused solely on me. I felt a rush of excitement, which quickly died as he turned sharply away. Biting my lip hard, I followed the others into the darkness of the trees, glad again of the coverage they gave me. I didn't want anyone to see my face.

On the way back to the pod, Jackson kept darting concerned

glances at me, but she knew better than to ask in front of Mason and Davis. When we reached the pod, she wasn't stupid enough to risk waking the rest of the girls with a conversation. Instead, she offered comfort by reaching out and squeezing my hand tightly before we slipped inside the pod door. I anticipated questions from her the next time the two of us found ourselves alone and out of others' earshot.

Once inside, we both stopped short. While the majority of the pod was sleeping as normal, something was different. We looked at one another and back at the shadowy space in front of us, eventually working out that the empty cot that stood at the back of the tent was now occupied. It was hopefully far enough from our own to ensure that our empty beds had not been noticed when the citizen had arrived. I felt sure if we had been caught out, someone would have woken the others to look for us.

But the cot, which had been empty ever since we moved in, now contained a sleeping figure. The woman in the bed looked a little sturdier than the average Patrol citizen, with a round face and jet-black hair which was slightly longer than the usual. She was asleep, but her rest seemed fitful, and she was currently tossing and turning so much that I was concerned she would end up on the ground. Jackson and I exchanged another worried glance before creeping back over to our own beds and slipping off the outer layer of our overalls.

Once we were settled, I looked back at the mystery woman. She seemed to have calmed now and was no longer thrashing around, but her face was pale in the moonlight and covered with a sheen of sweat despite the cool air. I had never experienced a new citizen arriving during the night before.

Disappearing, yes, removed by Governance or Shadow Patrol to be transported to Clearance when no one was looking, but never appearing. Wondering where on earth she had come from, I turned away from her and faced the other way in an attempt to focus on sleep. Jackson was already out cold, and I hoped I would follow very soon.

I slept badly, not quite having my nightmare again, but still feeling disturbed and exhausted when I awoke at first light the next morning. Usually I was one of the first up, but today my fellow pod members were rustling about and gathering their equipment for the day ahead well before me. There was more of an air of anticipation today. It took me a few moments, but eventually I realised that they were all eager to discover how many new recruits there would be, and when they would arrive. Thinking again of Cass, I hurried to join them. Finding out the result of the Trials, plus the discovery of who the new citizen in our pod was spurred me on.

Dragging on my overalls, I headed for the bathhouse for a hasty wash. When I got there it was almost deserted, most of the hustle coming from citizens hurrying to leave. Once inside, I filled a basin with water and, stripping to my vest, began to splash it over myself. As I did, I became aware of the presence of another person, although I couldn't actually see anyone.

"Hello?" I called tentatively into the empty space.

There was no answer, save for a tiny hiccup which might have been a sob. There was definitely someone else in here, perhaps in one of the stalls.

"Hello?" I tried again. "Are you ok?"

Getting no answer, I continued with my wash. Eventually one of the stall doors opened and a figure emerged slowly. It was my new podmate, the one who had arrived so abruptly. Her face was just as pale this morning and her eyes looked swollen and puffy. I turned slowly towards her, not wanting to spook her.

"Hey," I tried, keeping my voice gentle, "Can I do anything?"

Shaking her head no, she tried to pass me and head straight for the door.

"Do you– I mean I'm going down to breakfast now. Want to come with me?"

Turning, she looked back at me, the look in her eyes unlike any I had ever seen.

"Thank you, that's kind."

"Give me just a second then." I quickly finished up and emptied out the basin, pulling my overalls back over my shoulders and shrugging into them.

"You're in my pod I think," I tried as we walked out of the door together.

She nodded silently.

"Are you new?" No reply. I tried again. "Where have you come from?"

Again she remained silent, almost physically shrinking from my questions. I wondered why she had accepted the invitation to walk to breakfast with me. I made what would be my final attempt at conversation for now, going for the simplest approach possible.

"I'm Quin."

"Blythe."

At this we had almost reached the canteen, so I cut my losses and went for a smile to try and cement the tentative acquaintance. She tried to return it, but the expression didn't quite reach her eyes. We joined the throng of citizens making their way into the canteen building. Breakfast was being served as usual, but Carter and Reed stood on the podium at the end of the room, presumably waiting to address us all. Blythe seemed to know what to do and we lined up together to get some porridge. Once we had been served, we grabbed seats next to Jackson, being among the last Patrol citizens to arrive for the meal. Within two minutes the room was full of silent Patrol officers, staring intently at the podium.

Carter approached the front of the small platform and stared out at us all.

"Today we will publish the lists detailing how many of the citizens who completed the trials yesterday made it through to Patrol. I need to let you know that these citizens will be trained a little differently than usual, due to the large number coming up at once. Instead of living in the Annexe, they will be housed in special pods set up in one of the fields towards the rear of Patrol. Some of you will be assigned to duty there this morning. Others will be sent down into the Lower Beck to escort those citizens who are moving up here to the Patrol Compound. The Supers in the Lower Beck are being instructed on how to manage their teams with fewer citizens now that so many are moving across at once. We will be asking some of you to assist in the training sessions for the new recruits once they arrive."

Carter stepped back to allow Reed to complete the instructions. He moved forwards, his usual smug expression seeming even more pronounced than usual.

"We expect the next few weeks to be a challenge for everyone, but it is essential that we band together to support one another during this time of adjustment. There are other changes going on today, so be aware that there might be some movement of citizens which you are not used to. Bear with us while we make the changes and settle into new routines. Thank you."

The two officials left the stage quickly, not waiting to gauge the reaction to their news. There was silence for a few seconds, before the room erupted in a cacophony of whispers. I wondered about Blythe, thinking she might be a part of the unusual movement of citizens Reed was referring to. Jackson, who had cast a curious look at Blythe as we sat down, now leaned in closer, clearly wanting an introduction.

I was saved the trouble of giving one by the approach of three older Patrol citizens who I knew only vaguely. They all looked a little nervous as they reached us.

"Um, hey Blythe. How are you?"

Surprised, I turned to Blythe, my eyes asking for an explanation I knew she was unlikely to give. She surprised me by standing up and managing a small smile for the women who stood in front of us.

"Ok. Just about."

"Want to come look at the work assignments with us? Are you back on them yet?"

She shrugged, "Don't think so, but I'll check."

As she turned to leave she glanced back at me, "See you later Quin."

I found myself unable to do anything but nod. Once she was gone, I turned to Jackson who was staring after her.

"Who was that?"

"Her name is Blythe. That was all I knew about her until she started talking to them. I had kind of assumed that she was new, some kind of transfer from elsewhere... but they knew her. And talked to her like she knew Patrol. So she can't be completely new."

"No. She can't. Did she say anything about us?"

"What?"

"Did she notice our beds were empty when she arrived last night? She came in between midnight and two. Odd time to arrive."

"She didn't mention it. Don't think she's very well. She's so pale. But I think we're safe – think she's got enough of her own stuff going on to worry about us. She seemed genuinely nice. Though I guess you can never tell."

"So the mystery will have to wait then."

"I guess so, for now at least."

Chapter Eleven

We cleared our plates and headed out to the Jefferson Building along with everyone else. Mason and Davis were already there, but had not been successful in getting anywhere near the boards.

We waited several minutes for the crowds to thin out. Once we were able to see, the boards showed that Mason and Davis had been assigned to the erection of the new pods in the far field, which would house the new recruits. Jackson and I on the other hand, were part of a small team going down to the Lower Beck to bring up the transfers. I smiled. I didn't often get to work with Jackson, and spending time with her was always a pleasure. I was also keen to discover if Cass had been reassigned to Patrol, and perhaps make her transition a little easier if I could. The only down side to the assignment was the Super who had been put in charge.

"Barnes." Jackson sighed.

We both knew Barnes well from our training days, where he had been partly in charge of our own transition to Patrol, but most of the group had far preferred Tyler's style of instruction. He was all brawn and little brain, using his muscle rather than his wits to solve a problem. I hadn't seen much of him in the last three months and presumed he had been working elsewhere, perhaps on one of the many defence projects which had been put in place since the last storm. He hadn't been working with Cam, I knew that, but I hadn't crossed paths with him on any shifts either.

"We can cope with him for a morning, can't we?" I tried to sound cheerful. "There'll be lots of other people around to command his attention. We can just stay at the back out of the way."

We met Barnes and the others at the entrance to the woods around ten minutes later and set off for the Lower Beck. Usually, when citizens transferred there was a ceremony, but this time it seemed there would be neither the time nor the occasion for it. The transfers were not of the usual kind, and only moving between the Lower Beck and Patrol rather than all over the different Sectors of The Beck. And they were clearly being moved swiftly, with no time for fuss. The group I was assigned to had ten people in it, which made me wonder how many new recruits we were receiving. I presumed it would be a fairly significant number.

Ours was a mixed group in terms of gender and age, as though those in charge had tried to assign the most diverse and approachable team possible for the task. Among the group was Anders, a Dev recruit who had trained with us. Although Jackson and I had spent a lot of time with him initially, I didn't know him well. He was always fairly pleasant, but so quiet I never knew what to talk to him about.

I wondered if he knew Montgomery at all, or whether or not he might be able to answer some of the questions I had about the Dev Sector. I resolved to try and speak to him later and see how he responded. It would do me good to test my skills at reading people, in preparation for working out which of the new recruits we might trust enough to join the

Resistance.

We reached the Lower Beck Square in less than half an hour. Once there, Barnes, who had yet to speak to any of us, held up a hand and beckoned for us to gather round.

"Wait here," he said. "They'll come to us."

Our group stood around awkwardly, knowing now we were so far from Patrol we shouldn't be seen talking openly. Barnes offered no further guidance. Jackson and I exchanged glances, unsure what to expect. This was a first for most of the citizens here. Patrol usually only received a recruitment group of around ten people, hence the number of beds in the Annexe. The number of citizens about to be brought up to Patrol was a complete mystery to all of us except Barnes at the moment.

Around ten minutes later, citizens in various different coloured uniforms started filing into the square. Most of them looked at least a little nervous, as I had expected. There were fewer Agric citizens than I would have liked. Most of those arriving so far were men from LS or Rep. A few green overalls wandered in, and I was glad to see that there were some Sustenance staff too, to balance up the gender divide.

A jab in the ribs from Jackson made me refocus my attention on the entrance to the square. Among another small group of Agric citizens, small but unmistakable with her white-blond hair, was Cass. Our eyes met across the crowd and she could barely contain the grin on her face. I smiled back, wishing I shared her enthusiasm. Here she was, blindly assuming that she was joining her old friend in a better place, when I knew the truth. I wondered how I could protect her now. She had been safer in Agric.

Five minutes later there were almost a hundred new recruits standing around us. They gathered apprehensively in small groups, unsure how to behave. I marvelled at the sheer number of them, wondering how we could possibly house, feed and train this many new recruits effectively. Since her initial smile, Cass had avoided eye contact with me and I inwardly saluted her for being sensible. Clearly, she was learning to curb her passionate nature, and for that I was glad.

At last Barnes held up a hand to gain everyone's attention, a gesture which seemed unnecessary considering the silence which hung over the square. As he spoke, I remembered my first journey to Patrol from this very location with a small shudder.

"Ok. Hope you're ready, 'cos Patrol's definitely not easy. I'm Barnes. Let's get moving – training starts this afternoon."

Jackson and I exchanged amused glances. He had made a very similar speech to us on the day of our transfer. It seemed that things didn't change much. The recruits around us fell into a sort of ragged line, correctly assuming from Barnes' tone that he wanted them to demonstrate their obedience. I caught Cass's eye for a brief second and she rolled her eyes at me. Not a good start, especially if she wanted to gain Barnes' trust.

Within seconds we were jogging through the trees up the hill. Having had no guidance from Barnes, we spaced ourselves evenly throughout the group. I smiled some encouragement at those recruits who seemed particularly nervous, deliberately avoiding the front of the group where, predictably, Cass had positioned herself. Ever competitive. I had decided that we would both be better off if I was assigned to another group. Close enough to speak to her, to advise her where necessary, but not directly attached to her.

The run was a pleasant one, the sky fairly clear and a little pale sunlight making its way through the gaps in the trees. In no time we had reached the Compound, which was far busier than usual. Barnes held up a hand to stop us and we waited in the field for another Super to join us. The pattern the new recruits were following was the same as we had done three months ago. The only difference was the addition of the ten Patrol citizens to create additional support for Barnes and Tyler, who was just making her way across the field, clipboard in hand.

"Good morning," she began, her suitability for the role of trainer evident in her professional tone and calm manner. "Welcome to Patrol. Today you will be assigned to pods and given equipment, then taken back into the woods for some endurance training with Barnes and myself. You all performed well in the Trials yesterday, but there is still more work to be done before you are considered fit enough to become full members of Patrol."

Barnes stepped forward, his tone almost threatening, "It won't be easy, like I said before. Patrol is tough, and since there are so many of you, there will be even more pressure to keep up. We're not all as nice as Tyler here."

He threw a glance at her as he said this, as though challenging her to interrupt. She merely stared back at him and I admired her ability to resist being baited into a leadership contest. Barnes was extremely competitive and I had seen him corrected by Tyler on more than one occasion. Today he seemed angry, as though he had something to prove. The group before me waited to see how Tyler would progress from this point, sensing the open challenge in Barnes' words.

"Barnes is right, of course. Nothing about Patrol is easy, and adjusting to new rules and routines is never a simple task. We will try to make the transition as painless as possible for you, but do make sure that you think before you act at all times, as failure to follow the rules here has severe consequences."

She backed away, gesturing for Barnes to take over. He looked a little deflated, as though he had expected her to contradict rather than agree with him, and it was a few seconds before he managed to respond.

"For now, let's head into the Jefferson Building to collect equipment. Then you'll be shown to your pods."

Barnes made off without further hesitation. I found it difficult to hide my smile. Tyler knew exactly how to combat his arrogance and he was always on the back foot with her. He struggled to assert his authority and then when given the opportunity to take charge, often fumbled his words and messed it up. He was not a great speaker, and having marvelled at both Cam and Tyler's speeches the previous night, I knew that it was an essential quality for an effective leader. I wondered why he had been assigned the role of trainer in the first place.

We reached the Jefferson Building and went to collect equipment. The line was lengthy and even though the citizen on duty in the equipment store seemed to be prepared, I could see that it would take a while. I dropped back to the rear of the line and leaned against the wall, knowing that we would be here for some time. Tyler was standing nearby, a strange expression on her face. She beckoned me over.

"I need you to go into the Annexe."

"For more equipment?"

She shook her head, taking me by the shoulder and walking me a few paces away from the rest of the group. "There's someone in there. In a minute, Barnes is going over, to collect some extra supplies. I need you to get her out of there before he arrives."

"Why?"

"Don't ask please. There isn't much time. Just get there, persuade her to come out, and take her back to her pod."

"Ok. Anything else?"

She shook her head. "Once she's in the pod, try to get her to rest. Then head back here. You have around twenty minutes until you'll be missed, alright?"

I understood; if I wasn't back by then, people would start to ask questions. Still, the pod wasn't far from the Annexe and, assuming I managed to convince this citizen to leave, I could easily make it back before anyone noticed that I was absent.

I turned to go but Tyler stopped me with a cold hand on my arm. "Her name's Blythe."

I didn't have time to ask any more questions before Tyler turned away and hurried back to the equipment line. I wondered if Tyler knew that Blythe was in my pod, or whether it was simply a coincidence that I was about to meet this new citizen twice in the same day. Checking that Barnes was occupied, I jerked my head towards Jackson so that she understood where I was going, and slipped away from the busy store room.

Chapter Twelve

The rear of the Jefferson Building was deserted. From there I could reach the door of the Annexe within seconds. Peering in through the porch window I could not immediately see anyone, so I eased the door open and slid inside. The room was cool and dim, its familiarity comforting. The beds close to the entrance were empty and boxes of equipment were stacked around the walls in various places.

I wandered between the bunks, heading towards the back, where my old bunk was. I had never been alone in this room, I realised. Memories of my first conversation with Jackson, an argument with Cam, Mason's agony after being whipped for disobedience flooded over me. This was where I had lived when I realised the horrific truth about The Beck. A noise coming from somewhere at the side of the room startled me and I remembered that I was not alone at all. Blythe was here. And, like this morning, she didn't want to be found.

"Blythe?" I tried, knowing that she did not know my voice, but hoping that the fact I knew her name might hold some weight. "Blythe, Tyler sent me to find you."

Silence. I tried again. "It's Quin, Blythe. From your pod? We met this morning."

Again, nothing. "I know you probably don't want to see anyone, but Barnes is heading over here in a minute. That's why Tyler sent me."

A rustling told me that finally something I had said was getting through. I followed the sound and ended up rounding the edge of the final bunk on the left. Behind it, hunched against the wall, a blanket clutched around her shoulders, was Blythe. Her face was stained with tears and she looked paler than ever. She reminded me very much of Harper before her Clearance transfer, and my heart went out to her. I held out a hand.

"Come with me. I'll take you back to the pod. Tyler says you can rest there for now. You aren't needed for a shift anywhere?"

She shook her head.

"Ok. Let's go then, because Barnes might be here any minute."

She seemed to shake as she heard his name. Something about Barnes unnerved her. I realised that she had responded both times when I had mentioned him. Moving forward cautiously, I took her arm and eased her into a standing position. She winced as she straightened up, and I wondered if she was ill or injured in some way. It would make sense for Tyler to be protecting her if that was the case, but I didn't understand why Blythe was not on any of the work schedules. I had never known anyone to live in a Sector and not be expected to work. Shelving my questions for now, I offered Blythe my shoulder and helped her towards the door.

As we reached it I panicked when I realised that Barnes was already on the other side. Wondering if we could hide, I took a step back, but it was too late. As he stepped in through the door his expression was serious, focused only on locating whatever equipment was required from the Annexe. The second he saw us his face altered dramatically, going through numerous different emotions. I braced myself, expecting anger, fury, even delight at the prospect of finding someone breaking the rules, but instead I saw shock, dismay and finally pain as his eyes locked on to Blythe's.

"What are you– I heard you were coming back but…"

He trailed off, looking at the ground. I had never seen Barnes look so lost. I looked across at Blythe and saw a similar expression on her features. Immediately I felt awkward, trapped in the middle of a situation I didn't fully understand. After a lengthy pause, Blythe stepped forward.

"I got back last night. I won't be on the duty rota for a few days… you know… give me a chance to rest."

"Are you… are you alright?"

She attempted to nod and I was horrified to see her eyes fill with tears.

"You're not, are you?"

Barnes stepped towards her, putting a hand on her shoulder. She recoiled from his touch instantly and stared at the floor, her eyes dull and listless. Barnes' features clouded over for a moment but he rallied quickly. Stepping back, he looked instead at me.

"You came here to get her right? Tyler sent you?"

"Yes."

"Well do as you're told. Take her back to the pod. Get her to rest. You've got ten minutes – understand?"

His orders surprised me, firstly because he had deduced that Tyler had sent me out here, and also because he wasn't going to report us. Wasting no more time, I took Blythe by the shoulder and steered her out of the Annexe, leaving Barnes behind us.

It took us a few minutes to reach the pod. Knowing instinctively that we weren't supposed to be seen by anyone in charge, we took a path which led away from the general thoroughfares of Patrol. Blythe might not be on the duty roster, but she wasn't supposed to be wandering around aimlessly either. Not when we had so many impressionable new recruits here today. Again, I wondered where Blythe had been and why I hadn't come across her in the past three months if she was a Patrol citizen.

Once inside the pod, I helped her to her cot and she laid down. I felt awkward, wanting to offer her comfort, but not knowing what to say.

"Where have you come from?"

The words were out of my mouth before I could stop them and I cursed inwardly, knowing that I could easily frighten her into shutting down altogether and never telling me about herself. She looked up at me, shifting her body in the cot, patting the space she had left beside her. I moved closer and perched next to her, waiting to hear what she had to say.

"I was a Patrol Super. Am a Patrol Super." She seemed to shudder as she corrected herself. "A friend of Tyler's. I've been away though."

I waited quietly, knowing she could continue when she was able to. Her breath came in short gasps as she struggled to remain in control, but I was almost certain that the pain was mental rather than physical. I patted her hand awkwardly in an attempt to calm her.

"I've been away in Meds for almost two years now. I haven't been back to Patrol for so long. Not really sure how to act here anymore since- since-" she trailed off.

"Is it terrible there?" I imagined from her behaviour that

Meds was a difficult place to live, and remembered an Agric Super, Riley, a friend of mine who I hadn't thought about in a while. She had been sent to Meds when I had moved to Patrol, and had seemed extremely nervous. I wondered how much worse it could be than other areas of The Beck.

She shook her head, "No. Mostly it's wonderful. Good food, decent portions, not too much hard work to be done."

"Then why…?"

She sighed. "Don't worry about it Quin. You don't need to know at the minute. Just imagine I'm in recovery from something but will be back to normal again soon, ok?"

I didn't really want to leave it at that, but my ten minutes was running out and I knew I needed to get back. Any questions I had would have to wait for another time. I leaned forwards and tucked the blanket around her.

"Try to rest. It looks like you need it."

She smiled slightly. "I do. It's just that when I lie down, my brain can't relax. I lie awake for hours. I've been that way for a month now."

"No wonder you look exhausted! Why can't you sleep?"

She shook her head, "It's nothing, really."

Seeing her face shut down, I changed the subject. There was one more question I wanted to ask.

"And where does Barnes fit into this?"

She didn't reply, suddenly looking very sad.

I continued to press her, my curiosity getting the better of me. "I thought I was supposed to be keeping you hidden from him – like he would report us for being there, get us into trouble."

"Ah no. He wouldn't do that."

"But–"

She held up a hand which told me the conversation was over. "Shouldn't you be getting back now? Won't you be missed? I'm actually beginning to feel a little sleepy now. If you can let me get some rest, that would be great."

Her voice was still fairly gentle, but had a slight edge to it which told me it was time to go. I stood up, knowing she was lying about getting some sleep, but also that I wouldn't get any more information from her at the moment. Maybe if I left her in peace she would manage a short rest at least. I found myself wishing that I had one of the pills which Cam had given to Fin to help her sleep through the pain of her injured ankle. That would ensure that Blythe managed to get some much-needed rest and perhaps prepare her for being included on the Patrol rotas in the coming days. Because, I admitted as I walked back to the Jefferson Building, at the moment, I couldn't imagine Blythe managing a shift on the wall, in the Hydro Plant, or even in the canteen. And if she couldn't manage an ordinary Patrol shift, I knew exactly what would happen to her.

Chapter Thirteen

I returned to the Jefferson Building to find the groups of recruits being dispatched with their equipment to various pods. I was assigned to a group of girls which did not include Cass. Not knowing whether I was disappointed or relieved, I headed out across Patrol, leading the citizens in the direction of the rear fields. Jackson was nowhere to be seen, having already left with her own group. Our instructions were to get them settled, give them a brief tour of Patrol, then bring them back to the canteen for some food. After that, they would begin their first training session.

The group behind me seemed strangely quiet, until I remembered that this was normality for them. They were used to remaining silent wherever they could be seen or heard, and I was an unknown quantity to them. Also, with a mixture of green and tan overalls, there were clearly different Sectors in the group, and even within the same Sector, no guarantees that they knew one another enough to have developed any sort of trust. I myself had only been absent from Agric for three months, yet the faces in the green overalls were mostly strangers to me. I vaguely recognised two of them, but could not recall their names. They were certainly not from my pod.

I felt a strange mixture of power and sympathy. I held all the cards here for the moment, and was the 'experienced' Patrol citizen to them. I knew exactly how nervous they would be feeling, no matter how well some of them managed to hide it. Transfer was a terrifying process. It required a certain amount of guts, moving to an unknown place where things might be even worse than they had been before. A leap of faith was difficult. Far easier to remain where you were and feel safe, if perhaps unhappy.

We reached the field quickly and I was surprised to see the new pods there. Despite knowing that they were being erected by Mason, Davis, and others that morning, I had passed this empty field so many times that the unfamiliar pods looked somehow wrong. They were mostly in place already; the men working on them were almost finished, and the last pod would be completed before the final group arrived. I looked around for the Super in charge and my heart sank as I noticed it was Donnelly. My new confidence in my superiority as an experienced member of Patrol dissolved instantly when I realised that I would have to deal with him, if only for a few moments.

Telling myself I was being ridiculous, I took a deep breath and marched over. He stood surveying the final pod as it was being hammered into place, a superior look on his face.

"Hey Donnelly," I began, forcing the volume of my voice to be louder than it usually was. "Where am I taking these new recruits?"

He turned and a broad grin spread slowly over his face. Raising both eyebrows, his gaze swept over the girls behind me as though he were appraising their worth. It made me shudder as I looked at the group myself, every face displaying a different degree of embarrassment. A girl with jet black hair towards the back caught my eye. Her expression was quite different. She glared openly at Donnelly, and instead of fear or discomfort, her face was twisted in anger. She caught my eye and dropped her gaze immediately, but I had witnessed a fury in her which surprised me. I turned to face Donnelly, suddenly feeling extremely protective of the new recruits.

Stepping in front of the group, I cleared my throat loudly.

"Ah, yes." He returned his gaze to my face and I swallowed hard. He strolled across to me, consulting his clipboard officiously as he did so. When he was standing closer to me than was strictly necessary, he stopped and bent to show me the list which was in front of him. With the clipboard in my face, his shoulder was almost touching mine and I could smell his slightly sour breath, damp against my cheek as he spoke. I forced myself not to step away from him, knowing that would only demonstrate how awkward he made me feel.

"This is Group Three right? The pods are numbered according to the groups. Number three would be…" he trailed off, placing a hand on my shoulder and leaning across me as he pointed with his clipboard in the direction of a particular tent, "over there."

Through gritted teeth I managed to reply, "Thanks."

"No problem." He slid his hand down until it rested against my lower back and gave me a small shove in the direction of pod number three. Shuddering, I stepped out of his reach and beckoned to the group behind me to follow. As they did, he continued to stare. As the dark-haired girl at the back passed him, he shot a hand out and stopped her in her tracks.

"You." His tone was sharp and he punctuated the words with a finger which prodded the girl's shoulder. "Watch yourself, alright?"

She looked as though she might argue, but I stepped back

108

and took hold of her arm myself before she could. He refused to move as I pulled her away, and when I turned back a few seconds later, he was still staring after her.

Most of the group seemed uncomfortable, but the girl at the rear continued to look vengeful, resisting me as I attempted to lead the group away. Up close, I noticed that her face was pale and her eyes strangely bloodshot. I forced myself to smile as I led them to their pod, determined not to let my own discomfort show and to make the new transfers feel as welcome as possible.

Inside, the pod looked the same as all the others. I left the recruits to get changed and make up their cots, instructing them to wait until I was back before going anywhere else, and went to find Mason and Davis. I found them taking a short break before heading back to the canteen. They were both sweating and looked extremely tired, the long morning erecting the new pods having exhausted them. There was only a small team assigned to the job.

"Hey," Davis called with a warm smile as he saw me.

"Hey yourself."

I threw myself down on the ground beside him and helped myself to a swig from his canteen. Mason joined us a moment later, after stowing their tools in a large kit bag which would have to be carried back to the Jefferson Building. He looked around inquisitively as he approached.

"She's not here yet."

"Who?"

"Jac, who else?"

He smiled ruefully. I knew that he always wanted to see her, and his searching gaze was not hard to interpret.

"She'll be here any minute. In fact, she has to be around

here somewhere, she set off way before me."

Casting an eye across the field, I saw that most of the accompanying Patrol staff were taking the opportunity to grab a little rest before taking the newbies on tour around the Compound. Jackson, however, was nowhere to be seen.

"Where is she?"

Mason sounded worried, but I tried to console him, "She's here. Stop fretting."

A moment later she emerged from a smaller tent across the far side of the field. I knew in an instant that something was wrong. We waited until she reached us before tackling her about it, Mason being the first to question her.

"What?"

She looked at him seriously, not replying for a moment.

"Come on – what's up? You look–" he trailed off as though he were afraid to finish his sentence, as if the news she might have would be yet another crushing blow to our already low spirits.

"The equipment. Did you look at it Quin?"

I shook my head. "To be honest I just came straight out here. I felt so sorry for them all, not knowing what they've got themselves into. I needed some air, or else I might have blurted out something I shouldn't have."

"What, like 'Run for your lives!'" Davis joked, but the smile died on his face as Jackson continued.

"Well yes. Kind of. But I didn't mean the recruits' equipment. I was given an additional bag to haul up here. So were some of the others. Weren't you?"

"No. But I was one of the last to come up. Maybe there weren't any left."

"It was heavy. There must have been seven or eight bags.

They were different than the usual backpacks—made of some kind of tough material I'd never seen before—and I wondered what they had inside them… you know, after the harnesses…"

I thought back to the packs we had hauled over to Clearance on our first trip there. With no idea what we were carrying, we had delivered them to the Shadow Patrol in the Clearance harbour, only to return later that night to find them being fastened on to the Clearance citizens who were about to be dumped into the sea. The weighted straps we had carried had directly contributed to their drowning and although we'd had no knowledge beforehand, I knew that the terrible thing we had been a part of haunted us all.

"So I took the bag to Donnelly and he told me to stow it in one of the storage pods," Jackson pointed to the slightly smaller pods which had been erected at the side of the field. "Once I got inside there was no one else around, so I slid the top of my bag open." She leaned closer. "They're full of weapons."

"Guns?" Mason sounded excited at the prospect. Guns were not items we were generally familiar with here in The Beck. Mostly our defences involved knives and batons, with the occasional electric cattle prod or whip to cause even more pain. Guns were rare. We were told of them in Minors when we were educated about the workings of The Beck, but few of us had ever seen one.

The Beck had some guns, reserved from a time long before our community had existed, when they had been in much wider use. Here, they were reserved for emergency situations only, and left in the hands of Shadow Patrol, who were the only ones trained to use them. Bullets were difficult to produce, and Governance preferred our defences to be built on handheld, reusable weapons as often as possible. I couldn't see them simply assigning one of their most treasured resources to the inexperienced Patrol recruits.

"Not guns. No." Jackson shot him a cold stare. "There were some knives, obviously, but also… I don't know… some kind of bomb perhaps? No, that's the wrong word. Grenades maybe. Explosives, anyway. Small, roundish in shape, and an awful lot of them."

"And you said the bag was made of really strong material?" I asked, thinking back to the protective gloves Montgomery had insisted I wear when handling the pot.

"Yes. Thick and sort of smooth. Not like the normal ones." She raised an eyebrow at me. "You think the fabric was protective?"

I nodded, knowing that transporting the dangerous substance from place to place would require a lot of caution.

"What kind of damage can these explosives do?" Mason seemed torn between the potential danger Jackson had been in and fascinated by the concept of the new weapon.

"If it's something to do with the stuff Montgomery was making, then quite a lot." I sighed. "I'm frightened to even think about it."

"What are they going to do with them?" Davis' question was a practical one.

"Well presumably train the new recruits to use them effectively in combat. Not in The Beck I suppose. They do fine with the existing punishments they have in place already." Jackson looked directly at Mason. "How do grenades work?"

"You throw them. They explode on impact, and if they're filled with some kind of chemical, well…" Mason didn't need to complete his sentence. We could all imagine the wounds that might be inflicted by such a device.

"But this confirms Tyler and Cam's idea that the new recruits are going to be trained differently than we were." I fought to keep the panic from my voice, "They won't just be ordinary Patrol recruits."

"They'll be part of an army." Mason stated the alarming truth. "But the storage pods will presumably be guarded around the clock?"

"I suppose. It wouldn't make sense for the new recruits to have easy access to any weapons."

"Or the existing Patrol staff." I could see where Mason's brain was taking him. "I wonder how many weapons they have in there."

"Not so many that they wouldn't notice if some of them went missing," Jackson's tone carried an unmistakeable warning.

"You're right," Mason's rapid agreement with her surprised me, before he followed it up with a much more predictable reply. "We'd have to be careful."

"No. We are not taking weapons. Not knives, not explosives. Nothing, Mase. We'd get caught."

"Maybe. Maybe not. But don't you think it's important to build some kind of secret weapon stash which the Resistance could use when the time came?"

I chimed in before I could stop myself, "We need to tell Cam and Tyler about this. Governance might have more weapons stashed somewhere else. Perhaps in their compound. Or in Dev."

"And you think Dev are making them?" Again Davis asked the intelligent question, "They could do that?"

"Montgomery could. I've seen her lab."

"So we at least tell the bosses about it," Mason pressed the point. "And soon. How can we do it?"

"See who's on shift with one of them?"

"Probably. Or try to catch one of them during rec tonight."

"I'll do it." Jackson clearly wanted to take charge of the situation and not allow Mason to get carried away. "I think I have a shift on the wall with Cameron tomorrow."

She glanced at me as though she felt guilty even admitting it. Davis didn't miss the look, and scowled as he realised its significance. I pretended not to notice and carried on as normally as I could, hating myself for the jealousy which I felt at the knowledge that Jackson would be working close to Cam tomorrow. It wasn't as though she was interested in him. She'd be far happier spending the day with Mason. And being with Cam myself yesterday hadn't made any difference to our relationship. I promised myself for the hundredth time that I would try and stop caring about him.

"Great." My cheeriness was forced. "Better to tell him than Tyler."

"You realise he may already know," said Mason.

Jackson was quick to reply, "But surely he would have mentioned it last night?"

"Not necessarily. There wasn't a lot of time. Or maybe he didn't want us to know."

"What do you think he'll do about it?"

Mason shrugged, "Maybe nothing, for now. But you're a fool if you think he doesn't see the potential of access to a ton of dangerous weapons in terms of us standing up to those in charge."

I found I didn't really want to think about it. Pushing myself into a standing position, I turned to go.

"Quin!"

I forced myself to look back at Mason, keeping my expression as neutral as possible.

"If they're preparing for war, then we need to. It's just good sense." He shrugged as though he were sorry, but he didn't look particularly apologetic.

Facing the field full of new pods again, I strode resolutely towards number three, determined to give the best tour possible to my group of recruits. All the while I desperately tried not to think about the storage pod filled with deadly weapons, and the idea of us stealing them for use in a battle against Governance.

Chapter Fourteen

The tour took around an hour, and I tried to keep my mind occupied by appraising each new recruit for their suitability for the Resistance. Truth was, it was difficult to discover anything about them. They didn't speak. They followed me like sheep, aside from the dark-haired girl, who continued to brood close to the back of the group. Most of them looked afraid, as though some terrible punishment might descend upon them at any moment if they didn't do exactly as they had been told.

Once we had seen the Solar Fields, the central Patrol pods, the Annexe, and taken several paths through the upper areas of the woods, I brought the group back towards the canteen. We were almost there when someone moved alongside me. It was the dark-haired girl I had noticed earlier.

Out of the corner of her mouth, she hissed, "Is it true we can speak up here?"

I paused for a moment before replying, shocked at her audacity. It had taken me several days to feel confident enough to speak to a Patrol citizen without being spoken to first. "What's your name?"

She hesitated, clearly wondering if her question had been unwise. Eventually, she whispered, "Wade."

I glanced at her. She was not tall, but quite well built,

with sharp green eyes. Thinking back, she had been wearing Sustenance overalls when she had arrived. I wasn't surprised when she turned and met my gaze, a flash of determination in her eyes. Wanting to warn her to be more cautious, I moved my own eyes back to the path before answering. "To some extent, yes."

This girl was certainly rebellious, but I wasn't sure she'd be the kind of rebel that Cam and Tyler wanted on our side. She seemed too openly insubordinate, unable to hide her feelings. I wondered how she had survived so long in Sustenance without attracting negative attention. Like Mason and Cass, she was too passionate and would need to learn to curb her emotions if she was to be an effective part of a fight against Governance. She continued to walk next to me, as though working out whether she should reply or just wait. Eventually, I put her out of her misery.

"You can speak, yes. To other Patrol citizens and other Sectors in the Upper Beck. But not in the presence of those citizens from the Lower Beck, and not while you are still a recruit."

I felt her nod, "Got it." She dropped back into the group as silently as she had approached, seeming to decide that she had pushed her luck enough for today.

Minutes later we entered the canteen. I instructed my group to help themselves to one of the oaten biscuits we usually had around this time of day, noting their surprise at the extra rations and remembering my own reaction to it. Surely this was the key to working out who would make a faithful member of the Resistance: their reaction when they discovered the injustices which were rife throughout The Beck. I watched Wade closely.

Where others rushed to hide their shock, the expression of surprise flashing only fleetingly across their faces, she didn't seem to have the ability to keep her feelings a secret. I watched as shock, and then understanding, and finally disgust dawned on her face. Approaching her, I again felt the need to alert her to the dangers of her behaviour.

She turned to me before I got there, nodding as though we were old friends. I leaned close to her, first making sure that there was no one close enough to listen.

"You need," I whispered, "to hide it better. I don't know what's made you so angry, but letting it show so obviously will get you into trouble."

She leaned away from me, an open challenge in her eyes. "And what if I don't care?"

I leaned past her on the pretence of reaching for a cup of water. "You won't last very long."

Moving away from her deliberately, I walked to the rear of the canteen where Jackson was standing. Concerned as I was about Wade, I knew I couldn't afford to be sentimental. There were already too many people I cared about here, who I would hate to be hurt. I could not allow myself to attempt to protect someone who was showing signs of defiance before she even got started here. I needed to make sure that I wasn't associated with her in any way if she was heading for trouble.

"Alright?" Jackson sounded a little distracted.

"Yes. Though there's a recruit in my group who seems to have a death wish."

She looked more interested now, "Which one?"

I gestured quickly to Wade, who was standing alone, her gaze sweeping the room openly, although I wasn't sure if she was searching for allies or enemies. Eventually she made her way towards a small cluster of women who had not been part of my tour. I saw her nod at another girl, presumably someone she knew from Sustenance. My heart lurched when I saw Cass standing with them. She was staring right at me, and I wondered how long she had been doing so. I managed a small nod at her and she returned it, the ghost of a smile on her face. It was strange to see her dressed in Patrol overalls, and I realised now how difficult it must have been for her the first time she had seen me dressed that way. Familiar, yet alien at the same time.

I forced myself to tear my eyes from hers as people began to move out of the canteen. Our next instructions were to deliver the recruits to the entrance field for their training session. We then had duties of our own to complete and would leave them in the hands of others. I thought back to Fin and wondered if some of them wouldn't last the day. Gathering my own group, I herded them outside and we crossed the courtyard and headed for the field. Despite not really knowing any of them, I felt horribly responsible for their welfare, and as they were greeted by Barnes, Tyler, and some other Supers, I found it difficult to leave.

Returning to the Jefferson Building with Jackson, we checked the board to find that she was headed for the Solar Fields while I was needed down at the Hydro Plant. Well used to preparing for our shifts now, we gathered our belongings and headed off. As I reached the path into the woods I eased into a fairly rapid pace. The recruits had disappeared and there were few people around, those who weren't responsible for the new citizens having headed off earlier. I hoped that my lateness would not frustrate whoever I was taking over from at the Hydro Plant, and that people had been pre-warned about the alterations to the schedule for the day.

When I arrived, I was relieved to find that I was taking over from Dunn, a female Patrol citizen who was very laid back. She didn't seem in the least bit bothered that I was over an hour late, and waved away my apology.

"Will's already inside. Said you could take the first half of the shift on the gate, then switch ok?"

I nodded, and watched as she took off up the hill. I was pleased to be on shift with Will. The only issue with Hydro shifts was that the one guard was required to be posted inside the Plant while the other was outside the gates, so I knew there would be little chance for conversation.

Checking the gate was latched properly, I settled back against it. Shifts in Hydro were dull, at best, and any excitement which might have been provided by the Dev check which had been going on when Jackson had been here yesterday was gone. At least from outside the gates I could see what was going on in the Lower Beck. I enjoyed watching the Agric workers in the fields, remembering a simpler, if hungrier, time when the terrifying knowledge about Clearance was not weighing on my mind.

Agric looked as it always did. Behind it, there were some LS citizens moving livestock around, and a couple of Rep staff were bending over some fencing not far from where I stood. Eventually I turned the other way and watched the wall. From where I stood I could see a couple of sentries on the top, and a larger group of citizens further away who looked to be completing a section of the barbed wire extension to the wall defences. The wall had wire stretched along almost the full length of it now, and I wondered when the project would be complete. I considered how nice it would be to have Cam back up in Patrol more often once it was completed. Then, remembering my promise to get over him, I cursed myself for feeling that way again.

I passed the next hour leaning on the gate, observing life going on around me. I forced myself to keep my eyes off the wall in an attempt to prevent more unwelcome feelings about Cameron from entering my head. The first I knew of a problem was a piercing scream coming from the base of the ladder closest to the Hydro Plant. Instantly I was on alert and scanning the area close by for any potential threat. My hand went to the knife in my belt and I prepared to withdraw it if necessary.

Something was approaching the plant gate from the base of the wall. I squinted, trying to work out what it was, eventually realising that there were three figures coming towards me, one of them being either dragged or carried by the others. All the citizens were dressed in Beck colours, so I seriously doubted that this was any kind of ambush. More likely an injury of some kind. I flung open the gate to the Hydro Plant and waved at Will furiously.

She was by my side in an instant, knife in hand, crouched ready for combat.

"S'okay. I don't think we're under attack." I gestured towards the citizens as they came closer. It was now clearly two human beings carrying another, who was still shrieking loudly.

She relaxed a little. Now they were upon us I could see that two citizens, dressed in the familiar blue of Patrol and the dark green of LS, were carrying a second LS citizen. He was the one screaming. As they finally reached us I recognised Cam, but I didn't have a second to feel awkward as he began shouting instructions at me.

"Water! We need water fast!"

I was slow to react, but Will rushed back inside and began filling up one of the Hydro buckets from the river which cut straight through the centre of the Plant. I stood back as Cam and the other citizen carried the man awkwardly in through the gate. I couldn't tear my eyes away from the man's arms, which were an alarming shade of purple and beginning to blister horribly.

"Get in here now Quin, and shut the gate!"

I obeyed without question and hurried to Cam's side as he lay the man down on the ground as gently as he could. Now I was closer, I could see that the purplish stains covered both of his arms, one as far up as his shoulder, and the leg of one of his overalls was also stained with some kind of fluid.

"Scissors!" The order was barked at me and I sprang into action, lurching for the tool box which lay under the main Hydro operations panel. Will had returned with the bucket of water, which Cam was attempting to get the man to immerse his arm in. The second LS citizen was standing, a look of horror on his face. Cam glanced across at him, a worried expression on his face.

"Duff, get back to the wall. Back on duty. You don't need to stay."

The man's face was pale, but he tried to argue, "But I can't leave him. Can't I help?"

"No. Frankly you can't. You're in shock. Too close to Lewis to be helpful."

"What did you do to him?" Duff's voice echoed, too loudly, through the space. The fact that I had no trouble hearing either of the men was proof of their panic. The volume of the water usually masked voices and made it difficult to hear, but their shouts were loud and desperate.

Cam shot a pleading look at me. I understood instantly. Approaching Duff, I steered him towards the gate. He allowed me to, which I was grateful for. He was a tall man and I was sure if he had resisted I would have had little chance of moving him. Outside, I pulled the gate closed and let go of his arm. He staggered slightly and I caught hold of him again.

"Are you alright?"

He was breathing heavily and a sheen of sweat covered his forehead. For a moment he didn't reply, and then the torrent of words began.

"He was– we all were– testing. Testing the new substance out. Cam was demonstrating– He just– just…" his voice trailed off as the horror seemed to hit him anew. "He spilled some– dropped the pot…"

At these words I made the connection between the pot I had delivered to Cameron the previous day and the gloves I had been carefully instructed to wear. Clearly there had been some kind of accident with one of the pots and Lewis had been in the way. I thought of the horrible purplish stains and shuddered when I realised what I had carried. The screams continued to echo from inside the Plant and I knew Cam would need me back inside. I placed a consoling hand on Duff's arm.

"Look. Cam's right. He's your friend – Lewis, I mean?"

Duff nodded.

"Well then he means too much to you for you to be helpful. The best you can do is get back up there and leave me to look after him instead."

He stared at me doubtfully.

"I promise." I held his gaze seriously. "Promise, that I will stay and help him. I'll do everything I can. He'll be okay."

This seemed to make some kind of sense to him and this time he seemed a little steadier as I released my hold on his arm. Smiling with encouragement, I gestured towards the wall again. After a moment, he seemed to accept my word and began to make his way slowly back to his post. Turning to re-enter the Plant, I hoped I would be able to keep my promise.

Chapter Fifteen

I moved back through the gateway and was by Cam's side a second later, this time a little more prepared.

"What can I do?"

Will was still busy bringing additional buckets of water which Cam was pouring carefully over Lewis's wounds. His screams had lessened in volume and become more like sobs now, and he looked in so much pain that he might pass out at any moment. I prayed that he would. It would at least mean he wasn't in such agony.

"The scissors. And wear gloves." Cam gestured to Lewis' overall leg, which looked even stranger than it had before. Not only stained with liquid now, it appeared to be disintegrating in front of my eyes, melting into the man's leg and the exposed skin beneath looked like raw meat.

I hesitated, unsure of what Cam wanted me to do. He made a cutting motion with his fingers and pointed again to the man's leg. Finally comprehending, I grabbed a pair of protective gloves from the tool box. Sliding them on, I moved closer to the man's lower body, taking hold of the base of his trouser leg. As I pulled the fabric away from the skin, Lewis' screams grew louder. I jerked back, not wanting to hurt him. Cam scowled at me and pointed more forcibly at the leg again. I raised my eyebrows and held out my hands, hoping to convey my discomfort. Cam stopped pouring water for a second and leaned down closer to me.

"You have to remove the material. It's his only chance."

Hearing this, memories of Cam attempting to help Fin cope with the pain of her ankle injury flooded back to me. Of course he would try and help Lewis. He probably felt responsible for him as he was assigned to Cam's project. Cam would want to protect his team, not put them in danger. Add to that the fact that it had been Cam who spilled the chemical, and he'd be desperate to save him.

I leaned forwards again and took the piece of material between my fingers. This time, I pulled firmly on the clothing and managed to peel most of it back in one rapid movement. Lewis screamed loudly, but then stopped a moment later as the intensity of the pain lessened. His cries softened to moans and I was able to begin cutting the overalls upwards along the top of his calf, taking care not to let the fabric brush against his injured skin as it fell away.

I worked like this for several minutes, until I had cut the overalls as far as his upper thigh. The material was not wet there and I assumed the liquid had not reached this far up his leg. Stopping, I repositioned the scissors and cut around the trouser leg, managing fairly quickly to remove the whole lower section of the overalls, leaving his leg free of any obstruction. The job done, I glanced up at Cam to seek further instruction and found him gazing at me, unmistakeable respect in his expression.

I wasn't surprised when he looked away immediately, but it felt good that he seemed pleased with me for a change. Will arrived with another bucket of water and motioned to Lewis' leg this time, looking at Cam for approval. He nodded, and motioned that we should alternate the two buckets of water, sharing their contents between Lewis' leg and arms alternately. I glanced down at Lewis again, noting that his moans had stopped. His eyes were closed, and for a moment I felt panicked, but then his chest rose and I realised that he had simply passed out.

Cam hauled himself to his feet slowly, looking exhausted.

"Can you keep this up by yourselves for a few minutes? I need to contact someone." He freed his radio from his belt as he spoke and began heading for the gate before I had even managed to nod. It felt good that he trusted us to continue without him for now.

Looking back at Lewis, I had more of a chance to actually observe him. Now that his screams were silenced, things were calmer. Surveying his skin, how much of it was affected, the severity of the marks across his body, I didn't hold out a lot of hope. If there was no chance of a girl with a broken ankle recovering, how could someone so badly burned manage any kind of recovery?

Will brought the latest bucket of water over and paused for a moment. She looked exhausted. I realised that she had kept this up: leaning down into the fast-flowing river, hauling the heavy buckets of water up and carrying them across to Lewis, for a long time now. Still, she seemed resolute. But I wondered how much of her resolve came from how the difficult task allowed her to focus her energies on something other than the injured man who lay unconscious in front of us. As she paused to regain her breath and glanced at his poor, ravaged body, a haunted look crossed her face and she seemed to be biting back tears.

I wondered at the people she said she had lost. Was this

bringing back bad memories for her as well as me? Our eyes met for a moment and she shook her head sadly, as though she knew there was little hope for the man on the ground. Then she blinked hard and headed back to the river, determined to continue.

We kept it up until Cam returned. He stood behind me, a helpless look on his face. He was, most of the time, a strong, determined figure. I had never seen him look so defeated. I wanted to reach out and touch his arm, comfort him in some way, but was afraid he would reject my touch. Instead, I continued to pour the water over Lewis' ravaged flesh in the hope that it was doing some good.

Cam took over from Will, who collapsed gladly by my side and took turns with me bathing Lewis' wounds. I wondered what we were going to do ultimately, and where Lewis would end up. My bet was on Clearance, where he would be instantly transferred to the sick pods and stood no chance of recovery without treatment. I wondered why we were continuing with the water, and felt perhaps we were simply making ourselves feel better, refusing to admit that what we were doing for Lewis was only to distract us and reduce our guilt at a later stage. We had tried to help him, we would tell ourselves.

Not long after, I became aware of a fourth presence in the Hydro Plant. I looked up to see that Cam had stopped transferring the buckets to us and was instead conversing intently with a figure in white. Montgomery. Her calm, clinical appearance contrasted sharply with Cam's filthy, sweat-stained overalls. I watched as their conversation grew more heated, Cam gesturing regularly towards Lewis and Montgomery standing, almost immobile, seeming to appraise Lewis indifferently. At length, she approached us and waved me away sharply. Backing off, I stood next to Will as Montgomery leaned down to study Lewis' wounds.

Eventually she opened the satchel she had on her back and took a moment selecting something from inside it. I glanced at Cam as she drew a small vial of colourless liquid from inside the bag. Emotions raged across his face: anger, hope, and a desperation which terrified me. I looked away, back at Montgomery who was applying a small amount of the liquid to a patch on Lewis' arm. She painted it on with a small brush and sat back to watch its results. I saw nothing at first, but within a few minutes the colour of Lewis' skin was less angry and some kind of sheen had formed across the top of the patch, sealing it. I let out a sigh of relief, realising with a start that I had been holding my breath for some time.

Montgomery sat back on her heels, a strange smile on her face. Then she placed the liquid back into her bag and took out another vial and a tiny knife. To my horror, she bent over Lewis again and used the instrument to slice off a section of the injured skin. She slid it neatly into the vial and fastened a lid back on to it. Cam looked sickened at her actions, yet did nothing to stop her. Anger surged within me and I leapt forwards, unsure of what I was about to do. Before I could get very far I felt a hand on my arm and found myself being steered towards the Hydro Plant's control panel.

I realised it was Will, and caught sight of Cam's face as she manoeuvred me away. He looked furious, and I thought that perhaps it had been him who spurred Will to take action. Reaching the relative safety of the Hydro controls, Will took her hand away from my arm and bent over them, as though she were doing the usual checks.

"Stop it."

I had to stoop lower to hear her words. She glanced over at Montgomery, who was studying the sample in the jar as though it were not a piece of injured human flesh.

Will continued. "I don't think she noticed. What were you thinking?" Her expression was anxious, but kind. "Look, I can see how you're feeling, but if you try to make a stand you'll end up where Lewis is going. She's a Super. A Dev Super. Capable of healing wounds. Powerful." She looked at me meaningfully. "You don't want to mess with her."

Shaking my head, I realised she was right. So often I criticised Cass for her hot temper. Only this morning I had been warning Wade to hide her feelings to avoid being noticed. And now I was letting my own emotions get the better of me. A movement to my right caught my eye and I turned to see more Dev staff entering the Plant. Montgomery stood up and motioned to them. She spoke to the two men in white, pointing and gesturing excitedly as she did so. They moved off towards Lewis and began carefully shifting his unconscious form on to some kind of stretcher.

I hoped desperately that they were going to take him away and care for him, but felt doubtful of this fact as I saw Cam's face. An expression of hopelessness had settled over it. For a moment, he looked utterly beaten. Then Montgomery approached and leaned in to talk to him. I didn't like the smile on her face, the way she stood too close to him, her lips only millimetres from his ear. Cam had forced a neutral expression as she approached, and now he actually smiled. A strained kind of smile, but a smile all the same.

I looked down into the raging river again, desperately wanting to be somewhere else. The noise of the rushing water allowed me to block out what had happened momentarily.

I felt a hand on my arm again and knew that Will was attempting some kind of comfort. Presumably she thought I was still upset about Lewis, but now I actually felt worse. How could I stand here fighting jealousy while a man lay dying in front of us? My fists on the railings which flanked the river were clenched tightly and turning white. Will leaned down and loosened them slightly, freeing my grip from the bar as she did so.

The two Dev operatives were now hoisting up Lewis on the stretcher and making their way out of the gate. As Montgomery turned to go, she leaned in to Cam one last time and whispered something further into his ear. He actually laughed as she backed away, the two of them appearing to share a secret joke. I felt sick at the idea of it. Moments later, her willowy figure floated out of the gate, her overalls just as spotless as they had been as she entered. I glanced down at my own overalls, stained a dark scarlet with Lewis' blood, and felt my own anger return with a vengeance.

Will looked across at me, an expression of empathy on her kindly face. "You ok?"

I shook my head.

Without warning, Cam approached from behind and cut across us. "You both want to go? Your replacements will be here soon. I can hold the fort until then."

Will shook her head. "I'm ok thanks. I'll stay." She pointed at me, "She should go though."

Cam avoided my gaze as he replied, "Fine. I'll stay with you until you're replaced. Quin, go."

Wanting to scream, I backed away from them both, nodding my agreement. Seconds later I was heading out of the gate and racing past the Agric fields, my fists balled tightly in my pockets.

Chapter Sixteen

I kept up quite a pace, passing a number of Lower Beck citizens with my eyes firmly fixed on the ground, until I reached the safety of the square. Unless there was some kind of ceremony going on, people here were generally only passing through and I would probably not be noticed if I kept moving. As I turned the corner I saw to my relief that it was completely empty. I forced myself to slow my pace to a walk and found myself gulping huge breaths of air.

The thought of Lewis lying there, writhing in agony as the chemicals continued to ravage his skin, was seared into my memory. I recognised that some kind of survival instinct had kicked in while the emergency had been going on. That I had somehow managed to get through it. I knew from past experience that I was someone who could cope in a difficult situation, however now that it was over, I felt on the brink of collapse. I was dizzy, blood was pounding in my head and I almost felt as though I would faint. Staggering to the side of the square I held onto a wall, taking deep breaths to try and prevent myself from bringing up the contents of my stomach.

Poor Lewis had been in such pain, such agony. It had been utterly terrifying to watch. The power created by Montgomery's chemicals mixed in a particular way. It wasn't knives or whips or electrocution with cattle prods. Nothing tangible. It seemed a cowardly way to attack others. And while I knew that the substance inside the pot that I had carried to the wall was meant for our enemies, I couldn't help but imagine a situation where it would be used on people within The Beck itself. What was to stop Governance from using such poisons against its own citizens?

Having already witnessed the drownings, I knew how cruel Governance could be. If significant developments were being made in the Dev Sector, there was a distinct possibility that Governance would use the new discoveries as alternatives to eliminate unwanted Beck citizens. Would it be neater than drowning them? I imagined a situation where a large number of Beck citizens were fed a meal containing something deadly. Given water which was poisoned. Harper's face flashed in to my head and I thought again of Lewis. Leaning over the gutter at the side of the square, I heaved, until the contents of my stomach lay splashed all over the ground.

Straightening up, I felt better. It was just another reason which would strengthen my resolve to get out of here. And surely it was having the same effect on Cameron. But as I thought of him, my fury returned. He claimed he was building a Resistance. A group of people who could fight against the injustices suffered by everyone in The Beck. And I wanted so badly to believe in him.

But to be so close to Montgomery, who was the creator of the substance that had destroyed Lewis today? To accept the use of such a vile substance, knowing the damage it could cause? I knew that he had to participate in certain endeavours which he didn't agree with, in order to further the cause of the Resistance. I understood that, for the greater good, he had to ignore his personal feelings and pretend he was on board so those in Governance continued to trust him. But how far would he actually go? How many individuals would he be prepared to sacrifice, in order to save The Beck citizens as a whole?

Hearing some other citizens approaching, I forced myself to move off again, leaving the square and taking the path which led to the woods. I passed some Patrol Officers I recognised and forced myself to nod a greeting. Once alone again, the torment returned. What was hard to take was the fact that, deep down, I cared very much for Cameron. Despite the distance he had put between us since my induction into Patrol, despite the questionable things he was involved with, I found that I couldn't hate him. I was disgusted with myself for still caring about him, but there it was. After today though, I wondered how well I really knew him.

Maybe he didn't understand what Montgomery was capable of, I tried to tell myself. When she had taken Lewis with her, it hadn't been to help him. I had seen the fascinated expression in her eyes, and it had contained no compassion for Lewis. She did not look upon him as a human life, as precious as any other. She saw him as an intriguing reaction to an experiment. And Cam had been working with her for weeks now. Weeks of time spent in Dev, inside her laboratory. For a moment, it crossed my mind that perhaps they had even worked together on the substance in the pot I had carried to the wall.

But I couldn't believe that. I couldn't believe that Cameron was actually capable of creating a substance which was able to do so much damage to a human being. Lewis was only the first Beck victim. Who knew how many more there would be? More accidents involving Beck citizens who were simply following orders, entirely innocent of what was going on. I considered our enemies, those who came across from other places. We were told we had to fight against them. And maybe we did. Certainly, if they were trying to steal from us or hurt us we couldn't just welcome them in.

Yet I couldn't let go of the idea that maybe some of these people were just like us. I wanted desperately to believe that there were other societies out there who would not simply want to attack or steal from us. Other communities which were run differently from ours in The Beck. Run better. Places where citizens could be free and have a fair and equal chance at everything. I sighed. Cameron was trying to save us from the terrible society that we lived in. He had to consider all the options: fighting Gov, or running from them. In the past The Resistance had tried escaping from The Beck, but had so far been unsuccessful. We had no idea how many others were out there, or if they would be friendly. No doubt some of them would not be. At the moment, Cam was biding his time, trying to work out the best course of action. I had to believe that whatever he did he was trying to improve the situation for us. He had told me it was difficult; that sometimes his role required him to do things he didn't agree with. If he didn't do them, I wasn't sure who would.

I slowed my pace slightly as the incline became steeper and the path entered the woods. I hadn't gone far into the trees before I heard footsteps behind me. Pounding footsteps, from a person who was sprinting up the hill towards the woods at an extremely rapid pace. Stepping to one side, I waited for the runner to pass me by, not wanting to hold them up. At the last moment though, the footsteps slowed and came to a sudden stop. I turned, expecting it to be Mason or Davis, someone I knew from Patrol who wanted to run back up there with me.

Cameron was standing behind me, a wary expression on his face. Disgusted, I faced away from him and began to jog up the hill again.

"Quin."

I ran faster.

"Quin!"

Faster. His footsteps pounded behind me again and I knew he would easily catch me. I cursed his speed. I didn't want to see him or speak to him at the moment. I was still so angry and confused, I had no idea what I would say. But I had a feeling he wouldn't give me much of an option.

He caught up and we jogged alongside one another for a while, saying nothing. I certainly wasn't going to start the conversation. He stayed in step with me until we reached the edge of the woods, where he slowed his pace. I kept going, pulling ahead, until he spoke.

"Quin. Can we talk?"

I stopped in my tracks, no longer able to contain my ravaged emotions. When I turned he had disappeared, but upon closer inspection I saw that he had simply retreated behind a crop of trees, presumably to avoid us being seen in conversation. I strode behind the trees to find him waiting, a guilty expression on his face.

"I'm so sorry you had to be involved back there. Will you let me explain?"

"Will you stop trying to shield me from all the evil in The Beck please Cam?" I spat the words at him, "I'm not a Minor and I don't need protection. I need the truth."

"I know." He was quiet for a second and held up his hands in a defeated gesture. "I just wish there was some way I could spare you knowing about some of the horrendous things which go on."

"We've been through this! You said you wouldn't shut me out anymore. I want to be a part of this Resistance, whatever form it takes. You have to trust me."

"I know."

"You'd tell Tyler, wouldn't you?"

He nodded.

"And what about Montgomery?"

He looked confused, "Montgomery?"

I turned away, not wanting him to see my jealousy.

"Look Quin, you deserve an explanation. I can't tell you everything… but I'll tell you what I can." He stepped towards me. "How's that?"

I shrugged, not wanting to reply. He lowered his body to the ground and sat resting his back against a tree, motioning for me to follow. I didn't.

"Fine. Have it your own way."

"I will." I cursed how childish I sounded and a moment later I slid to the ground next to him, feeling him visibly relax beside me.

"Look, Montgomery is a brilliant scientist. Better educated than you or I. She's been developing a range of chemicals for different useful purposes around The Beck. A lot of those are for defensive use."

He paused, as if waiting for a reaction. I stared at the leaves on the ground around us.

"Ok. So Gov had me working with her, planning the potential uses for the deterrent paint she gave to you yesterday – in the pot you brought over to the wall?"

I managed to nod.

"Well it's nasty stuff, hence the need for gloves. I'm not

certain I agree with its widespread use, but..." He trailed off, seeming at a loss for a moment. "Anyway this afternoon, while we were painting a coat of it on to the barbed wire above the wall, there was an accident."

I couldn't prevent myself from interrupting. "What does it do?"

He looked at me, his face clearly grateful that I was at least reacting to what I was being told.

"It's nasty. It burns the skin horribly. But it's meant for our enemies. Gov instructed us to strengthen our defences against the people who want to attack us, so we have done as they asked. It means that the wall is not only higher because of the wire, but it will also savagely burn the skin of anyone attempting to scale it. And deter others from trying, obviously. It further secures The Beck against attack."

"But it's no good if it's used to burn the skin of The Beck citizens, is it?"

"No. It's not. But what happened today was an accident, I promise you."

"And what if the people attempting to get here over the wall are not enemies? What if they simply want to reach out to us?"

"Look Quin, there may well be people out there who are friendly and would want to work with us, but they're not all like that. We have to be sensible. We know people from the outside have attempted to steal from us in the past. Gov want to stop this from happening. They feel that the wire and the paint are a sensible extra layer of protection for our society, and who am I to argue with that? They put me in charge of the job, which means they trust me. Can't you see that I need them to believe I'm working with them? No matter what my beliefs are about people outside the Beck, the task on the wall has the added bonus of getting me inside Dev and communicating with some of the people there."

I sighed. "You certainly seemed to know one person well."

Again he looked at me, confused. "Do you have something you want to say?"

I shook my head no and gestured reluctantly for him to continue.

"So I got to know Montgomery. She's brilliant, and we might well be able to use her, or at least the things she is making, in our Resistance efforts. So I've been trying to keep her onside. Getting along with her. Because although I don't like her or trust her, the Resistance might find her skills very useful in the future. We can't afford to make an enemy out of her."

"Clearly."

He ignored my sarcasm. "So when the paint was spilled over Lewis today, I brought him to the Hydro Plant because it was the closest place with an accessible water source. When I radioed for help, the crew who turned up came directly from Dev. Montgomery has developed a serum which treats the burns inflicted by the paint. It kind of eases the pain and swellings. Lewis was badly hurt, had burns over a large percentage of his body, but I was hoping that Montgomery would have enough of the serum and be prepared to use it to help Lewis."

"And she did. Sort of. Was she taking him back to Dev to heal the rest of his burns?"

He hung his head, afraid to even meet my gaze. "No."

"Where did she take him then?"

He continued to look at the floor.

"Cam?"

"Well I don't know for certain."

"Don't try and hide it from me. You're lucky I'm even speaking to you right now."

"I know."

"I don't understand you. You kiss me. Then you ignore me for weeks. Then you say you want to protect me. In a way you don't seem to protect anyone else."

I waited for an answer, but none came.

"Cam – where did she take him?"

"Oh she took him back to Dev. But she refused to tell me what she was going to do with him."

"I don't understand."

"Only that she didn't have enough serum to heal him entirely."

"Then might she have enough to heal him partly? Could she make more?"

He shook his head. "I don't think so. It takes time, and a lot of ingredients, to create. Some of them are incredibly difficult to come by, and she won't be able to get enough together in time to…"

"You're lying to yourself. It's not that she can't. It's that she won't. The Beck won't. The life of a single citizen is not worth it."

"Well isn't she right? Can we justify the cost of producing a large amount of the serum just to save one life?"

I stared at him. "Are you serious?"

He remained silent.

"Do you seriously believe that Lewis' life is worth so little?"

"No. Of course not. You just watched me trying desperately to save his life?"

"I did. But now you seem happy to abandon him."

"No. That's not what I'm saying. I'm just saying that The Beck won't allow him to live. And I have to think of the Resistance. I'm in a good position now. They trust me. I have access to so much more than I had a year ago. Things that will make a huge difference to us when we're ready to face up to those in charge. But not yet."

We stared at one another, clearly at an impasse. Cam reached out a hand and took hold of mine, very gently.

"Look Quin. You have an amazing capacity to care for others. And you're tough. It's what I love about you. But you miss the bigger picture. If I try to fight them now, for Lewis, for a single life, I will lose. They'll send him off to Clearance anyway and possibly me alongside. And then where would we be? As it is, I'm trusted by those in Governance, I have allies in most of the Upper Beck Sectors, and I'm privy to so much useful information. You have to be able to see how great that is for us in the Resistance when we fight them in the future."

Ignoring the way my heartrate had increased at Cam's touch, I forced myself to shrug. "You didn't really answer my question."

A puzzled look crossed his face.

"What is Montgomery going to do with Lewis?"

He sighed. "I'm not sure. I wasn't lying when I said she wouldn't tell me. But I think she's curious to see the effects of the healing serum. We've never had anyone suffer burns to that extent before."

I jerked my hand away from his. "You mean she's using him to test the stuff? Experiment on him?"

He didn't reply. Unable to take in the implications, I leapt to my feet.

"I can't– can't believe you'd condone this!"

"I don't–"

But his words were lost as the image of Lewis stretched out on a table with Montgomery leaning over him filled my head, his screams of agony silenced by the sound-proofed chambers of the Dev Compound. And Cam, knowing it was happening and doing nothing. I took off up the hill through the woods, running as fast as I could, trying desperately to block out the uncomfortable thoughts. I could hear Cam calling after me, and was desperate for him to follow, to grab me and pull me into his arms and tell me it was all going to be ok.

He didn't.

Chapter Seventeen

That night as I walked back to the pod I felt totally drained. Since I had returned to the Patrol Compound I hadn't stopped. There were extra duties linked to the arrival of the new recruits, which meant that all Patrol staff were having to take on short, additional shifts guarding the field with the new pods in it or supervising the recruits as they went from place to place. Until they completed their Patrol Pledge Ceremony, they had to be closely guarded and were not trusted to roam freely around the Compound. After dinner, I sat for two dull hours outside the pod I suspected contained some kind of terrifying explosive created by Montgomery.

I realised that in the chaos of the incident with Lewis, I had failed to tell Cam about their existence. I also wondered if we would often be placed on solo shifts from now on. With so many new recruits there were simply not enough of us, and certainly not enough Supers, to cover all the different duties if we were doubled up as we usually were. I considered the fact that solo shifts might make it easier to steal some of the weapons for ourselves, then dismissed the idea, wondering how on earth we could safely conceal such dangerous items.

When I reached the pod it was fairly quiet, most people having already washed and collapsed into their cots. Jackson was still awake.

"How was your shift?"

I busied myself changing out of my overalls and rearranging my blankets for a moment before replying. "Eventful."

"Oh! How?"

"It's a very long story, but," I lowered my voice to whisper level, not wanting the others to hear, "there was an injury on the wall and we had to try and deal with it."

"What kind of injury?"

"Burns."

Jackson's eyes widened in the darkness, "You mean from the–"

"Yes. It's horrible stuff."

There was a pause as she took the information in. "And the citizen injured?"

I shook my head. "It was pretty bad. He was taken away."

"Clearance?"

"No." I didn't want to say the words, knowing what they might imply. "Montgomery took him to Dev."

Jackson was not stupid. She took a moment to let my words sink in, but understood their negative implications. "That's terrible."

I didn't answer.

"Was Cameron there?"

"How did you–?"

"Your face. You look sad as well as angry. Like he let you down again."

"Well he did."

"How?"

I hissed at her, "What do you mean how?"

"Ssshh." She cast a cautious glance around the pod, but no one seemed to have stirred. "Are you angry that he didn't try and save this man?"

I nodded.

"I knew you'd feel like that. Can't you see? Cam has to let it go. He's working towards an enormous goal here. He can't afford to put one citizen's life above everyone else's."

"That's what he said."

"Well then he's right." She paused, her expression softening, "Quin you always expect so much from people. It's what makes you who you are, but your expectations are so hard to live up to. Life's far from perfect. Cam is trying to improve things for everyone. And at times that's going to mean there has to be some kind of sacrifice."

I hated that she was repeating the exact same sentiments as Cam had earlier. Coming from her they were more difficult to dispute.

"What happened to this guy is terrible. Tragic. But if Cam had tried to help him, he would have lost the trust of those he has worked so hard to gain, and probably would have ended up in Clearance himself. How bad were his burns?"

"They pretty much covered both his arms and one of his legs."

"That sounds awful, but you know The Beck wouldn't spare a thought to try and help or heal him. If he had only been a tiny bit injured then maybe it would have been worth trying to help him, but as it is..."

She trailed off, not finishing the sentiment. I thought about Fin being dragged off to Clearance. Lewis had been as badly injured as she was, probably worse. Would he have been able to return to health if Cameron had risked his life to save him? I knew that he wouldn't. Sooner or later he would have ended up in Clearance and any fight would have been for nothing.

I sighed. Jackson' reasoning was hard to challenge. She was calm and rational and, above all, right. I only wished that I could have recognised this when I was with Cameron.

"Are you ok?" Jackson sounded concerned.

"Yes. Just realising that you're right. And I was awful to Cam. I ran away while he was trying to explain."

She reached across the small space between our beds and squeezed my hand. "He'll understand. Eventually."

I wished I agreed with her. Managing a small smile, I turned over and faced the other way. Within a few minutes I heard her breathing deepen and knew she was asleep. I closed my own eyes and drifted off, praying that I would manage to rest free from my nightmare tonight.

When I woke up, it was still dark. Too dark for it to be morning. Something seemed wrong. Jackson was still sleeping soundly in the cot next to mine, and a glance across at the others told me no one was out of their bed. A rustling from the doorway of the pod alerted me to a presence outside. My mind ran through the possibilities. It was unlikely to be Mason, since Jackson usually arranged when they would meet and would certainly not allow herself to sleep if they had plans. None of our other podmates had people visiting them at night, to my knowledge. I wondered for a second about Cass, who had been caught sneaking to see me once before. I hoped she had not decided to try it again so soon after being transferred here.

When the canvas was pulled back, a shaft of moonlight fell across the beds closest to the gap. The figure in the doorway stepped inside and headed for my cot. I tensed for a moment, but as he came closer I relaxed, realising who it was. Cam was by my side in seconds, his stealthy footsteps sure of their progress through the tent. He didn't speak, but beckoned me to follow him. After a moment's hesitation, I did.

Once we were outside the pod, he set off in the direction of the woods. I moved with him, unsure as I did of whether what I was doing was a good idea. When we were safely under the cover of the trees, he handed me a spare set of overalls which I slid into, thankful for their thickness in the cold air. Only then did he speak.

"Will you let me show you something?"

Feeling far calmer after my conversation with Jackson, I knew that I had forgiven him for his earlier betrayal. Hoping that this would lead to a reconciliation of sorts between us, I nodded.

"Are you up for running?"

Despite my earlier tiredness, the brief period of rest had refreshed me, and I also felt intrigued by where he was taking me.

"Yes. Let's go."

We set off, racing down the path together. We stayed side by side, although he couldn't have been running at his fastest pace, or I would never have kept up. A companionable silence settled between us and I could tell that he was happy that I had agreed to accompany him. But at the back of my mind I was aware that there was still some tension within him, suggesting that what he had to show me was not something I would be comfortable seeing.

When we reached the Lower Beck, Cam slowed down and took the path which led toward the Dev Sector. At this point I began to wonder what we were doing here. Just before we were in sight of the Dev gates, he ducked into the trees at the side of the path. He looped around until we were

148

standing at the back of the Compound, behind the fence through which we could clearly see the Zone Three building, where Montgomery's lab was situated. Only then did he turn to look at me.

"Are you ready for this?"

"For what?"

"I thought about what you said today and realised that you were right."

"No! Cam – I was talking to Jackson. She calmed me down. You were right. There's nothing we can do for Lewis that won't get us both into a ton of trouble. And we need you. The Resistance needs you. I get it now. You don't have to be a hero. Not for..."

"Not for you?" He smiled wryly in the shadows. "Well it's not just for you. Maybe a little, but you're not the only reason I'm doing this. And," his expression changed, "we're not here to be heroes."

"Then why are we here?"

He sighed, "Do you trust me?"

I nodded.

"Ok. Well you'll see. But you have to promise not to try and stop me."

He took a set of bolt cutters from the bag he carried on his back. Within seconds he had made two small cuts through the wire and lifted a section of it for us to crawl beneath. From there it was a quick sprint to the doorway of the Zone Three building, where he took a pass from his pocket and used it to open the door.

"Won't that identify you?" I hissed in the darkness once we had slipped inside. "Why cut the wires and then use your pass?"

He held the pass up to my face, shining a dim shaft of light on it from his lantern. The pass belonged to someone called Randall. Stolen or borrowed, if the Dev guards tried to work out who had broken in here tonight, they would be looking for the wrong person.

I followed Cam down the corridor, passing Montgomery's office and stopping at the next door along the hallway.

"There's rarely anyone working in here at night," he said.

"Have you been here a lot?" I asked tentatively, curious to learn more about the Dev Compound and how closely Cam had been working with Montgomery, despite my fears.

"A few times. Mostly I only came here to pick things up from Montgomery. Usually when I visit Dev I go to Zone One, where they hold meetings."

I sighed with relief. It didn't sound like he had spent hours working on projects with her then. She was the scientist; he was the man who put her experiments into practice.

"I attended a few discussions about new ways we could be protecting our assets here. They were interested in hearing my ideas. That's where I met Montgomery. She was another of the people they consulted, only where I was practical, she was theoretical."

Turning his attention to the door, Cam bleeped us access, again using the fake identity card. It struck me that Randall must be fairly senior if he had access to Montgomery's lab. The door swung inwards silently, revealing nothing but darkness. Grabbing my hand, he pulled me into the space beyond. Once inside, he let go of me and secured the door.

As our eyes began to adjust, I could see we were in a room much bigger than Montgomery's office. This one had a lot more free-standing equipment within it and seemed to be better equipped for larger experiments than the room next door. Cam flicked a switch and the room was lit by an eerie glow.

"I don't want to risk putting all of the lights on. We'll keep to the emergency ones, they'll give us plenty of light for what we have to do."

I was unused to lighting which was instant. In Agric everything was done by hand, our only lights provided by flame-lit lanterns. The greenhouses were the only area of Agric which benefitted from the Hydro Plant's electricity, a generator constantly keeping them at a steady temperature. In central areas such as the Canteen and the Assessment Buildings power was more commonly used, but even then only for certain periods of time. The ovens in Sustenance were powered by electricity for their operations in the hours preceding a meal, but these were turned off once citizens had eaten, and the Assessment Compound only required power when the tests were taking place.

In Patrol we had more electricity usage, where the main buildings had power for most of the day and the pods were sometimes lit in the dark early mornings and late at night by battery-powered lamps. But here in Dev, it appeared they had round-the-clock access to electricity for whatever experiment they were currently completing. I marvelled at how important this Sector was considered by Governance. And it wasn't just the lights which required power. The entire room was filled with noises which could only be created by machines: constant bleeping and whirring sounds filled the air.

Now I could see better, I looked for the source of the noise. My eye was drawn to a raised table towards the rear, with a number of machines humming gently around it. Each one had a display of some sort with various numbers flashing up, recording something. On the table itself was a figure covered by a sheet. I realised immediately who it was. Cameron, less daunted by the room than I was, had already made his way to the table and was bending over it cautiously.

Dreading what I would find when I joined him, I inched my way slowly across the room, telling myself I was only being cautious, but knowing all the while I was simply putting off the moment when I would see Lewis up close and discover what Montgomery had done to him.

Chapter Eighteen

"Is he-"

Cam turned to look at me, his eyes sad. "Dead? No."

"That's good."

He didn't look as though he agreed.

Lewis lay, covered with a white sheet which ran from under his chin to his toes. His face was pale, but otherwise he looked fairly normal from where I was standing. I had begun to believe he might survive after all, when Cam placed his hand on the top edge of the sheet. Respectfully, he took the material between his finger and thumb and began to peel it slowly back, revealing the rest of Lewis inch by inch. I bit my lip to avoid crying out as I noticed the horrendous burns which still branded him. His upper torso was unaffected, but both of his arms were a lurid purple colour, the edges of the burnt sections of skin beginning to flake and peel away. I shuddered at the sight of his ravaged body.

"How is he not awake? In pain?" The question had plagued me ever since I had realised it was Lewis. "Surely that hurts. He should be screaming like he was earlier."

Cam pointed at a metal stand next to the bed. Some kind of see-through bottle half full of liquid was fixed to it, and my eyes followed a tube from the bottle which snaked down towards the bed and ended taped firmly to a point on Lewis's

153

arm where it fed into his body. The clear tube stood out starkly against the alarming scarlet markings of the burns caused by Montgomery's chemicals.

"Some kind of drug. It's fed constantly into his system and keeps him unconscious."

Removing the sheet from Lewis's body in reverse only revealed the same: his leg was also badly damaged. Angry scars stained the majority of the skin, aside from several small patches where it looked slightly less inflamed and was a different colour.

Cam pointed at them. "That's where she's applied the healing serum."

"But she only used it once this morning."

"So we were right. She's used it again since he was brought back here. And perhaps different strengths. Look at the differences between the patches."

I bent closer and began to see what Cameron meant. Some of the patches of skin looked almost normal, whereas others were a slightly darker colour, but looked like they had started to heal. One of them was almost black in colour though, and the skin on this small section had begun to disintegrate. I recoiled in horror.

"She's testing different substances on him!"

Cam nodded. "Different strengths at least. You were right. And it's barbaric. I had to check, but…"

His voice trailed off, a note of desperation entering his tone. "What?"

"Well I wanted to find out if this was what she was doing, but I didn't want to believe it. I had a plan if this were the case, but I was hoping so badly that I wouldn't have to put it into practice."

I waited, knowing that he would go on.

"But I guess I'm going to have to."

"So what's your plan?"

Cam reached inside his backpack again and pulled out a small bottle.

"I've been paying more attention to Montgomery than she realises. This is a dose of the same thing that's inside that bottle."

"So?"

"It's a far stronger dose." Cam hesitated, as though he were waiting for me to react.

It took a moment, but I thought about the liquid which had the power to suspend a human body in sleep. I knew that horror was etched on my face as the realisation dawned on me.

"You mean…?"

He nodded sadly. "When you said you didn't know how I could live with myself if I let Lewis be used in some kind of experiment, you wanted me to save him." He took a deep breath. "Well I can't save him."

My eyes filled with tears as I realised what Cam was suggesting.

"But you can stop her from experimenting on him."

"Yes. You understand how?"

I thought for a second. "I get it now. Jackson made me see… you were right about staying focused on the end goal." He looked at me hopefully as I continued. "I think maybe we have to face up to this. But this… tonight… well, I didn't expect it. You're… trying to stop Lewis' suffering. You didn't have to do – you could have left him here. You're risking so much."

He grabbed my hand, "But you were right too. I have to at least try something. I couldn't stop thinking about what you said. His suffering–" He hung his head. "But this was the only solution I could come up with."

I squeezed his hand. "I think it's the best we can manage."

He returned the squeeze and then, letting go gently, turned to face Lewis. He hesitated for a moment, devastation carved into his features. Keeping my gaze on his, I stepped forwards and pulled the sheet back down over Lewis' body, smoothing it out carefully until he looked exactly as he had earlier. I moved to the top of the table and placed my hand against his cheek, which was still warm. With the cover across him he looked like he was just sleeping. Cam's haunted eyes followed me, their expression unchanging despite my attempt to show him support. I could see what this was doing to him.

A sudden thought crossed my mind, "Won't Montgomery know?"

Cam seemed to jerk out of his trance. "Know?"

"Know that his drugs have been tampered with."

"Hopefully not. The fact that she's testing the different serums on him tells me she doesn't know what their effects will be. I'm hoping she just assumes that he either died of his injuries or one of the drugs affected him badly."

"OK. What do we have to do then?"

He looked across at me, his face bleak, yet determined. "This isn't 'we', Quin. It's 'me'."

"Oh no."

"Yes. I don't expect you to participate."

"Then why bring me along?"

"I brought you because… because…" his voice softened, "I can't bear to have you think badly of me."

I bit back the tears that threatened my eyes at this comment. "Well I don't. But you can't do this by yourself." I stared at him. "I don't want you to."

Ignoring my plea, he dropped his gaze from mine, moved towards the metal stand and took down the bottle containing the liquid. He twisted a dial on the side of the container, detached the tube and held it aloft, looking around for somewhere to place it without the remaining liquid spilling out.

"You see," I said, coming forwards to stand beside him, "You do need me."

I took hold of the tube gently. At first, he wouldn't relinquish it. I could sense the battle raging inside him. Eventually he let go and allowed me to stand next to him, the tube gripped tightly in my fist. For a moment, he didn't move, clearly racking his brain for some way to proceed that didn't involve me. Finally he turned his attention to the bottle, turning it right way up and unscrewing the top smoothly. Placing it on a tray to one side of the trolley, he took the smaller bottle from his pocket and tipped its contents into the existing container. Within seconds he had refastened the top and took the tube back from me, securing it and replacing the refilled bottle on the stand.

We stood back.

"Is that it?"

He shook his head. "No. I have to turn the dial to start the feed into his system again."

"Do you want me to–?"

"No. You've done enough Quin."

We stood together, staring down at Lewis. He looked peaceful again now his wounds were covered, and it was hard to imagine what we were about to do to him was necessary.

"Tell me there's no other way." Cam's voice was choked. I had never seen him like this before. I moved closer, taking his hand in my own.

"There's no other way."

Tears were coursing down my own face without me realising that I had started to cry. Cam let go of my hand. He stepped forwards and took hold of the tube, closing his eyes. A moment later, he turned the dial sharply. Then, with a deep breath he returned to my side, taking my hand again.

"I hope you're at peace now, Lewis," I whispered, feeling the need to say something, though I wasn't sure what was appropriate. "We're so sorry."

We stood for what seemed like forever, but it could only have been a few minutes. Lewis' face didn't alter, his body remained still, but eventually, the slow, regular bleeping of the machine increased in pace until it was racing. It became a relentless high-pitched shriek which reverberated around the laboratory, a desperate echo of the searing pain inside my head. The unbearable sound seemed an inappropriate way to mark Lewis' passing and I knew Cam agreed as his body went rigid. I tightened my grip on his hand as a new terror struck me.

"Montgomery might get notification of this! Might be checking on him. Cam – we need to go."

For a moment, he didn't move and I thought I was going to have to hit him to break him out of his stupor. But slowly, he tore his eyes away from the table and turned to look at me. I was alarmed by the intensity in his eyes as he squeezed my hand until it began to hurt.

"Don't let go."

Together we backed away from Lewis, Cameron replacing the bottle in his pocket and pulling out the Dev pass. He waved it over the control panel at the entrance and the low clicking noise told us the door was now unlocked. Easing it open, we peered out. There was no one in sight. We slipped through and pulled it shut behind us, creeping down the corridor to the exit as fast as we could without making any noise.

Within seconds we were out of the Zone Three building and crossing the empty yard. The compound remained silent as we passed through the open space and headed for the broken fencing. Sliding under it, Cam re-secured it behind us and we took off up the hill, running faster than I thought possible. No sirens cut through the darkness around us, there was no sound of racing footsteps, or voices raised in anger calling after us. Soon we were in the woods, under full cover of the trees, and still we did not stop. We moved as though we could outrun our guilt. The fear and devastation at what we had done spurred us on, chasing us through the dense trees.

Cam stopped when he reached the clearing close to the Patrol entrance and leaned heavily against a large tree at the side of the path. I slowed to a walk and approached with caution, not knowing how to broach the subject of what we had just done without angering him.

When I was a metre away from him I stopped altogether, with no idea of how to respond to the look of utter desolation he wore. We stared at one another, unmoving, for several seconds before he managed to choke out some words.

"I never– I didn't–"

Closing the final gap between us, I wrapped my arms around him, holding him as tightly as I could, as though I might rid him of his sadness if I could get close enough. Dry sobs racked his body. I could feel them beginning, erupting from somewhere deep inside him and sending shudders through his entire being.

When he let go, it happened suddenly. Leaning away from me slightly, he bent his head towards me and I knew he would kiss me. But after weeks of waiting for this moment, I felt bitter regret at what had led to the contact I craved. I tried to pull away, not wanting the tenderness I had previously felt with him to be tainted by the tragedy that we had just witnessed. I didn't manage to resist for long.

He pressed his mouth closely to mine. His kiss was so unlike it had been the last time. He was hungry, desperate, breathless, as he deepened the kiss and moved closer. He pressed himself against the entire length of my body, his arms, vice-like, imprisoning me against him. I cried out as his lips crushed mine so fiercely it hurt. Behind it all I was painfully aware of his despair. His desire to kiss me so aggressively was only motivated by his need to escape the terrible events of the past few hours. In the back of my mind, I was devastated that it had taken such shattering circumstances to bring us back together. Despite this, my own breaths grew shallower as I allowed myself to be swept away by the strength of the feelings coursing through me, also welcoming the chance to forget.

Chapter Nineteen

After several minutes locked together, our lips moving over one another's intensely, the pain returned. Slowly, the horror of what had happened with Lewis crept back into our thoughts, and the contact between us was broken. To begin with, the desperate embrace had been enough to erase the depressing thoughts, but eventually our kisses were no longer enough to rid us of the guilt. Cam was still leaning into the tree, but I felt him withdraw. I stepped away in response, sensing that we needed to put a little distance between us.

Touching a cautious hand to my bruised mouth, I winced slightly. The embrace had been far more powerful than our previous one, but it had been filled with anger too. I found myself studying his face breathlessly, trying to work out what to say to mend the damage. Coming up short, I remained silent, not wanting to make the situation any worse.

Finally, it was Cam who broke the silence. "I know what we did was… was necessary. I just can't feel good about doing it."

I nodded. "Have you ever…"

He cut across me, "No. I have never had to kill another human being before. Not even an enemy. And Lewis wasn't–"

"You didn't kill him."

He remained silent.

"You didn't. You can't hold yourself responsible."

161

"I can. And I do." His voice had taken on a different tone now, which matched the rough intensity of his embrace.

"But–"

"No." His words allowed no argument. "No Quin. I just administered a drug which ended a man's life."

"Yes, but it was the kindest–"

He cut across me. "Maybe, but that doesn't make me feel any better."

I shrugged, not knowing how to comfort him.

"And I'm sorry." His eyes were fixed on the ground now and he refused to look at me.

"For what?" I dreaded his answer.

"For this… for what just happened between us."

"Sorry because you hurt me, or sorry because it happened?"

He sighed, "Both."

I turned back to face Patrol. The sun was beginning to rise, and a faint light leaked through the trees into the clearing. It was almost morning. Trying to hold on to some kind of hope, I breathed in deeply before turning back to Cam.

"Ok. You're sorry. It's been a difficult night." I paused, willing him to look up at me, just once, before I left him. "What happened with Lewis was awful, just awful."

He continued to study his feet. His face was impassive, a shield. I had no idea how he was feeling, but I pressed on, not knowing what else to do.

"But I'm not sorry."

Still, he didn't respond. I waited another few minutes, hoping he would at least look at me, smile, react in any way. He didn't. Before turning to leave, I made a last attempt to reach him.

"I'm not sorry. I'll never be sorry."

Delivering my parting shot without breaking down took everything I had. After I finished speaking, I took off immediately in the direction of Patrol, not wanting to see Cam's lack of reaction. I was racing again, as fast as my feet could carry me. I listened, desperate again for Cam to call me back, but the air was silent other than the rustling of the trees in the light wind.

Back at the pod, everyone was still asleep. I had perhaps an hour before I needed to be up and ready for duty, and I knew I needed sleep. Lying down on my cot without bothering to remove my outer overalls, I let the exhaustion invade my body and was away within seconds.

When I woke, Jackson was standing over me, her face etched with concern.

"What happened to you last night?"

I stared up at her, feeling nothing but an overwhelming urge to let myself drift back into unconsciousness. Allowing my eyes to close again, I tried to turn away from her enquiring gaze.

"Quin!" She shook me none too gently. "You have to get up. It's late!"

I heard a moan escape my lips and found I wasn't capable of stringing words together to explain my behaviour. Giving up on speech, Jackson leaned down and pulled off my blankets. Placing an arm around my neck, she hoisted me into a sitting position.

"Look. You're coming with me. Now. We don't have time for you to mess around. If you're ill we can deal with it, but we have to go."

Finally, her words sank in and I realised the necessity of getting up. If I didn't report for duty it would be noted, and questions would be asked. Hauling myself off the bed, I allowed her to lead me out of the pod to the wash tent. We limped the short distance together. Once there, she stood me in front of a basin and splashed the water over my face and neck. The cool liquid began to bring me round.

"Sorry." I managed to mutter. "I can't tell you now."

"No, you can't. There's no time. We have to get you up and moving, then down to the canteen in the next five minutes."

Straightening up, I threw a final blast of water over my head and shook myself free of the drops of liquid. Inhaling deeply, I forced my thoughts away from Cameron and the events of the previous night. Walking with what I hoped was purpose, I left the wash tent and began moving towards the canteen. Jackson followed, and as our feet traced the now familiar route we took every morning, I felt her push something into my hand. Glancing down, I saw a small cube of sugar in the palm of my hand. I had no idea how she had managed to steal it; sugar was a real luxury saved for special occasions, even in Patrol, but I was immensely grateful. Hoping it would provide me with the extra energy Jackson intended it to, I pressed it into my mouth surreptitiously as we passed the pods closest to the Jefferson building and entered the canteen.

Once inside, we collected our daily ration and went to sit with Mason and Davis, both of whom looked concerned by our late arrival. Thankfully, although they had noticed we were later than usual, no one else seemed to. We were able to gulp our breakfast down rapidly and catch up with the rest of the Sector. The canteen seemed more cramped and much warmer than usual. I realised that the new recruits had joined us and were seated at several additional tables which had been crammed in at the rear of the room.

"Ok?" Davis enquired of me towards the end of the meal.

I found myself glad of his concern for the second time in as many days. Managing a small smile, I nodded.

"Sure?"

"Well not really, but it's nothing I want to talk about at the moment," I whispered, loudly enough for only him to hear me.

Underneath the table, he reached over and squeezed my hand, a gesture which I would have usually appreciated. Today it only reminded me of my unsuccessful attempts to comfort Cameron, and I pulled away, ignoring his hurt expression. An awkward silence fell as we cleared away the plates.

Once we had finished, we headed for the work assignments board to check where we had been placed for the day. I was desperately hoping for light duties, fighting the exhaustion which threatened to overtake my body as I stood waiting for the other citizens to move. Among the group I noticed Blythe, who looked paler than ever but was, it seemed, due to begin proper shifts again today. She looked even less capable of work than I was.

The crowd thinned out as people began to hurry away to prepare for their assignments. Finally reaching the front, I looked at my pod list and found my name. Instead of the usual listing, the text next to my name stated simply 'See Super for duty assignment.' I had never seen this before, and glanced around for a Super who could tell me where to go. There were very few people around now. I began to panic that I wouldn't be able to find anyone to help me in enough time to prepare myself.

I wandered into the main thoroughfare of the Jefferson building and saw a familiar figure hurrying towards me. Tyler.

The look on her face told me that she was the Super I needed to see. As she reached my side she looked serious, and jerked her head for me to follow her back outside. Once we were away from the building and out of earshot, she turned towards me.

"Cam said you'd be tired and need some extra rest today."

I looked at her, wary of how much she knew and unwilling to answer before I worked it out.

"I've managed to find you an assignment with me in Meds. Now it's usually only Supers allowed there, but with the way things are at the moment– the new recruits taking up so much of everyone's time and energy– it's been allowed, since you'll be with me. I've told them I need extra help shifting some equipment around."

"Meds?"

I was surprised. Meds was a closely guarded compound, and Tyler was right that only Supers, and certain female Supers at that, were permitted on guard there. Once we left the Meds Sector at the age of five, the place became a distant memory to most of The Beck. Most remembered little about it. We knew it was where babies were brought into the world and the youngest children were cared for. We knew that certain Supers were assigned to the Sector to live and work for different periods of time before they were returned to their original Sectors. But what went on there was a real unknown.

"Yes. Meds. It should mean that I can find you a bed for a couple of hours and you can actually rest."

"Thanks," I managed, grateful that Cameron had at least realised how tired I would be this morning. Clearly he wanted to ensure that I was given a chance to recover from the events of the previous night. It didn't make me feel any better about the way we had left things, but at least he seemed to care a little about me.

"I have a couple of things to do before we leave. Go and change into a fresh set of overalls and meet me at the entrance to the woods in ten minutes."

She was gone before I could respond. Making my way back to the pod, I considered the situation. Meds, like Dev, was another Sector which fascinated me. I wondered, despite my tiredness, if I would be able to take a look around, or whether I would simply be assigned to a room to sleep in or an entrance to guard. I thought about Riley, a Super from Agric who had really helped us when Harper was ill. She had been transferred to Meds at the same time I moved to Patrol. I wondered what the three months there had been like for her.

Jackson stood anxiously at the entrance to our pod. I knew she was looking out for me.

"Where did you go?"

"My assignment – Tyler gave it to me."

"Where are you today?"

"Meds."

I watched as her eyebrows shot up. "Meds! Really? Why?"

"Remember when Mason was whipped and needed to take it a little easy? Cam and Tyler made sure that he was able to rest that day and didn't put too much pressure on him–protected him?"

"Uh-huh."

"Well let's just say I didn't get a lot of sleep and Cam has made sure I've been assigned somewhere that Tyler can make sure I get a little extra rest."

167

"Really? What happened last night?"

I shook my head. "I can't get into it now. It was awful." I had to pause and breathe slowly to prevent memories of the previous night from overwhelming me. "I promise I'll tell you, but not now."

She accepted this quietly. "Ok. But be careful today." She too paused, as if she were unsure whether or not to continue. Then, quietly, she said, "He must care a lot about you Quin."

Now the tears came, and I was unable to stop them.

"Quin! I'm sorry – what did I–?"

Moving past her into the pod, I began to rummage under my cot for a fresh pair of overalls. Anything to allow me a moment to regain control. Jackson followed me, clearly even more concerned than she had been a moment ago. She waited patiently while I slipped out of one pair of overalls and into another. When I was ready, I turned to face her again.

"Sorry. It's just– well I don't think he does care that much about me, not in that way at least."

She reached out and squeezed my hand. "I'm sorry. We can talk later ok? He's right. You'll feel better after some rest."

"Where are you today?"

"Mason and I are with the new recruits. Weapons training." She turned to leave.

"Jac?"

"Yes?"

"Will you– I mean I haven't had a chance to check on Cass. I know you don't know her, but I wondered–"

"Yes, of course. I'll see how she is if I can."

I managed a small smile, "Thanks."

She returned the smile and disappeared out of the pod. Reaching down to collect my dirty overalls for drop-off at the laundry, I noticed I wasn't alone. Blythe lay quietly on her own cot, so pale and silent that neither Jackson nor I had noticed her. As our eyes met, I could see that she had been crying.

"Are you ok Blythe?"

She nodded.

"Can I help you at all?"

With a shake of her head this time, she pushed herself up to a seated position. Brushing off her overalls, she didn't take her eyes away from me.

"Did you say you were assigned to Meds?"

"Yes."

A look of agony crossed her face.

"Blythe, are you ill? Can I get you anything? I'm with Tyler today, perhaps she could–"

"No. She couldn't. But thank you."

I needed to go, as did Blythe, who surely had a shift somewhere too now she was back on the duty rota. But something held me there for a moment longer, the sad expression in her eyes made me wait.

"Quin. Tell Tyler– tell her–" she broke off for a moment and I thought she might start to cry, but at the last moment she bit her lip and managed to continue. "Tell Tyler to check on Perry please. Like she did the last time."

"Right. Perry. I will."

Feeling terrible for leaving her but knowing that I had no choice, I turned to go. At the last moment, wanting to give her some support, I stopped.

"Blythe, where is your shift today?"

"I'm on a canteen rotation. Light duties to begin with." She gave a short, humourless laugh. "Help me to recover and get

169

back to it!"

I wondered what she meant. In The Beck people were not usually given the luxury of recovery time from illness, not officially anyway, which was why my own shift today was so surprising. But I couldn't worry about that now. I waited another moment, holding Blythe's gaze.

"Don't worry Quin." She stood up as she spoke. "I'm going. I won't miss it."

I comforted myself that the canteen was the closest possible rotation she could have been given. She was now standing as though she was ready to leave, so I had to trust that she would see the sense in attending her shift. Attempting a smile, I set off to meet Tyler. The exhaustion I felt had abated somewhat while I had concerned myself with Blythe's situation, but now I turned my attention to myself again, I knew that I desperately needed rest. Plodding through the pod field on my way to the woods, I prayed that the bed I had been promised in Meds would be accessible, and that I could use it for at least a few hours without being caught.

Chapter Twenty

Tyler and I headed through the woods together in silence. I had no idea how much she knew about what had happened with Lewis the previous night, and didn't want to give anything away just in case. She was wrapped up in her own thoughts and didn't question me. We walked down the usual path until we had made it almost halfway to the Lower Beck. At this point, Tyler changed direction abruptly and moved off down a path I had not encountered before. It was almost hidden from view behind a large crop of willow trees, and I suspected this was purposeful. Citizens were curious, and signposting the entrance to a Sector they wanted to keep fairly private was not a good plan.

The path wound through the trees on a fairly level plain until we reached a section where it sloped upwards fairly steeply and plunged into some thicker woodland. Like Clearance, the trees hid it from view and if I hadn't been following Tyler I doubted I would have believed the path led anywhere at all. We hiked upwards for a while in silence, making our way through the dense trees which I was certain completely concealed us. At the top, I was surprised to see a parcel of land which was almost flat, and flanked by more cliffs, far steeper ones, on all sides. The space was filled with two small buildings and a number of pods similar to the ones in Patrol.

I did not recognise the place at all. It was completely unfamiliar to me, despite me knowing that this was where I had been born. Confused, I turned to Tyler, who had anticipated my question.

"Meds has two sections. Area Two, the second one, you would remember. It's where the older babies are taken once they're weaned. You will have lived there from the age of one until you were around five years old, before you moved to Minors. This is Area One, where the very youngest and most vulnerable of our society live."

"But how? I didn't even know they were two separate places."

"It's purposeful. They know we remember little from the ages of birth to five, so they allow most citizens to believe that Meds is all one place. Think back though – can you ever remember seeing a new-born baby during your time in Meds?"

I thought for a second, casting my mind back. "Well no, but I always assumed they were kept separate from the toddlers and the older children."

"And that's what they count on us believing. It helps to keep this place more of a secret. Protects it." She pointed to the two buildings as we approached them. "The one on the left is for the assigned recruits during the conception process and their gestation period." I blinked at the new terminology. Tyler laughed, "Never mind. You'll understand later. The one on the right is where the babies are born and reared until they are ready for transfer to Area Two."

A thought struck me. "Blythe asked me to pass on a message."

172

Fear clouded Tyler's features as I mentioned Blythe's name. I continued cautiously, unsure of her reaction. "She asked if you could check on Perry. Like you did last time."

Tyler turned away without replying. "Let's go."

I followed, my feet just about managing to keep up with the rapid pace that Tyler set.

"Will you?"

"Will I what?"

"Check. On Perry."

"Yes." She sighed, "I will."

With no further information forthcoming, I tried again, desperately curious. "Who's Perry?"

There was no reply. We were close to the first building now and I wanted to discover who the mysterious Perry was before we encountered other citizens and the chance was gone.

"Is she another Super? Transferred here? A friend of Blythe's? She just transferred back from here, didn't she?"

"Yes, she did." Tyler pushed open the door to the first building, the one she had said housed the Supers who lived here before the babies were born. We entered a building much smaller than the Jefferson, and not unlike the one I had been inside in Dev. The walls were whitewashed and a hallway led away from us with a number of doors leading off it.

Tyler knocked quietly on the first door. A voice from within called something, and we entered. Sitting behind a desk in what appeared to be some kind of office was a woman dressed in the vivid turquoise overalls of the Meds Sector. She smiled as we entered.

"Hey Tyler."

"Hey Ellis. Quin here is with me for the day, but I wondered if the den was free?"

Ellis nodded, pulling a key from the desk drawer beside her and handing it to Tyler. "Yes of course. I'll make sure it's not used for the whole morning if you like?"

"That would be brilliant. Thanks. I'll take her down there now."

"Wait." Ellis stood up and reached into a fridge behind her. "Take this, she looks like she needs a little looking after."

She handed a package of something to Tyler, who accepted it with a smile and moved away.

"Thanks," I added, speaking for the first time. It seemed like Ellis was trusted and I wanted to show my appreciation for the care she was showing me.

She looked straight at me for the first time. "No problem Quin. You look like you need a little support today. Just make sure you follow Tyler's instructions and you'll be able to rest here safely."

She sat back down at the desk and continued with her work. Tyler led the way out of the door and walked me down to a room at the far end of the hallway. Unlocking it swiftly, she slipped inside and motioned for me to follow. The room was only a little larger than the office we had just been in, but contained a bed and a couple of comfortable looking chairs.

"I don't have much time – I was supposed to take over from the current duty Super five minutes ago." She pointed at the bed. "Rest. Get some sleep. I should be able to leave you here undisturbed for a couple of hours, but then you'll have to vacate the room and help with some of my duties, ok?"

"Ok. Will no one come in here?"

"They shouldn't. We can trust Ellis. She's helped us before. I'll lock you in and no one should disturb you. If they do, they won't be able to get inside, and Ellis will be able to warn me if someone comes looking for the key. Use the time to rest." She handed the small package to me. "Enjoy these. I have to go."

Abruptly Tyler left the room. I heard her turn the key in the lock and for a moment I panicked a little about being imprisoned. Reasoning that she was only trying to protect me, and that it was Cam in fact who had wanted me to have this chance to rest and recover, I sat down on the bed. Unwrapping the package, I discovered something which looked a little like the oatcakes we received in Patrol, although they were a slightly different colour. There were two of them. Taking a tentative bite, I discovered they were far sweeter than the ones I was used to. Within minutes, I had consumed them both, relishing their sweetness as it filled my exhausted body. Then, unable to do more, I lay down. As I drifted off to sleep, I wondered if Cam was managing to rest in the same way, or if he was battling on with his duties on the wall project, shutting all his grief and anger away inside himself. I shuddered at the thought.

When I woke, the room was just as quiet as it had been previously, and I wondered about the peace which seemed to reign in this hidden corner of The Beck. A gentle glow of light filled the room, filtering through some kind of material which was fastened over the small window at the side of the den. The bed I lay on was larger than the cots I had witnessed in any Sector, and I felt fantastically rested, despite the sadness which returned the moment I remembered the events of the previous night.

Straining my ears, I began to hear soft sounds, the shuffling of feet and muted tones of conversation. This building housed the Supers who were on temporary transfer from their usual Sectors. It seemed like a lovely environment to inhabit, yet

I wondered what lay beneath the surface. I was too used to finding out the terrible secrets hidden in our community to believe that this small section of Meds was as good as it seemed. I thought about Blythe: her sadness and her reaction to Barnes. She had just returned from a year or so here. What could be so bad about it? Or was it, I reasoned, simply that she yearned to be back here because it truly was the paradise it appeared to be?

I pulled myself to my feet, stretching the kinks out of my muscles as I did so. Walking to the window, I released the catch which held the material in place. As it released, I was able to pull it aside and see outside. The room I was currently in appeared to face the rear of the compound. Behind the building was a small, grassed area, where several women dressed in long white tunics were hanging washing out on a line. Their clothing was unusual. I had never seen anything like it before. Instead of trousers which enabled their legs to move freely, they wore a kind of skirt which covered both legs in one section and billowed out around them, travelling down to their ankles. It made them look ethereal and beautiful.

Other women were sitting on the grass together in various poses, and I began to notice the differences in their shapes. While some were as slender as the typical Beck citizen, others had stomachs which swelled out in front of them, to differing degrees. They were, I realised suddenly, carrying children. New lives, babies, who would be born into The Beck to replace the citizens they had drowned in Clearance because they were no longer useful. The thought filled me with horror. Not that I resented the presence of the babies, they would be entirely innocent, but the thought that we as human beings were so totally replaceable was horrific. And the idea that these babies were being born into The Beck, with no concept of the life that lay in wait for them, made me furious.

There was a noise at the door and I dropped the window cover quickly, guilt plastered on my face as I returned quickly to the bed. The door opened slowly and Tyler peered in.

"How are you? You look better."

I tried to smile. "Yes – these beds are like nothing I've ever known."

She chuckled. "They certainly know how to treat the citizens who are sent here. Meds is a nice Sector to be assigned to," she paused for a second, and worry clouded her face, "well most of the time anyway."

"It seems like it."

"Want something else to eat? The food here's better too."

"Definitely!" I stood up quickly and took a step towards her.

She laughed again. "Someone's hungry! Ah – and you've obviously tried and liked the cookies." She smiled at my confused expression. "The food in the package? They're delicious, aren't they? Well, I guess all that sleep has brought you back to your usual self." She became serious for a moment, placing a hand on my arm, "I'm glad. I was worried you'd completely lost your spirit this morning."

Feeling slightly uncomfortable being so close to Tyler, I shrugged awkwardly and stepped past her into the hallway. She followed me out, making sure to lock the door, and I waited while she returned the key to Ellis. Once she had, she led me through another door to a canteen, which although much larger than the room I had left, was nowhere near the size of the canteen in either Agric or Patrol. Clearly there were fewer people to feed in Meds.

Tyler motioned to a bench close to the door and we sat

down opposite each other.

"It's almost lunchtime," she said, "They'll all be here soon."

"Lunchtime?" I queried.

"They get three solid meals a day." Tyler grinned ruefully, showing she didn't resent their extra rations, "another way they try to soften the idea of a Transfer here. The extra food is necessary though."

"Why?"

As she responded, the door opened and a group of women entered, their long tunics flowing behind them. They appeared to glide across the room and congregated close to what I presumed was the serving hatch.

"They're growing babies. They need all the strength they can get. Even if they didn't simply deserve additional rations for that, Governance wants all the babies born as fit and healthy as possible, and that begins with how well they grow inside their mother's body."

I nodded, speechless at the idea of a new life growing inside my own body.

"It's a great place to live. So many advantages. The women here are treated really well. But it has its downsides too. That's why I prefer to simply do the odd shift here. Experience the advantages for a little while without any of the agony."

As I was about to question her about the agony she spoke of, a figure appeared behind the hatch with a large tureen of something which appeared to be steaming hot. My attention was distracted and I felt my stomach rumbling.

"Hot food? In the middle of the day?"

Tyler snorted a laugh at my disbelief, "Yes. Hot food. In the middle of the day."

I was astounded. In Agric we had only been allowed two

meals per day, morning and evening, unless there was a very special occasion or reason for extra rations to be assigned. Even in Patrol, where we did get rations in the middle of the day, it was usually only bread and fruit, certainly I had never eaten anything hot unless it was porridge at breakfast or the evening's stew.

"Coming?" Tyler pushed herself to her feet and stood waiting expectantly.

"Really? We can eat too? I'm not carrying a baby."

She burst out laughing again. "No. But I told you – it's an advantage of working a shift here."

"But I haven't done any work!"

Tyler took my hand and pulled me gently towards the serving hatch. "I'll make sure you do some this afternoon then, happy?"

I let her lead me to the front of the room, passing by a short girl who seemed almost as round as she was high. She smiled shyly at me, while I tried not to gape at her huge belly. I felt Tyler behind me, impatiently moving me towards the food. At the hatch, I took a bowl of delicious smelling stew filled with a number of vegetables I knew had to have been brought up from the Agric greenhouses at this time of year. The stew also contained meat, a huge luxury, and not the kind of scraggy, stringy meat we often experienced in Patrol, but huge chunks of what looked like beef, swimming in the thick brown gravy of the casserole. Add to that a large, soft bread roll which even contained some butter, and I was in heaven by the time I spun round to return to my chair.

As I did, I almost ran headlong into two people standing in the queue behind me. With a start, I recognised one of the figures. Clothed in the same billowing gown as the other women, deep in conversation with another Meds citizen, was Riley. The last time I had seen her she had been out of her Agric bed illegally (just like me) the night before her transfer. And she had seemed quite terrified of the move.

Chapter Twenty One

I stopped and stared at her, remembering the trepidation with which she had approached her Transfer. Now, watching her face, she seemed serene, calm, happier than I had ever known her. Meds must not have been so bad after all. I found myself curious, wanting to speak to her and find out what had happened to her since her move. Concerned that she wouldn't recognise me, or that I had no right to speak to her as a visitor to Meds, I hesitated. She hadn't seen me yet.

As I wavered, she glanced across to see what was holding the queue up and her eyes met mine. For a second she seemed confused, unable to place me, but then a smile blossomed on her face.

"Quin!"

Her greeting was loud and exuberant, not a sign that we should be nervous of speaking in public. This area of Meds was becoming more like heaven, the more I learned about it. Delicious food, the chance to rest in comfortable beds and now the ability to converse just as freely as we did in Patrol, perhaps even more so.

"Hey Riley, how are you?"

My reply was a little lower in volume, and her grin broadened at my caution.

"Good thank you. Let me get my food and I'll come and sit

with you. Where are you…?"

I looked around for Tyler, who was waiting impatiently by a table close to the rear of the room. Nodding towards her, I checked that Tyler understood, and continued towards her, feeling the line of women behind me grumble at the delay.

Within minutes I was tucking into the delicious food. It was far superior to that which we got in Patrol, which was in turn better than the food in Agric. Further evidence of the inequalities of our society, although I could forgive Governance for providing better rations to expectant mothers who surely needed the extra sustenance. It made sense to provide the next generation with the best chance of health and strength, qualities which were essential for survival in The Beck.

When Riley joined us, she beamed at me and nodded a silent greeting at Tyler, who returned the gesture slightly less enthusiastically. We sat and ate for a while in silence, enjoying the good food, the warm and comfortable surroundings, the peace which infused the room. All the women here seemed content, whatever stage of pregnancy they were in. Some did not look to be carrying a child at all, others had stomachs which swelled gently, and a further set drifted like over-inflated balloons around the room.

When we had almost finished eating, Tyler broke the silence.

"How do you two know each other?"

Riley grinned again, "We're old buddies from Agric."

"Buddies?" Tyler's tone was curious.

"Friends. Allies. You know what I mean Tyler."

I started at Riley's easy mention of the Patrol Super's name. How did she know her? And then I realised that Tyler had mentioned loving the shifts up here. There could not be too many women living in Meds at any one time: presumably it wasn't difficult to remember all of them.

"You two know each other?"

Tyler was quick to answer, "Not really. I met Riley a couple of months ago when she moved up here. I know most of the citizens here by name at least."

Riley continued, "Tyler's one of the good ones. We like it when she's on shift."

Tyler fought a smile and I found myself grinning too. Riley had always been a very positive Super, preferring to praise citizens rather than doling out the endless sanctions and cruelty favoured by others. That didn't mean she was naïve. She understood the severity of the punishments here, she just tried not to let them get her down. She had been an endlessly supportive figure during my friend Harper's illness in Agric.

Tyler stood up abruptly. "Time for me to continue my shift. I'm going over to the ward. Riley, bring Quin over to me when you've both finished."

I realised that, despite the gruff way the order was given, Tyler was attempting to be supportive and leave the two of us alone to catch up. I turned to smile my thanks, but she was already several steps away, her back rigid and her step rapid. Sighing, I turned back to Riley, unsure that I would ever be able to work Tyler out.

"How're you finding the rations here?" Riley's grin was back again, and broad.

"They're unbelievable. Who would have known that such food existed?"

"I know. Makes me want to stay here forever…" She trailed off, sounding sad all of a sudden.

"What's wrong?" I ventured to ask.

She shook her head briskly, "Eat up! Might as well take advantage while you can. Who knows the next time you'll be up here." I opened my mouth to argue but she held up a hand. "Not now. When you've eaten I'll take you the scenic route to the ward. We can talk then."

I accepted her explanation and focused on finishing my meal. She was right that it made sense to take advantage of good sustenance while it was available to me. As someone who was only up here as a favour, I had no idea if I'd ever set foot in Meds again.

Once we were finished, we cleared our plates and headed outside. Riley led me around the edge of the building and we ended up in the area I had been looking out at earlier. It was empty now, except for a couple of birds which flew off hastily, startled at our sudden approach. Riley took a seat underneath a tree and motioned for me to follow suit.

The sky seemed a lighter grey than usual and the trees provided shelter from the breeze of the day. The small grassy area was warm and pleasant, seemingly designed for relaxation and peace. I was beginning to realise how difficult it would be to lose all this if you were transferred up here and then sent back to your old Sector. I also wondered how those moving back to their previous Sectors didn't spread the word about how wonderful it was up here.

Riley's voice cut through my thoughts. "How's life in Patrol?"

"It's... different." I managed.

"I'll bet it is," she snorted a laugh, but there was no mirth in it this time. Her voice softened, "Have you seen Cass at all?"

"Yes. Actually she had herself reassigned to Patrol. Tried

out in the recent recruitment drive."

"You don't sound happy about it. Surely it'll be nice to be together again?"

"I suppose." I took a deep breath, "I'm just worried she'll get herself into trouble."

She nodded. "I remember that temper of hers." Her voice dropped even lower, "And what about Harper?"

I turned away, forcing my voice to remain calm. "Clearance, as you know. We went over there as part of Patrol training. It's awful."

"You saw her?"

I found I couldn't answer her, so nodded tightly and changed the subject. "What about you – here? You seem happy."

She considered me closely before answering. "I am. But only... only because I don't allow myself to be anything else." I stared at her, confused. "It's lovely here. Perfect, almost. But I know I'm only here for a little while. So I try to enjoy it and forget about the time when I'll have to leave and go back to Agric, or somewhere... somewhere else."

"Clearance?"

She nodded sadly, "Maybe."

"But why?"

She shrugged. "A large number of the women who live here don't cope well when they return to their old Sectors. We're made to take a vow of secrecy when we arrive, to prevent us from sharing too much about the Meds Sector. Citizens tend to think the lack of information means that life here is awful. I certainly believed that. You saw me the night before I came here. I was terrified. But when you get here you realise it's the exact opposite. It's extremely difficult making the transition in reverse."

"But why? Are the women too used to the luxury?"

"No. That's not it. What happens to us here can be amazing, but it can never have any kind of happy ending. In fact it can drive you crazy."

I thought suddenly of Blythe, and began to understand. "Riley, do you know a girl here called Perry?"

She frowned, puzzled. "No. There's no one here with that name."

"Are you certain?"

"Yes. I know everyone. There aren't many of us."

"What about a citizen called Blythe? Did you know her?"

Recognition dawned on Riley's face. "Yes. I certainly did. But how– oh, I see, she's back in Patrol now?"

I nodded. "Yes. I met her recently."

The clouds darkened Riley's face again. "How is she?"

"Well I don't pretend to know her very well, but I'd say… not good." She waited for me to continue. "She seems… unhappy. I've seen her crying. She's pale… she looks exhausted. They gave her a rest period when she first came back–"

"That's normal."

"But now she's meant to be back on normal duties and I'm not sure she'll cope with them. It's like she's forgotten how to function in Patrol."

Riley sighed. "A year is a long time to be away."

"How can I help her?"

"You probably can't. Tyler will try. She knew her before, I think. Blythe was a really good Super in Patrol, from what I hear, but…"

"But what?"

She hesitated, seeming unwilling to respond at first. "I told you. What happens here changes you. Hurts you."

"But you said life here was amazing!"

"And so it is, but leaving here... leaving them behind is... well... difficult." She bit her lip and looked away.

"Them? Do you mean the friends you make here?"

She shuffled a tiny bit closer to me, taking my hand in hers. "Do you understand why we are brought here Quin?"

"I... I think so."

Taking my hand, she brought it towards her. At first I thought she was attempting comfort, but she gently steered my hand towards her stomach. As I made contact with her body, I couldn't stifle a gasp. Beneath the loose gown, the flesh swelled out just a little. At first I flinched away from her, but she smiled gently and I found my hand drawn back to the warm, comforting bump.

"Are you...?"

She nodded, "Yes. Only a little bit. It takes nine months for the baby to grow and be ready, but they think I'm around two months gone."

I had assumed that Riley had not been here long enough to be carrying a baby, but here she was, her body clearly demonstrating the presence of a tiny person growing inside her.

"I'm very lucky. It doesn't work so quickly for some. In fact, for some it doesn't work at all."

"What happens to those women?"

"They get sent back to their old Sector." She shrugged. "As long as they keep their mouths shut about life here they can generally go back to their old way of life."

Riley's hand still rested with mine on her stomach. She sighed. "In a couple of weeks, I'll start to feel the baby moving.

It hasn't happened yet – it's too early – but I've seen it with other women. It's magical. That a life is growing inside you and you can feel it getting stronger every day."

I didn't know what to say. I was finding it difficult to take in everything that she had told me, everything I had witnessed so far today in Meds. She smiled, sadly this time, and removed my hand.

"It's difficult to understand if it isn't happening to you." She hauled herself to her feet, taking a little more time and care getting up from the ground than she used to. "Let's get you to Tyler. I think you're supposed to be helping her this afternoon rather than talking to me."

She moved off towards the second Meds building, which I assumed contained the ward Tyler had spoken of. Reaching the door, she pressed a buzzer not unlike the one I had seen on the gate in the Dev Compound.

"I'm not allowed in. Access for mothers only, and those in labour of course."

I didn't have time to ask her what she meant as the door swung open, revealing an older woman in turquoise overalls.

"This is Quin. Tyler's expecting her?"

The woman nodded. "I'll take her in."

Riley turned to leave, embracing me quickly. "Hope you never get assigned up here Quin. No matter how good it looks." And then she was gone.

The woman inside motioned impatiently for me to follow her and made sure I pulled the door completely shut behind me before she led me into the hallway. The building was similar to the one I'd been in this morning, except the entrance hall was small and there were only a couple of doors leading off it. I understood why as soon as she opened one of them and led me inside. The ward behind it was huge: much larger than the canteen in the other building. It housed several beds ranging along the walls, each of which had a small crib at the base.

The woman didn't stop here, however, but led me between the beds to a smaller, curtained-off section at the back of the ward. She thrust the heavy material aside quickly and motioned for me to enter. The space did not contain more beds, but was filled instead with cribs. Tyler was standing over one at the far end, and beckoned me over as the Meds citizen hurried away.

I hesitated before walking towards her, not knowing what to expect when I reached the crib she was standing over. As I looked down into it, I couldn't help but smile at the tiny human figure lying clothed in white blankets. As if it sensed the approach of a stranger, the baby opened its mouth and began to wail loudly, so I almost didn't hear Tyler's introduction.

"Quin," she said, her voice tinged with sadness, "this is Perry."

Chapter Twenty Two

I stared at the tiny child in the crib. It took a moment or two, but eventually my brain caught up. "You mean–? The baby…" I trailed off, unable to finish the sentence.

Tyler nodded, "She's Blythe's."

I reached out to the child lying tangled in the blankets, her feet kicking away as though she was fighting to escape their constraints. My hand looked giant next to hers, and she screamed even louder as it came close. But once I touched her, stroking a finger over the smoothest skin I had ever felt, she stilled, wriggling her own fingers as though she were trying to reach out for me.

"How old?"

Tyler paused before she answered, working it out. "She'll be about… about 9 weeks now."

"So up here in Meds, once the baby's born…?" I trailed off, unsure that I wanted to discover the answer to the question in my head.

"The women are allowed a short respite period once their babies have been delivered. Mostly this is spent resting and recovering their strength, but they feed the babies themselves for some of that time. Then, when judged fit, they're sent back to their original Sector."

"And their baby?" I was afraid I knew the answer.

"Stays here."

"Oh. I thought maybe Blythe was ill. But she's…"

"She's… grieving. Women feel a huge attachment to their children. I think it's inbuilt… natural. Getting over the separation from their babies, well… it's not easy."

And finally what Riley had been saying sunk in. She was pregnant herself. She would live here in relative luxury until it was time for her baby to be born. And then she would be expected to have the child and leave it here.

"We've got work to do." Tyler moved away from Perry's crib. "Let's talk as we walk."

She circled the small area, checking each crib briefly before returning to my side. Reaching into Perry's crib, she lifted the child out and cradled her gently in her arms.

I followed her as she moved out of the curtained area, rapidly passing through the main ward and out into the hall again. Choosing the second door this time, she entered the other main section of the building, which was filled with more babies, and two additional Meds staff, each one seated on the floor with a particular child. The room was filled with sights and sounds that were alien to me: some of the babies calling out, making sounds which were not yet words; some crawling about the softly matted floor; some sucking greedily from bottles of milk.

Both women looked up as we came in. One of them smiled a welcome, the other was less friendly. Tyler moved through the room, stepping carefully between the small bodies. She paused when she reached the more pleasant of the two.

"Hey, Perry's due a feed. Can I leave her with you?"

The citizen nodded. "No problem. I'm almost done here. She can be next."

Tyler smiled in response and placed Perry down on the floor gently. She yowled a little as she was transferred to the mat, as though she felt the abandonment, missing the warmth of Tyler's arms.

"She'll be fine," the woman registered the look of concern on my face. "I'll get to her in just a minute."

Tyler frowned at me, as though I should not have been judging the way things were run here, and I felt a little aggrieved at this, not having actually voiced my thoughts. But perhaps she was right. I knew I had to work harder on keeping my facial expressions neutral. Who knew which of the Meds staff could be trusted? I wasn't really supposed to be up here, I reminded myself. I forced a pleasant expression on my face and followed Tyler as she left the room.

"We need to patrol the perimeter now, and then Ellis wants some supplies shifted from the stores to the canteen. You ok to help? Not as tired now?"

I stretched, knowing that my earlier sleep had done me the world of good. "I'm fine. Just tell me what to do."

We headed outside and proceeded to walk the outer limits of the Meds compound. It was flanked on all sides by dense trees and sheer cliff faces, and I seriously doubted that anyone trying to access this place would be able to do so without being spotted and stopped very quickly. Still, the walk gave us the chance to discuss the Meds situation in more depth. I waited a while before asking my first question, despite feeling intensely curious about the Birthing system. Tyler seemed lost in her thoughts, and I wasn't sure how much she was prepared to share with me.

"So… Blythe. She'll never see Perry again?"

Tyler's face said it all.

CHAPTER TWENTY TWO

"I never– I never realised what it meant… never thought about it properly."

"Few people do. Governance work hard to keep information about Birthing fairly mystical to the rest of The Beck. They only report the positives: new children birthed, the amount of good, strong Minors coming up to The Beck once they turn fourteen. And they talk as though Governance was responsible for the production of every new citizen. But they get away with it. Children rarely have conscious memories before the age of three or four, and by that time they are safely housed in the older Meds Compound. They forget about their first year here. And the babies are well looked after. Just not by their own biological mothers."

I questioned her, "Biological?"

She frowned. "Yes. Meaning genetically linked to the woman whose egg they were born from."

I only just understood this, vaguely remembering some of the basic science we had been taught in Minors. "You mean they're a product of their mother."

"And their father."

"Father?"

"The egg requires fertilisation. Here, it's all done by special selection. The women chosen for Birthing are considered prime specimens, and so are the men whose seed is taken for use in the fertilisation." She glanced at me for the first time since we had started walking, almost smiling at my puzzled expression. She stopped walking and looked at me with some sympathy. "It's confusing I know. The way we create babies here is fairly… scientific. It wasn't always that way. But Governance makes sure that all citizens are incapable of producing offspring before they join The Beck's main community. And when they are selected for Birthing, they reverse the process temporarily."

"But how?"

"Do you remember them giving you an injection when you left Minors?"

I nodded, recalling the sharpness of the needle, in amongst the battery of other checks completed before we were permitted to transfer.

"Well that's how they control it. It's a dose of a drug which remains in your system indefinitely, and prevents you from producing any eggs. Then, if and when you are selected for Birthing, they administer a second drug which counteracts the first."

It was a lot to take in. I thought of Blythe's pale face, her sadness, the baby left here in Meds. No wonder she was finding it difficult to deal with life back in Patrol, if all she could think about was Perry. I feared for her future if she couldn't find a way to deal with the terrible loss. I started walking again, knowing I would be more comfortable asking the questions I wanted to ask if I wasn't looking directly into Tyler's eyes.

"What about the father?"

She hurried a little to catch up, "What about him?"

"No one knows who he is?"

"Nope." She paused, and then sighed, "But once the woman is returned to her Sector, no one knows who the mother is either."

A thought struck me. "But once the child turns fourteen and joins the main community, don't some of the mothers try to find their child?"

"Well no, actually. The babies are given names at birth but

these are changed when they go through to the second tier of Meds. It means their mothers will never know who they are, at least not from their name alone. It's sad, but Governance feels it's necessary."

"But wouldn't the mother recognise her own child?"

Tyler looked surprised. "From a couple of weeks after the birth? Babies look very different from the teenagers they have grown into when they enter The Beck. The Meds staff are kept very separate, so there's no real connection between the two Meds Sectors and Minors. That way even the staff themselves can't be sure they know that a baby they cared for is the same teenager who enters Beck life at fourteen. Plus the Meds staff don't really mix with the rest of The Beck. They have no real need to. Life is good here and they have it better than many other citizens. They know it, so they avoid stirring up any kind of trouble."

"And no one's ever worked out later on?"

"Not that I'm aware of. Think about it though. A lot of the women don't make it back in The Beck once they've given birth. Many end up in Clearance, some transfer to other Sectors in an attempt to start afresh." She shrugged helplessly, "And who knows which Sector a Minor will be sorted into? The chances of there being a connection made with any certainty are very slim."

"There's no way of finding out then?"

She shrugged. "There must be records. I can't believe that Governance wouldn't keep some kind of track on who gives birth when and to whom. They will be tracking the children's progress, seeing how many of them do well as they progress in Minors and then into the Beck at large. I suppose if someone were to get access to the relevant records…" I thought of the Resistance's recent meeting and the records Harris had given Cam access to. "…it might be possible. But extremely dangerous. And for what? So we would know who our offspring are? What good would that do us?"

"None, I suppose. But still, to think that Blythe has you checking in on Perry now. She obviously wants to know she's ok… making progress… But once she's in the older section of Meds you won't be able to keep track of her any more, will you? What will that do to Blythe?"

Tyler's face clouded over. "I have no idea. She's barely hanging on even now. We're trying to support her, but… I'm so frightened for her. I try to imagine how she must be feeling, but I'm not sure I manage to. It's just… just so difficult for Beck citizens once they become mothers."

"And what about fathers? Are they completely unaware of their children? I assume Perry's father could be… literally any of the men in The Beck?"

"Only those who are Supers."

"Have to prove what they're made of before Governance permits them to reproduce, hey?"

She nodded, looking uncomfortable.

"So Cameron, Barnes… They could potentially be the father?"

"They could. It's best not to think about it." She looked thoughtful. "I think Blythe would be happy if she thought Perry did belong to one of the men she knew. If Perry turned out to be Barnes' child, she'd be over the moon."

"Really?"

"Really. They were together before she left for Meds."

"Together?"

"Yes. A couple. Like Jackson and Mason." She sighed, "I

know Barnes comes across as a fool sometimes, but his heart's in the right place. And he has found it extremely difficult being without her for this past year. He desperately wants her back but..." her voice trailed off.

I waited, "But...?"

"I'm not sure she can cope with it right now. Managing day to day without Perry is hard enough."

"That's horrendous."

She nodded. "Yes, but there's little we can do about it for now. You know how they treat those who defy Governance."

I thought of Clearance and the drownings and shuddered. "I do."

"So for now all we can do is learn as much as possible about the system. Hope the information makes us more able to fight it in the future." She stared at me intently, "Do you understand Quin?"

I nodded, biting back tears. We had circled the perimeter of Meds three times now and were standing back in front of the main buildings again.

"Right. We need to move those supplies before we can head back to Patrol. You ok to help?"

I nodded. Glad of the chance to distract myself from the disturbing discoveries of the past two days, I followed her. The rest of the afternoon was spent transferring crates of supplies between various store rooms and the canteen and then patrolling the ward, watching over the tiny figures lying in the cribs and speaking to some of the expectant mothers who were preparing to give birth. I marvelled that their bellies didn't explode, they were so huge. Over the course of the afternoon, one of the women began breathing harder and harder, and occasionally crying out, the volume of her calls increasing as time went on. As we left, additional Meds staff hurried in and rushed to the woman's bedside.

Tyler smiled, "There goes another."

"Another what?"

"Baby. She's going into labour – next time I come up here one of those empty cribs will house a new baby."

"And another woman will be returning to her Sector utterly miserable."

She didn't answer. Ducking past me, she gathered up two backpacks and, passing one to me, headed out of Meds.

Chapter Twenty Three

It did not take us long to get back to Patrol, though our return journey was almost completely silent. I was trying to work out how I felt about the entire Meds system now I knew how it worked, and Tyler seemed lost in her own thoughts, perhaps fretting about Blythe and her desperate unhappiness. Back in the compound she left me and took the packs into the Jefferson Building, while I went straight to the canteen. Jackson and Mason were already there and I joined them once I had collected my tray, feeling guilty about consuming my second hearty meal of the day. I wasn't even particularly hungry, which told me how satisfying the Meds food had been.

Jackson's face flooded with relief as she spotted me. She and Mason exchanged a strange glance at my approach, and he was the first to speak, his voice a forced normal.

"Hey Quin. Good to see you."

I forced a grin. "How was everything here today?"

"Usual." He returned the smile, but it didn't reach his eyes.

"What's wrong?"

There was silence for a moment, while the muted chatter of other citizens swirled around us. Jackson looked increasingly uncomfortable.

"Jac?"

Mason checked no one was within earshot and leaned in close. "You asked Jac to check in on Cass."

My blood ran cold. "Yes?"

Jackson put a reassuring hand on my arm, "She's ok. It's just…"

"Just what?"

Mason took over again. "Jac and I were both on shift with the new recruits today. They were training with knives – remember, like we did?"

I thought back to the early training session, the first we had with Cameron.

"It was with Donnelly though. He wasn't… he isn't as helpful a teacher as Cam, and the session didn't run all that smoothly."

"Was anyone hurt?"

"No. Nothing like that. But… Cass seems to have formed a friendship with another recruit. And while Cass herself is mostly keeping her head down, her friend is… well, attracting attention, shall we say. She was determined to get a rise out of Donnelly every chance she got."

My heart sank. I knew that Cass was lonely. She had made her reasons for coming up here quite plain. She missed my friendship and wanted to work alongside me again. But her transfer had, as yet, not proved to bring us together at all. In fact, if Governance were moving ahead with a programme to create a squad of highly trained Patrol Officers meant for the sole purpose of fighting against an enemy from across the water, then there was a very strong chance that we would never work together. I was an ordinary Patrol citizen, trained in a range of tasks. Cass would be trained for one thing only. To kill.

This in itself was bad enough, but I had hoped that Cass

would impress her trainers, and there might be a chance of her transferring across. But if she was making friends with the wrong people, people headed for trouble before they even made it through the first few days of training, then her chances of that were increasingly slim.

"Who is this friend of hers?"

"She's called Wade."

It instantly made sense. I had already witnessed Wade's defensive attitude. I inwardly cursed my headstrong Agric friend. How could Cass have been so stupid? To align herself with someone so volatile was suicide.

"She's the one who was in my original tour group. I told you she was trouble."

"You were right. It looks like she's come up here with the express aim of demonstrating her hatred for the system. She's bent on defying her trainers anyway." Jackson sighed. "I don't know how she's survived so long in the Lower Beck to be honest."

We finished our meal just as Davis wandered in. He gave us an exhausted wave as he collected his food and soon collapsed into the seat next to me. For a few minutes he didn't speak, doing nothing more than filling his mouth and swallowing until his hunger was more sated.

As we were preparing to leave, he finally spoke. "Productive day, everyone?"

We all murmured various responses, few of them positive.

"How 'bout you Davis?" Mason looked shrewdly at him, "You don't look so good."

"Shift at the wall." He wiped a hand across his forehead. "Exhausting. Cam was a real pig today."

"Really?" The question had come from Jackson. I knew only

too well what might have caused Cam to be less than content today.

"Yup. Yelling at us the entire time. And he kept us later than he should've to finish a particular section. Don't know what's got into him. Must really have Reed and Carter on his back about getting the extra security measures completed."

I stood up abruptly. Questions about the Birthing process and the issues with Cass had driven the events of the previous night from my thoughts, but now they returned with a vengeance. Cam had arranged for me to spend the day resting and recuperating from the horrors of our experience in Dev, but he had been given no such reprieve. Clearly, exhaustion, and his guilt over Lewis' death had affected him today. I wondered where he was now, and if he would get the chance to recover properly tonight.

Pushing my chair under, I muttered a vague apology and headed off with my tray. Outside, it was raining hard. I hunched my shoulders against it and was just crossing the courtyard when Jackson caught up with me. She didn't speak, but took hold of my elbow, steering me in the direction of The Annexe. Once inside, she pulled me to the furthest bed from the door and hauled a blanket from it, placing it on the floor and pulling me down beside her so that we were out of sight.

"Ok." She said without further preamble. "Spill."

I burst into tears. Shifting forwards, she shuffled close enough to stretch her arms out and pull me to her. We sat like that for several minutes, until my sobs abated and she was able to pat me awkwardly on the back and move away.

"You needed that. Now will you tell me what's going on?"

We sat together for the next half an hour or so. I poured

out the whole thing in a jumble of words, conveying what I had learned about Meds and Birthing, the trip to Dev with Cam and, eventually, Lewis's death. I left this until last, almost afraid to hear her reaction, terrified that she would judge us. When I had finished and looked into her eyes though, I could see that all she felt was sorrow. Tears streamed down her face and she hauled me into a second embrace that felt as much for her own comfort as mine.

"Just when I think it can't get worse." She sighed. "Poor Cam. Imagine having to make that kind of decision..." She paused for a moment as if wondering how to continue. "That's why he treats you the way he does. I'm certain. He cares about you – he just has so many people depending on him. That's a lot of pressure for him, and, I think he's trying to shield you from it."

I didn't answer.

"I mean it. I know you don't believe it because sometimes he ignores you, but it's not like me and Mason. We're the same status. Cam's a Super. Plus, he's in charge of the Resistance. He doesn't have time for a relationship." She smiled sadly, "But that doesn't mean he doesn't want one."

She took my hand in hers, waiting until I looked up and met her gaze. "Look, I've seen the way he looks at you. If he didn't have all that pressure weighing on him, you'd be taking walks in the woods at night just like us. Don't tell me you haven't thought about it?"

I looked at the floor, knowing that I was blushing. She pressed on. "But because he's the kind of guy who wants to change things, for everyone, for the better, he can't act like everyone else. Even when he'd like to. Trust me. I've enough distance to see that he's trying not to hurt you." She smiled gently. "He often fails. But he's trying."

She looked up towards the doorway. "We'd better go I suppose. We're lucky no one's missed us. Better check the boards, see if any of us has a night shift."

It was unlikely that, after a full day shift, we would be assigned to work this evening as well, but as security had been increased since the last storm, the rotas had demanded more and more of Patrol citizens. Some days we were now required to do a full day shift in one location followed by a shorter shift in the evening as well. On those days we were close to collapse by the time we made it to bed, and more than one citizen had been caught sleeping on duty. Jackson took my hands and we pulled ourselves to a standing position, the burden of knowledge weighing heavily on us once more.

"Mind if I tell Mason about this?"

My reaction was instant, "Of course not."

"Although I might leave out the part about Lewis. I worry sometimes. He gets so angry. I know one day he's going to say something he regrets. When Wade was talking back to Donnelly today I tried to stop her. Mason seemed like he wanted to encourage her behaviour, even though he knows first-hand what it can lead to."

I was surprised. "He didn't seem like he agreed with her attitude when he was telling me about it before."

She laughed without mirth. "Only because I reminded him how dangerous that kind of attitude is. He listened, for now, but I worry one day I won't be there and he'll forget and let his mouth run away with him."

I squeezed her arm, wanting to support her the same way she had me. She smiled, and we headed to the door together, pausing to check that there was no one watching before slipping out into the damp evening.

After checking the boards and realising that neither of us were on shift until the following day, I headed back to the pod. Jackson went to find Mason, and I knew they would want to be alone. Thinking about them together made me recall my conversation with Tyler about Blythe and Barnes. It made me incredibly sad to think that a relationship which had brought some happiness to Beck citizens had been so cruelly ruined by circumstance.

I wondered whether Blythe would ever get over the loss of Perry, and if she would ever be able to talk to Barnes about what had happened. It would be difficult enough for her to explain how she was feeling to another woman, but to make a man understand what she had been through, when clearly there was no comparison, struck me as an impossible task. And Barnes was not the most sensitive of citizens either, in fact it surprised me that he had managed to function as part of a couple at all. Still, the expression on his face when he had encountered Blythe the other day had stayed with me. He had seemed truly concerned about her.

Wandering past the wash tent, I wasn't looking where I was going and almost ran headlong into a figure lurking behind the pod. He turned at my stifled cry and I recognised Cam with some relief. To begin with, his expression was so vulnerable I almost flung my arms around him, but a second later it became the blank mask it so often was. Retreating hastily from the intended embrace, I wobbled slightly before I could regain my balance. He threw out an arm as if to steady me, and then withdrew it just as quickly. We stood, awkwardly staring at one another.

"Were you looking for me?"

He looked at the ground, refusing to meet my eyes, "Yes."

"And?"

There was a long pause before he answered. "I wanted to see how you were." He forced his eyes up to mine, looking directly at me for the first time. "After–"

"I'm ok. The rest did me good. Thanks for sorting the Meds shift out for me."

"It's no problem. You needed it."

"And what about you?"

He turned away again. "I'm fine."

"That's not what I heard."

He stiffened, defensive as ever. "What did you hear?"

"That you were a bit of a slave driver today. Staying busy to keep out the demons?"

"Maybe."

"You need some time too. Can you rest properly tonight?"

"Think so. Nothing on the schedule for me at least. Possibility of a storm approaching, but no certainty as yet. I'm hoping it will pass us by." He sighed, rubbing his lower back.

I dared to take another step closer to him. "You look exhausted. To say nothing of what's going on inside your head." I reached up to his cheek hesitantly, remembering the way I had boldly kissed him once. I wondered what had happened to that girl.

He started visibly at my touch but didn't back away, closing his eyes instead. I glanced around. No one was anywhere near. Hesitantly I closed the final gap between us and stood, my body lined up against his. Circling him with my arms, I held him the way that Jackson had held me. For now, the intensity of the previous night was gone, replaced by a simple need to be close to one another. I felt the tension slowly leave his form, his body sagging into mine as he allowed himself a brief moment of respite, knowing that someone understood his pain and guilt.

"I wish we could go somewhere together."

I tensed as I spoke, wary that my comment would drive him away. With relief, I felt him nod his head against my shoulder.

"Not to… you know…" I felt my face flaming, "Just to be together, like this."

I felt him retreating from me slowly and my heart sank. But when he finally looked into my eyes, his expression reflected my own.

"Quin, I can think of nothing… nothing I'd like more right now, but…" his voice trailed off, full of regret.

"Least we want the same thing," I smiled through my disappointment, "even if it's impossible."

"One day Quin, maybe one day." Pulling further from me, he held my gaze. "Thank you. You can't understand how much better you've made me feel." He grimaced. "I've got to go. Couple more tasks left before I get any rest, and if I'm going to survive tomorrow I need at least a little sleep. Sorry I can't stay with you."

"At least you came. Worth it, even for a couple of minutes."

He backed away. "Tomorrow?"

I nodded, feeling a tiny bit more hopeful. A moment later, he was gone.

Chapter Twenty Four

Left alone outside the pod, I found my head was spinning. No matter how hard I tried, I couldn't work him out. Kissing me like his life depended on it; rejecting me in anger; turning to me for comfort: Cameron was consistently confusing. Knowing I would struggle to sleep for a while now, I decided to walk to the new recruits' camp and see if I could find Cass. I was extremely concerned about her poor choice of associate and fearful of what it might lead to. Perhaps it wasn't too late to talk some sense into her. Yet even as I thought it, I knew that if Cass had made up her mind about having Wade as a friend, there would be nothing I could do to talk her out of it.

The camp was quiet as I approached. I wondered at first if the recruits were asleep already, but as I passed the citizen guarding the weapons tents, I heard faint sounds on the far side of the field. Nodding a greeting to the guard, who I didn't know well, I picked my way in between the pods, until I reached the source of the noise. The rear of the field was flanked by trees, and the recruits appeared to be involved in clambering up them in the near-darkness, presumably some kind of exercise in stealth.

They had to be tired after training all day, but here they were, being forced to continue into the night. At the edge of the wood I came across a Super called Mitchell, who I didn't know well. He stood, leaning casually against one of the trees, paying the recruits little attention. I could see other shadowy figures standing on the ground at different points underneath the trees, and from the scuffling and whispered curses, more of them already above my head in the branches. I tried to saunter up casually, as if I were a curious observer and not someone on a mission to speak to a specific recruit.

"What's the aim?" I asked Mitchell, who looked thoroughly bored and unsurprised at my approach.

He smiled. "There are weapons strapped to the trees at various heights and locations. They're working in teams to locate and secure them."

"How much longer are they expected to look?"

"Until they're all found and handed back to me."

"And if they can't find them?"

"They'll be up there a long time," he smirked, "I think most teams are almost there now though."

Patrol had always tried to test its recruits to their limits, but this seemed a little counter-productive. To make the recruits work all day and then continue into the night with a task that seemed nearly impossible was unfair; allowing them the bare minimum of sleep before beginning more intensive training the next day was certainly not sensible. Perhaps it was designed to weed out the weaker citizens, but if forming an army was what we were attempting, it struck me that we would need every recruit we could muster. Eliminating them during these early training stages would just reduce the numbers in our ranks. And while I wasn't a huge fan of the plan to form an army, surely if there was an enemy to be dealt with, the larger our forces, the better.

"Mind if I observe?" I made the request sound casual,

disinterested, but I needn't have worried. Mitchell did not seem to suspect anything.

"Fine by me. In fact, I need to…" he adjusted his trouser belt meaningfully, "could you keep an eye out for a minute or two while I relieve myself?"

"Sure." I forced my voice to remain neutral, relishing the moment or two I might have to enter the trees without observation from a Patrol Super.

He wandered off towards the crude bathroom tent which had been hastily set up for the recruits to use. I didn't waste any time, but headed into the trees. The near darkness provided good cover and there were so many recruits that it was easy to get lost in amongst them. I found I was able to slip in and out of the citizens without being identified, hearing snatches of whispered conversation around me.

"How many did we need to find?"

"Has anyone completed it yet? I don't think…"

A muffled cry from above our heads, followed by a curse.

"Parker, you ok?

A groan, followed by a short pause. "Yes. Just scraped myself."

"Find anything yet?"

I realised that there were more groups deeper in the woods and left the fringes to search further in. I had yet to hear Cassidy's voice, and knew I would recognise it the second I heard it. I also found it difficult to believe that Cass would remain silent during such a task, extremely driven as she was. Sure enough, as I reached the base of a large oak tree, I overheard a conversation where one party sounded familiar.

"We've got five now. That's enough. Let's go." This was a voice I didn't know.

"No. What if there are more out here?" Cass' strident tone demonstrated that she was no less competitive than she ever had been. "If we can get more than five, we'll definitely come out on top."

A loud sigh. "Cassidy, it doesn't matter."

Another unfamiliar voice, "I'm so tired. We need some sleep!"

"And let another team beat us? Have the Supers thinking someone else is the best? No thanks."

"Please Cass?"

I heard nothing more than a snort up in the trees. The recruits on the ground were collecting together a number of different sizes of knife, a length of rope and a baton, all eager to return to their pods for some much-needed rest. I knew Cass wasn't coming down until she had found another prize to secure her team's win, and smiled in pity at the recruits who had ended up on her team.

A moment later I heard her triumphant shriek, and felt the tree tremble as she slid effortlessly to the ground, another large knife hooked through her belt She thrust it into the hand of the waiting recruit at the base of the tree without noticing me.

"Ok weaklings, let's go. We have more than we need to impress Mitchell over there, if he hasn't fallen asleep!"

I heard a few muffled hisses, as though some of her team were annoyed with her, but at least one recruit chuckled, appreciating her audacity. As the group turned to leave, two sets of footsteps thundered towards them. They were instantly on their guard. Two figures appeared. Both male, presumably separated from their team. They ran as though they were being chased, stopping only as they almost collided with the other group. Breathless, they sized up the competition, their eyes roaming over the weapons Cass's team had located.

"How many've you got?"

"All of them. We're done." Cass swept past him, the others following.

"Any idea where there might be any more? We've looked everywhere. Parker scraped her arm pretty badly too." The recruit sounded desperate. "Honestly, I don't know what they'll do if we don't have all five."

I found myself suddenly sympathising with them, their task seemingly almost impossible to complete as darkness fell. I watched as Cass paused for a moment, glancing behind at her group. Quickly, she turned back to the man standing beside his teammate, staring hopelessly into the trees as though at any moment a gun might tumble, fully-loaded, into his arms. I could see her assessing the situation, making a decision.

"See any other items anywhere else?" The remark was directed at the rest of her group, who murmured various negative responses.

The recruits from the other team moved onwards through the trees, looking for other areas which had not yet been examined. Reluctantly Cass stepped towards her own teammate and grasped hold of one of the smaller knives.

"What are you–?" he protested as he realised what she was doing. "No! I thought you wanted to impress them."

Clearly he didn't know Cass well. Because the Cass I knew wanted to win, but also hated to see others suffer. I remembered a bread roll, secreted inside her overalls on Assessment day, which had given Harper the strength to focus on completing the written test. It was so Cass. I knew exactly what she was going to do.

"Hey!" She called the other pair back. "Have this."

Proffering the small knife in her hand, she thrust it at the other recruit and was off, racing through the woods as though she hadn't already done a full day's training followed by a night exercise. I watched the relief flash across the man's face as he realised what it was, and felt incredibly proud of my friend. Both teams set off back towards the meeting point.

Not wanting to approach Cass while she was in training, I hung back and watched the teams report back to Mitchell, who seemed pleased with most of them. I noticed Cass slip away from her group and find Wade, who was standing towards the rear of the crowd. Only one team was without all five items, and they were sent back into the forest with the threat of no rest until the final item was found. I keenly felt their desperation as they trudged away. Before they were out of sight however, a voice rang out across the group, stopping them in their tracks.

"They had four weapons out of five. It's dark. Can't they be allowed some rest now?"

It was Wade. I could see from Mitchell's expression that he had dealt with her more than once and was more than a little tired of her. He turned towards her abruptly.

"Reed's orders. They failed to complete the task."

"But it isn't fair!" Wade seemed determined to defend the other group and have Mitchell bring the task to an end. "They could fall in the dark, hurt themselves. How do you expect to turn out fit and healthy recruits if you set them tasks like this?"

Mitchell looked in no mood for argument. Pulling something out of his belt, he advanced towards her.

"Look. Orders are orders. I'm just following them." He held up the weapon, a small version of the cattle-prod I had seen used as punishment before. "Do I really need to convince you to leave it?"

Wade looked like she would argue further, but Cass put a calming hand on her arm and pulled her back. It seemed like a role reversal of my own relationship with Cass.

"No Mitchell, you don't. We're going to bed now."

He lowered the prod, fastening it back on to his belt and waving an impatient arm at the failing team. Disappointed at the lack of reprieve, they set off into the woods again. The rest of the group wandered off towards the wash tent, some heading straight for bed, clearly too exhausted to wash off the day's grime. Cass and Wade walked in step with one another, their heads bent together. Mitchell watched them go, his expression exasperated.

I waited until they were mostly gone, and headed back to Mitchell, not wanting him to think he had left the recruits in the charge of someone irresponsible.

"Hey, they misbehaving?"

He grunted. "Wish they'd just do as they were told. What did you think?"

I wasn't sure what kind of information Mitchell was after, and decided to stay as neutral as possible.

"Not sure. They were all working hard to get the task done."

"They always do before bedtime and meals." He sighed. "I'm supposed to report back on progress each day. Don't know what to tell them about those two." He jerked his head towards the retreating backs of Wade and Cass.

"Are they performing badly?"

"No. Just too much to say for themselves, 'specially the dark haired one."

I gave up on remaining impartial and tried to defend my friend. "The blond one was working really well in there. Looks like a real leader."

He nodded appreciatively. "She is. Very impressive physically. She's just a bit too close to Wade – the dark haired one. Everyone has said she's difficult. Donnelly was furious with her after the session today. Not sure she'll last." He sighed and turned away. "Final evening checks call. Thanks for the support back there."

I knew I had got away with coming across as merely a curious citizen. Making as though I would return to my own pod, I slipped behind the wash tent and waited for Cass to emerge. It was several minutes before she did. Spotting her blond head ducking out of the doorway, I was relieved to see that she was alone and wasted no time.

"Cass!"

She turned, her eyes roaming wildly to discover where the voice was coming from. Locating me, she made as if to turn, but I signalled for her to stay where she was. Always good at picking up on cues, she dropped into a crouch and busied herself for a moment with her bootlace.

"Go into your pod as though you're going to bed." I kept my voice low. "Wait until people are asleep, then meet me under the tree where you found the last knife."

Realising I had been watching her, she looked startled, but managed a slight nod to demonstrate she understood. A moment later I watched her disappear into the folds of a pod towards the rear of the field. It was a good distance from the sentry tent, so I was fairly confident she'd be able to sneak out without being noticed. Then there was nothing left for me to do but to head back into the woods and wait.

Chapter Twenty Five

There was no sign of the final group, who must have headed deeper into the trees in search of the final lost weapon. I sat at the base of the agreed tree and waited. It wasn't long before Cass arrived.

"You sure everyone was asleep?"

"Everyone that counts," she replied.

I frowned.

"I mean everyone who would blab to the Supers."

"I hope you're right. You haven't been training with these people for long at all. How do you know who you can trust?"

She tossed her head and flung herself on the ground next to me, "I know."

We were silent for a while. I felt slightly awkward being with her after so long apart, and clearly she did too. I began to wonder whether she was still angry with me for abandoning her in Agric when she flung herself towards me in a clumsy embrace. Smiling into her hair, I returned the affection, knowing she struggled to admit her feelings. Cass was a fierce and loyal ally, yet that was what worried me.

"Are you ok?" I managed.

"Mostly, yes. I'm doing well with all the training so far…"

"So I saw."

"You were watching me!" She sounded pleased as we eased

away from each other reluctantly.

"I came to see how you were. Thought you'd be in bed. When you were busy, I hung around and waited."

She smiled. "I did well?"

"You know you did. Especially giving up your extra weapon to support the other group."

"I made some friends too. Not like you– but– well I'm trying. I know we won't be able to work together all the time."

I hid a grimace before launching into what I knew would be difficult. "Look Cass, about these new friends…"

But before I could get any further, the sound of footsteps rustled in the trees close by. I wondered at first if it was the other team returning, but soon realised the person was approaching from the direction of the camp.

"Cass!" The voice was hissed and urgent.

Before I could stop her, she responded. "Over here."

I leapt to my feet, instantly on guard. Seconds later we were joined by Wade. My heart sank.

"What're you doing out here? I was worried." She glanced mistrustfully at me.

"It's fine. She's with me."

"Quin, this is Wade. Wade, Quin. You already know all about her."

"I wish you didn't." I paused, not wanting to come across as too harsh. "Wade, go back to bed."

Cass placed a hand on my arm. "Let her stay Quin. She's my friend."

"That's the problem."

I could see Cass's face settling into the familiar stubborn frown. Desperate to save the situation, I tried a different tack.

"Look. Trust me Cass, you have the makings of an excellent

Patrol recruit. And while the rules up here are a little different, make no mistake: disobey and you'll be out like a shot."

Her face remained mutinous.

"Cass, I've heard from two others today that Wade here," I shot her a sideways glance, "no offence, but, you're attracting a lot of the wrong attention."

She shrugged, "I know."

I turned my attention to her. "Doesn't it bother you? You're a promising recruit yourself, if you don't ruin it. Don't you know what you're risking?"

"I know exactly what I'm risking. Thing is, I don't care."

Cass put a hand on my arm to prevent me from exploding. "Listen to her Quin. She has her reasons for behaving like this."

Now Wade turned to Cass, a furious expression on her face.

"You can trust Quin. I promise." Cass shot me a pleading look.

In spite of my anger, I was curious. I forced myself to settle back down on the ground underneath the tree, taking deep breaths as I did so.

"Ok Wade, let me have it. You've got five minutes before I have to get back to my own pod."

I thought that she might sit down next to us to tell her story. Instead, she began pacing back and forth, her hands twisted tightly together in front of her.

"I haven't always been like this. I know I'm getting a reputation for being trouble. Honestly, I don't much care." Her voice dropped, becoming softer as she continued. "I used to have a close friend, Marley. We grew up together in Sustenance. Supported each other. Followed the rules, most of the time at least, and did our job fairly well. We were doing ok until… until…"

She stopped talking, as though she had no breath left to continue. Despite the threat she currently posed to Cass, I couldn't help but identify with the deep affection she clearly felt for her friend.

"Go on." I tried, gently.

My words seemed to jerk her back to reality. She looked up, her gaze burning into my own as she continued.

"We had a small fire a few weeks ago. In the canteen kitchen. Nothing too bad, but worse than any we've had previously. Marley was close by when it started. Got injured trying to douse the flames. Not that she got any kind of thanks for it, as you can imagine. Never mind that she stopped the fire from spreading."

Wade's tone was bitter as she continued. "Now usually we deal with fires ourselves, but as it was more serious, they called in some Patrol officers and some of the Rep citizens to assist with the clean-up. They were with us for around a week, helping out. Most of them were ok with us, but the Super assigned to the project wasn't."

I glanced at Cass and back to Wade. "And the Super was?"

"Donnelly."

I failed to mask my feelings, and I could see that Wade knew I shared her negative opinion of the Super.

"One evening I was helping Marley with her clean up duties. The pain from her burns was pretty bad, but obviously she couldn't admit to it. Donnelly came in and queried the fact that we were both working on the same job. I was additional, I hadn't abandoned my own post to help her. I wasn't supposed to be on shift at all!"

She beat a fist against her palm and I saw the fury which

had first brought her to my attention back on the tour. But I had begun to understand the reason for her anger now, and didn't interrupt any more.

"So he questions us, pressures her to answer him, and she's so weak. Weak from trying to carry on as normal with all the burns, and weak from hiding the pain that she's in. She burst into tears. Sort of collapsed. I'd never seen her so low. And he slapped her. Slapped her hard across the face and threatened her with Clearance if she wasn't up to the job."

She was breathing hard now, and her pacing had become rapid and furious. I prompted her, knowing she needed to continue with the story, to get it all out of her system.

"What happened then?"

"He stalked off of course. Shoulders thrown back, chest puffed out, stupid smirk on his face. You could tell he'd enjoyed hitting her, you know?" She bit back tears. "I watched him go. There were a lot of people out there, you know? It was meal time, and we were still managing to provide citizens with some kind of lunch, despite the damage to the kitchen. So the room was full of Agric citizens. Packed. And he strode through, staring down his nose, like he's Governor Adams or something. And I snapped."

"What did you do?" I dreaded her answer.

"I followed him. Grabbed a jar of vinegar on my way out – we keep a stock of it in the kitchen, you know? Anyway, I opened it up. Threw it into his face. And while he stood there, rubbing his eyes, screaming in agony, I told him what I thought of him. Called him a coward for slapping a girl. Called him Adams' lapdog. Total humiliation. In front of the entire canteen. He didn't like it, as you can imagine. Rallied pretty quickly, and I caught more than just a slap for the attack.

By the time I got out of the canteen I was in a pretty bad way." She winced at the memory. "Most of Agric saw me being beaten that day. But I thought it was worth it, if I'd managed to at least show some kind of resistance to his bullying."

She smiled with satisfaction, the happiest expression I had ever seen on her face. Seconds later though, the grin began to fade, and was replaced by guilt and a sadness which I realised had been buried beneath her anger until now.

"Well I thought that was it. That my public beating had been enough for him." She sighed. "I was wrong. He wouldn't let it go. Not the fact that all those Agric women had witnessed him screaming like a child and accused of being a coward. And I could have coped if he'd just taken it out on me. Even if it meant Clearance, it would have been worth it. But he found a better way to punish me. The next evening when Marley and I were both on duty in the kitchens doing the late evening clean up, he came in with some others. His eyes still looked sore. We were on our own – it's not a demanding assignment. Looking back, I think Donnelly arranged it so that we were the only ones there. But he didn't come for me. He went straight for Marley. Grabbed her by her arms, right where she had been burned. She screamed, and I went for him, but his friends held on to me while he beat her."

She was almost sobbing now, tears streaming down her cheeks as she spoke of her friend.

"It seemed to go on forever. He didn't stop until she was curled up on the ground, like a child, with her hands cradled over her head. Her skin looked like it had been flayed in places. Like raw beef. And then he turned to me and laughed. Said no one got away with making him look small. He punched me once, right in the face, and they left, taking Marley with them."

"The fire damage was repaired the following day. The Rep guys went away and Donnelly came to see me one last time before he left too. He told me that Marley hadn't survived the attack… but… but…" she struggled to continue, taking a deep breath, "but that it didn't matter, because she'd been headed for Clearance anyway – because of her burns. And that I deserved all the pain that her death would cause me. Because I had humiliated him. He knew his revenge would be more effective, see, if he hurt the person I was closest to, rather than getting at me. He said his attack on her was justified, because it had taught me a valuable lesson about who was in charge. And that was it. He was gone."

There was a pause, and Wade finally stopped pacing and stared into the darkness of the trees behind us. I tried to find words which might convey some kind of comfort, but struggled.

"That's terrible Wade, really."

Cass spoke at last. "Isn't it awful? I mean, I thought what happened to us with Harper was bad Quin, but this…"

Wade seemed to shake herself out of her stupor, furiously scrubbing tears from her cheeks. "So now you get it. I vowed that I'd find a way to get here. To Patrol. And find him."

I tried to reason with her. "Ok, so you've managed it. You've found him. Now what? You continue to cause trouble in training sessions? How far do you think that will get you?"

"I don't honestly care." She shrugged. "I just need to be here long enough to make sure that his life's not worth living. I'm biding my time, working on finding out the best way to do that."

"But he's a Super." I fought to keep my frustration from

showing. "He's respected by a lot of people here. Governance likes him. He's strong, fit, clever. And you're a lowly new recruit. How do you expect to make his life a misery? Up here, he definitely holds all the cards." I thought about the plans for training up an army. Wade would become cannon fodder and Donnelly would sit back and laugh. "Don't think he's forgotten you. He can just as easily make your life hell you know."

"Oh I'll find a way to get to him Quin, don't you worry."

"You're mad."

"Think what you like." She turned her back on me, looking instead to Cass. "Look what I kept hold of."

I looked down at the object in her hands, afraid of what I might see. Clutched firmly in the grip of her right hand, clearly stolen during the training exercise, was a long, thin knife.

My anger returned. "What were you thinking?"

"I was thinking that I can defend myself now. If I need to."

"Against who?"

"Against anyone who tries to stop me."

"Stop you doing what?"

"I don't think I'll tell you anymore. Let's just say I'm working on a plan." She glared at me before turning to Cass. "Thought you said she'd be on our side."

Cass elbowed me none too subtly. "She is, aren't you Quin?"

"That depends." I paused, choosing my words carefully. "I'm on your side in terms of understanding how terrible you must feel, losing your friend. But believe me, you're not the only one that this has happened to. And if you keep hold of that knife, they'll know. The weapons have all got to be accounted for before the nightshift hands over. Once the other group gets back with the final weapon Mitchell will do the checks and discover it's missing."

"They won't get back with the final weapon though, will they?" She held the knife aloft triumphantly.

"You mean?"

"Yup. They hid the exact amount of weapons for each group to find five. I found six."

"So you're telling me there's a group out there right now, searching in the dark for a weapon which you're holding in your hands? And they won't be allowed to return until it's found?"

She had the grace to look a little shamefaced. "It can't be helped. I tried to persuade Mitchell to let them come back." She shrugged helplessly, "It's just that I haven't been able to get hold of a weapon yet. They guard them so closely."

"Exactly. So the best you can hope for is to keep it all night until the other group returns empty handed. Once the guards realise what's happened, they'll search everyone. What do you think happens when they find you with it?"

She went to interrupt, but I put up a hand to stop her. "Look Wade, I'm sorry you lost Marley. But you're strong, you're fit, you could do well in Patrol. Maybe, in the future, there will be ways to fight back... fight the system. But not like this." I softened my tone. "Take it to the group searching in the woods. Now. Then perhaps you can all get some rest and live another day to work out how you might get your revenge on Donnelly. Without dying in the process." I gestured at the knife. "This'll only lead to you being sent to Clearance or worse."

She continued to stare at me and I knew my words had not had the right kind of impact. She seemed hell-bent on self-destruction. I just hoped she wouldn't drag Cass down with her.

"I'm going to get some rest. You coming Cass?" Wade had clearly dismissed me now.

Cass hesitated, and for a moment I thought she would leave. Eventually she spoke. "Be there in a minute."

Wade nodded begrudgingly. Tucking the knife back into her belt, she pulled her shirt down to cover it and stalked away.

Chapter Twenty Six

Once we were alone Cass shuffled closer, until her arm lay against my own. It brought back memories of nights we had spent together on the wall top, where the extent of our rebellion lay in sneaking out of the pod at night for a few hours. Now rebellion involved stealing knives and administering fatal doses of drugs. Part of me longed to return to my former innocence.

"She's not so bad you know."

I remained silent.

"I think she used to be like us, but losing her closest friend, well… it hit her hard. Watching her attacked like that. The Super who did it, Donnelly, ran our training this morning. He's a nasty piece of work. I don't know how Wade managed to get through the session without going for him."

"Look, I know Donnelly, and I agree. He's awful. But he's a Super. You have to at least act like you'll obey him."

"Why though? He treats people like dirt. Enjoys causing pain. I don't blame Wade at all." I could feel her clenching her fist next to me. "I don't know, if I saw you or Harper being treated like that, I'd–"

I cut her off. "You'd what? Exactly what would you do?"

She stared at me, bewildered by the fury in my voice. Cass knew the sensible, calm Quin. The one who took precautions, thought things through, made sure we tested out the routes we took when sneaking out at night, who weighed up the citizens we could trust. She had no idea how much I had changed since my move to Patrol. She had not seen me since I had visited Clearance, witnessed the drownings, watched Lewis die.

"Because, Cass, although it's not quite the same, our friend was taken from us too. Yes, Harper was hauled off to Clearance rather than being beaten to death. But we let them take her. Just like every other citizen would have. We didn't do anything to stop them. We all tell ourselves that life in Clearance isn't so terrible, because it eases our guilt."

"Well is it so terrible?"

I turned to look her straight in the eye. "Yes!" I hissed the word at her, wishing I could scream it. "Yes. It's terrible. They're fed less than we are, they sleep on the floor, they work long hours in a hot, stifling environment, until they drop from exhaustion."

"But how can Harper manage that? She's ill!"

"Yes she is, but they don't care. Because there's an endless supply of fodder for the Clearance Sector. More and more dispensable, disposable citizens who can be herded over there to replace those no longer able to work."

Cass' voice shook as she responded. "But is Harper still…"

"Alive? Well she was the last time I saw her. But that was a while ago. Who knows whether she still is? And even if she's managing for now, they'll probably assign her to be exterminated at the next Assessments anyway." My voice cracked as I forced myself to continue, to reveal the horrible truth. "They drown them, you know. The useless ones. And the rebels."

A fleeting look of devastation crossed Cass' face, but then the stubborn part of her took charge. I could see the change in her eyes. This was what I had feared, and was the reason I had not told her about Clearance before now. I cursed the anger which had made me blurt out the truth.

"Well what can we do to stop them? Wade's got the right idea. At least she has a plan!"

"Did you not hear what I just said? They drown people from Clearance. Both the sick and those they discover defying them. Just like Wade. And you, if you continue to associate with her. They throw them on to boats wearing weighted harnesses, then sail out into deep water and toss them overboard."

Her face was a tangle of emotions. Agony at the discovery of what could happen to Harper. Fury that Governance could sanction such horrific measures to control the population. And a desperation that terrified me.

"Cass, stay away from Wade. I'm serious. If she is discovered hiding that knife, it'll be straight to Clearance, and if you're associated with her, you'll be sent too. And if she tries to use it..."

Cass stood up suddenly. I felt instantly cold as she moved her arm away, leaving my skin exposed to the cool night air.

"Get some rest Quin. I'll see you."

"Cass, please. Show me you've listened to what I've been saying. Trust that I'm your oldest friend and I've been in Patrol longer than you. What Wade is doing is going to end badly, I'm telling you."

She turned before she moved back in the direction of the pods. I felt like she was a million miles away. "I listened Quin."

And I found myself staring at her retreating back, knowing the fact that she had listened meant nothing if she chose not to follow my advice.

It didn't take long to get back to my own pod, skirting the edges of the Training Field to stay out of sight of the guards on the night shift. A driving rain had set in, perhaps the edge of the storm Cam had been referring to, and I was soaked by the time I got there. Collecting some fresh overalls, I went to the wash tent to clean up and change, knowing all too well the dangers of sleeping in wet clothing.

The wash tent was deserted, but as I headed back to my pod I saw Mason bidding goodbye to Jackson. Their kisses seemed so affectionate and uncomplicated, and not for the first time I envied them their simple relationship. I was in my cot by the time Jackson came to bed, humming slightly under her breath as she crept around me. Not wanting to spoil her mood, I faked sleep rather than tell her the events of my own evening. Within a very short space of time, I was asleep for real.

My dreams were not pleasant that night. I heard babies crying out for absent mothers and saw knives flashing silver in the darkness. I woke up to the sound of a scream ripping through the peace of the compound. To begin with I dismissed it as part of my dream and lay there, trying to calm my nerves with deep breaths. But as I adjusted to the gloom of the pod, I heard it for a second time. As the others around me began to stir, I realised it had come from somewhere close by.

Jackson sat up in the bed beside me, rubbing her eyes and looking around. "What's going on?"

I shook my head in confusion. Now we could hear footsteps outside, and voices raised in alarm. Along with the rest of the pod, I made my way outside.

It was still raining, and the night was dark, but some

people were carrying lanterns and we followed them. The disturbance was coming from a pod on the other side of the field. We were too far away; the driving rain and crowds of people made it impossible to work out what had happened. Elbowing Jackson, I jerked my head to the left and together we took a more circuitous route, moving around the edge of the field and attempting to approach from the other side, where it was much quieter.

There were still a lot of people milling around outside the pod, even from this direction. No one seemed to be in charge, and most citizens were taking advantage of the lack of organisation, crowding forwards to get a look at what was happening. Moments later an air horn rang out above the general clamour, startling everyone. The crowds parted automatically as a dark figure strode through the area. Director Reed. Once he reached the pod in question, he turned to the crowd and held up a megaphone, his commanding voice echoing across the field.

"Back to your beds! I only require a few Supers to assist. The rest of you go. Now!"

Well aware of Reed's reputation, most citizens began reversing their progress and moving off in small groups, occasional backward glances betraying their continued curiosity. Satisfied that he was being obeyed, Reed ducked his head inside the pod and disappeared from view. Jackson and I began to wander slowly back across the field, our previous diversion allowing us to take a route that led directly past the pod. A figure was emerging as we passed. I recognised her as she approached.

"Will!"

A look of recognition dawned on her face as her eyes met

mine. She nodded tiredly.

"Is that your pod? What's going on?"

She shook her head. "Not here. We've all been asked to leave so they can investigate." She took my arm and steered me back toward my own pod. Jackson followed closely behind. Waiting until we were too far away to be overheard, Will bent her head low and continued.

"Bad news. One of the new recruits sneaked into our pod just now. We were all asleep. Whoever it was had a knife. They–" she stopped speaking suddenly, a look of disbelief crossing her face.

"They what?"

"They stabbed him. Right in the chest."

I felt a dread come over me and let Jackson ask the question I feared I already knew the answer to.

"Stabbed who?"

"Donnelly."

"Damn! Really? Is... is he dead?"

Will rubbed a hand across her forehead. "He wasn't when I left him, but he was in a pretty bad way. I'm not sure what they'll do. I mean, he's a well-trained Super. They won't want to lose him at a time like this, but..."

Jackson's voice dripped with sarcasm. "You can't imagine them doing anything drastic to save him."

"No. I can't."

"What about the recruit?" I blurted out.

"Gone."

"Then how do they know it was a recruit?"

Will regarded me closely before answering. "The knife sticking out of his chest was one of those used in their training exercise tonight. They think it was missing from the weapons store."

"Did anyone see anything?"

"Don't think so. We just woke up to hear Donnelly scream-ing." She took a deep breath. "There was blood everywhere. So much blood."

We had reached the entrance to our pod now. I could hear a low hum of voices debating what might have happened drifting from the interior.

"This is us Will." Jackson showed her usual concern for others. "Where are you sleeping?"

She pointed at the buildings in the distance. "They've sent us to the Annexe. We're all headed over there now."

"Right. Glad you have somewhere to go. Hope you manage a little sleep at least. Night then." Jackson disappeared into the pod.

Will placed a hand on my arm as I turned to leave. "Are you alright Quin?"

"What do you mean?"

"Well you seem... disturbed by what's happened. I mean, more disturbed than other people are."

I sighed. "I'm ok. It's just a shock."

"Were you close to Donnelly?"

I snorted, "No. Hardly. I mean, not that I wanted this to happen, but..."

"But he's not the nicest person, is he? Try sharing a pod with him." She paused, staring hard at me. "Look, Quin, want my advice? Whatever you know, keep it to yourself. Things have a way of getting sorted out, for better or worse. Just don't let yourself get stuck in the middle of it all."

Leaning forwards, she gave my arm a quick squeeze before heading off towards the Annexe, clasping her arms tightly around her own body. I went back inside and clambered back into my cot, exchanging a worried glance with Jackson. I didn't dare tell her what I knew while others were listening, but was terrified that the consequence of the attack on Donnelly might directly affect Cassidy. Wade had clearly taken my warning to heart and decided to act quickly. I hadn't bargained on quite how determined she was. To attempt to kill Donnelly in his pod as he slept seemed an incredibly bold move. I could only pray that Cass had been nowhere near when it had happened.

Realising I was working myself into a state where I could barely breathe, I forced myself to inhale and exhale slowly, closing my eyes to calm the disturbing images flashing across my brain. Jackson cleared her throat quietly and I opened them again. Her eyes shone in the darkness, understanding my terror, promising support when we were able to share the news in private. I reached out a hand across the small gap between our cots and, not for the first time, we held on to one another as we fell asleep.

Chapter Twenty Seven

When I woke it felt like an ordinary day, until we emerged to discover that Donnelly's pod was being guarded by Shadow Patrol officers. This was not a usual sight. Shadow Patrol usually only wore their black uniform over in Clearance, and the sight of it on home turf sent a clear message. Governance was extremely concerned about the events of the previous night.

There was a strange atmosphere in the canteen at breakfast. Where I had assumed everyone would be buzzing with rumours about the previous night, the room was oddly silent, as though citizens were frightened that talking about it might associate them with the gruesome business and bring them under unwelcome scrutiny.

We were joined by Mason and Davis as usual, but other than exchanging curious glances with us, they followed the herd and remained quiet. It felt as though we were all waiting for something. Some kind of announcement, letting us know what had happened. I knew from experience that Governance lied to us on a regular basis, so there were no guarantees that what we were told would be the truth. But until we were given something to take away and interpret, the sense of frustration was overwhelming.

We didn't have long to wait. By the time the majority of

citizens were seated, Reed had entered the canteen, followed by Governor Adams. There was no sign of Superintendent Carter. The two men stepped on to the stage at the side of the room and waited for silence, before realising that they already had it. All eyes were turned towards them, waiting for some kind of news.

Adams stepped forwards first. His voice, usually calm and pleasant, shook a little as he began. "You will be aware that last night there was a disturbance within the compound. We believe that one or more of the new recruits from the Lower Beck stole a knife during a training exercise yesterday evening. They concealed this from their Supers and, at some point during the night, sneaked out of their pod and made their way into the main Patrol pods. They targeted a specific pod and, upon entering, made their way to one of our Supers, Donnelly."

At this he paused for a moment, glancing around the room to see how the news was being taken. Most citizens seemed fairly shocked; certainly Mason and Davis had not known what Will had already told us. But I could feel there was more to come.

"The recruit used the knife to viciously attack Donnelly, stabbing it into his chest more than once." Again he paused, before delivering the final blow. "I'm afraid to say that, despite efforts made by several citizens to assist him, Donnelly died in the early hours of the morning."

This time the shock was audible. There were gasps and cries from the group around the room who seemed disturbed to differing degrees by the news. Mostly death in the Beck was hidden from view. People who were about to die were simply sent away to Clearance, and most citizens attempted

to erase these people from their memories, at least outwardly, and pretend they no longer existed. It was less painful.

As someone who had witnessed the violence of the drownings which took place in Clearance, I had seen more death than most. I knew that the method Governance chose to dispose of those citizens no longer useful to Beck society was far from gentle and kind. No matter how much they tried to persuade Beck citizens that the harsh system was necessary to keep us alive, I knew that the truth was far from fair. But keeping citizens in the dark was what Governance did. It made me wonder why they were telling us about Donnelly's death now.

Adams stepped back and allowed Reed to take over. As usual, he had delivered the initial statement. Now he would leave the sanctions to one of his second in commands. I wondered what decisions had been made about those responsible, and how they would be punished. And where was Carter? She was usually the one who would convey such edicts to Beck citizens. While Adams was the face of Beck leadership, Carter and Reed were the muscle.

"The crime that occurred last night was a terrible one, and one which will affect us for a long time to come," he began. "Donnelly was a respected leader, and many of you will have worked alongside him during your time here. We believe we know the recruit responsible for Donnelly's death. She is still missing. Rest assured that the remaining recruits are all being questioned about the matter as we speak. Donnelly's killer will be identified swiftly and dealt with harshly."

Now I understood where Carter was. She was just the woman for the task of questioning the vulnerable recruits, who had probably been denied sleep. I was willing to bet

they were being pressured into sharing what they knew as we sat there listening to Adams and Reed speak. I closed my eyes briefly, hoping that Cassidy would remain calm under Carter's questioning, and not fly off the handle in misguided defence of her new friend.

Reed droned on, explaining that things in Patrol had to remain as normal as possible. That certain citizens would be taken off their usual duties to assist with the process of finding the culprit responsible for the crime, but that the rest of us needed to continue with the normal routine. Most citizens seemed to have stopped listening, the shock of the sudden announcement clear from their shared expression of disbelief. When Reed finished speaking and left the room, the only certainty was his instruction to continue as normal, so citizens began to shuffle out of the room slowly and head for the Jefferson Building.

We followed suit. The strange silence that had dominated the canteen remained with us as we moved to the work boards, but I knew that those of us on shifts with trusted friends would talk of nothing else once away from the building. The lists on the wall had been hastily amended, large crossings out marring the usually neatly handwritten schedules. Jackson and I found our names had been erased from shifts in the Solar Fields and on the wall, and added to a separate list at the bottom of the board, that simply said 'Clearance Duty.'

My heart sank at the words. I had not been back to Clearance since the drownings, and knew that my nightmares would not be improved by revisiting the scene. Still, the listing was vague. Ordinary Patrol citizens often guarded the gateway to Clearance yet did not have to enter the compound itself. A note at the base of the board instructed us to collect

some equipment before we left.

Bidding goodbye to Davis and Mason who were both on wall duty, we walked through the building and made our way up the stairs to the equipment store. We reached the desk to find it unoccupied.

"Hello?"

Jackson's voice carried through the space, but there was no answer. The desk was filled with various piles of equipment, but we had no idea what we were required to collect, and didn't dare to take anything without permission.

"I'll go and see if anyone's back there." Jackson gave my shoulder a squeeze, "Look, the sooner we get going, the sooner you can share whatever it is that's eating away at you."

I frowned.

"It might just help, you know."

She sidled past the counter and headed through the doorway into the depths of the room beyond. I had no idea how big it was, but Patrol required a lot of equipment, so I assumed that the space behind the door was large enough for a person to get lost in.

Peering around the upper floor, I wondered what else was housed up here. Reed's office, certainly, but there were other doors off the hallway which obviously led to different rooms. I wandered aimlessly down the hall, wondering if I might discover something useful for the Resistance up here. I had a reason to be on this floor: if anyone caught me up here I could claim I was searching for the equipment attendant.

Most of the doors were closed, but at the very end of the hall, one stood a little ajar and I could hear voices coming from inside. Edging closer, and checking carefully that there was no one around to catch me spying, I strained to hear the

words of the citizens inside the room.

"Security isn't good enough... that someone could just break in... no one saw anything... don't understand it."

The voice was female, and familiar. I realised with a start that it belonged to Montgomery. With all the fuss over Donnelly, I had completely forgotten that Lewis' death would have been discovered, and that presumably Montgomery would have something to say about the fact that her pet project had been ruined. I wondered who she was complaining to, and whether or not her grievance would be taken seriously.

The voice who finally replied to her was also familiar, and sent a chill through my entire body.

"...sorry... understand your concern... must have been shocking... we can increase security, put another guard on the gates... circle the Dev perimeter... make you feel any better..."

It was Cam. The Super Montgomery was complaining to, was the very person responsible for the break in and for ensuring that Montgomery could no longer test her chemicals on Lewis. I marvelled at how calm he seemed in the face of her anger.

Her voice dropped as she replied, so I inched a little closer to catch more of the conversation.

"...feel far better if it was you... know I can fully trust you, you see... especially at night." Her voice had taken on a teasing tone I had not come across before. "...after what happened here... murdered in my bed..."

Unable to stop myself, I closed the final gap between myself and the door and peered cautiously through the space. I found myself looking into a small office. Perched on the edge of the desk was Montgomery, her pristine-white overalls completely alien in the dusty, cluttered room. She was staring up into

Cameron's eyes, a smile on her face which suggested she wasn't in the least bit afraid. As I watched, she leaned in even closer.

"I know. I can alter the schedule... make some changes," Cam was saying, "We can't have our star scientist feeling frightened, can we? Not when you're on the verge of making such potentially life-changing discoveries..."

His voice trailed off in a suggestive manner, and I watched in horror as he also leaned in towards her, casually trailing a hand across her cheek.

I backed away in horror, fear forcing me to remain silent whilst I fought against the tide of revulsion coursing through me. I made it back to the equipment store just as Jackson emerged with the Patrol citizen who was on duty.

"Here," she said, motioning to two large backpacks on the floor at the side of the desk. "This is what you need."

I turned on autopilot and took hold of one of the bags. It was not overly heavy, but quite unwieldy. As I struggled to secure it on my back, there was a noise at the end of the corridor and the door to the office I had just been listening at was flung open. Montgomery strode out, a smug expression on her haughty features. Behind her walked Cam. As he ushered her along the hallway and down the stairs, he caught my eye. Shock flashed across his face for a second, but was quickly wiped away as Montgomery turned to say something else to him. My final view was of him glancing back up the stairway at me, a look of horror marring his handsome features.

Chapter Twenty Eight

I followed Jackson out through the Jefferson Building and across the field into the woods, where we took the less familiar path towards Clearance. It had started raining heavily, and we bent our heads against the downpour. I was numb, and felt completely unable to put my concerns into words. My friend trudged along beside me saying nothing, seeming to understand my need for silence. On top of everything that had happened over the past few days, I couldn't make sense of what I had just seen. And now I had to face a shift in Clearance.

I had not been there for several months, and most of the time, I was glad of that fact. Selfishly, it was easier to assume that Harper was still alive over in Clearance, but not witness her suffering. There was little I could do about it at the moment anyway. Also, the horror of the drownings haunted my dreams so regularly that I dreaded to think what might happen when I saw the place again for real. This morning, however, there was no escaping it.

The trees loomed around us and the sky was dark, making the path through the woods more gloomy than usual. We passed several extra Patrols clearly searching for Wade. Jackson attempted to nod at them as they passed, but the rain prevented any further communication and I was grateful for it. My stomach was still churning by the time the woods began to thin out and we reached the pass which led to the hidden entrance to Clearance. The rain was lighter, but continued in a steady drizzle which coated us from head to toe in a fine, damp mist. Ahead of us stood two Shadow Patrol recruits who looked bored. They brightened up immeasurably at the sight of us.

"Hey. What's going on? Lot of noise coming from Patrol last night."

Jackson took the lead, sensing that I was still not up to communication. "One of the new recruits went a little crazy. Stole a weapon. Crept into a pod and stabbed one of the Supers. Donnelly. He's dead."

Her explanation was brief and to the point, but she couldn't prevent the news from being shocking. It was several moments before either of them managed to choke out any words.

"Donnelly?"

"Yes."

"No way."

Both guards looked horrified at the news. They exchanged concerned glances before hastily gathering their backpacks from the small hut behind them.

"Thanks for the update. We'll get off now." He nodded abruptly as the two of them stomped off rapidly in the direction we had come from.

Remembering our own backpacks, I managed to stammer some words before they had gone out of sight. "Hey! We have equipment for delivery. Don't you need to stay until we're back?"

"Nope." They were simply calling back over their shoulders now. "One of you'll have to take it through alone."

"But–"

They were almost out of sight now and I realised it was useless. We watched as they vanished into the trees, feeling more than a little abandoned. Ditching my backpack on the ground, I grabbed my water bottle and took a long drink, tired after the long trek. It was warm, despite the constant rain, and we had worked up quite a sweat.

Ducking into the cabin, Jackson fumbled with the straps to her pack. "He's right. One of us will have to take the packs through. The other needs to stay here on guard duty. Can't risk leaving the pass unguarded today with everything that's going on."

"Great." I managed.

"I didn't dare earlier, but wanted to know…" She was desperately unthreading the straps to her pack to allow her access to the contents. I knew why she was looking. The last time we had come through to Clearance we had unwittingly carried the harnesses built for weighing the drowning victims down as they were thrown overboard. A moment later she had the top open, and a pile of worn, ripped Patrol overalls spilled out on to the ground. "Thank goodness. Just old uniforms. They must recycle them."

I shared a relieved smile with her. Neither of us had wanted to play any part in the deaths of innocent citizens for a second time.

"Do you want to go through? Or shall I?" She frowned, "Have to admit, after Fin, I don't relish the thought."

"I'll go."

"You sure?" She stared into my face intently. "You don't seem like you're doing too well today. Want at least to tell me what happened before you go?"

I sighed. "Not sure where to begin really."

"Try. Like I said, it might just help. We have time."

I ducked inside the hut with her, removing my outer jacket and hanging it up to dry. The two of us settled on the floor together, figuring that we could still see the path down to Patrol if anyone came from that direction, and the chance of someone heading out of Clearance was unlikely.

"Pretty sure I know the recruit who attacked Donnelly."

"Wade."

"You too?"

"Well I worked with her yesterday. I told you – I knew something wasn't right about her. The way she spoke to Donnelly in particular."

"I went over there last night after I left you. Saw them finishing their training session and talked to Cass. Wade joined us. She'd stolen a knife, Jac."

Jackson's mouth dropped open. "Really? So it was definitely her then!"

"It's my fault." I dropped my head.

"What do you mean? It wasn't you plunging a knife into Donnelly's chest."

"Maybe not. But I tried to persuade her to return it. Hand it to the other team so that she wouldn't get caught with it."

Jackson stared at me, confusion clouding her features.

"I told her they would miss it that night. That she wouldn't get away with keeping it for long. I'm certain she didn't plan to do anything this fast. I must've frightened her. She thought that if she didn't act now, she wouldn't get the chance to at all."

"So you think by telling her she'd be discovered before the night was through, she decided to carry out her plans early –

last night?"

"That's exactly what I think."

"Wow. Well you might be right. But–" she held up a hand to quell my protest, "She would've done it sooner or later, with or without your warning. This is not your responsibility."

I loved Jackson for her steadfast support of me. But I knew I hadn't finished yet. I forged on, knowing I needed to get the rest of it out before I broke down completely. "And then… just now in the Jefferson Building…"

"I knew something else had happened. Was it Cam?"

I nodded, barely able to go on. "I overheard him and Montgomery talking. She was angry about the Dev break in."

Jackson's face broke into a grim smile. "And she complained to Cam about it? She really has no idea what kind of person he is, does she?"

"No. Can you imagine, going for help from the very person who invaded your compound in the first place?" I laughed without mirth, then remembered the rest of their exchange. "But that's not what bothers me."

"Then what?" Her voice was gentle, coaxing.

"She was leaning into him, asking for his help. She didn't even look scared, but she was acting like she needed him to protect her personally."

"So Montgomery likes Cam does she? Know what I think? She's pretending to be frightened to persuade him to spend more time with her. Flirting with him, acting like she needs him. You know, making him feel like he's strong and powerful, and that she's vulnerable. So he'll feel flattered. Do what she wants him to."

"But he…"

CHAPTER TWENTY EIGHT

"Don't tell me, he looked like he was enjoying it?"

I could do nothing but nod.

"Ha! Don't you worry about it. Cam's got his head screwed on the right way. He might like it. But he doesn't like her."

"How do you know?"

Jackson shuffled a little closer to me, until she could loop an arm through my own. "I've told you before Quin, I've seen the way he looks at you. It's not Montgomery he wants to spend his evenings with."

I considered this for a moment, biting my lip to prevent the tears from soaking my cheeks again. "But you didn't see them. He leaned right into her too. He was stroking her cheek, comforting her."

She thought for a moment. "Because he's not stupid. He knows Montgomery. She's clever. She holds a lot of power here in The Beck because she knows about chemicals and medicine. She's useful. He doesn't want to get on the wrong side of her. And, maybe he makes it look like he wants to kiss her, but that's all. It's an act, I'm certain of it."

I sighed, feeling a little better for sharing the burden. Perhaps Jackson was right. It didn't seem like something Cam would do, pretend to have feelings for someone. It seemed manipulative, calculating. But so was Montgomery. Maybe Cam was just playing her at her own game. If she liked him, it was a clever way of getting close to her. She was just getting what she deserved. As usual, I felt slightly more at ease after listening to Jackson. Glancing outside, I could see another group of Patrol recruits marching through the woods, searching for Wade. I straightened up and attempted to gather my thoughts. Jackson pulled herself on to her feet and waved a hand at the distant figures confidently.

"You'd better get going. And I need to be more visible outside the guard hut. Not a good idea if we're not doing our job well today. Not with Reed and Carter on the warpath."

Her mention of our leaders made me think of Cass again, and I began to worry afresh. But there was nothing I could do for her at the moment. I needed to make like the perfect Patrol citizen and get the task done. Looking at the backpacks, I realised that I would have to make a double trip over there. They were too large and bulky to carry at the same time. Sighing, I shouldered the first pack and set off.

It took me all the courage I could muster to pull aside the curtain of fronds which hid the Clearance entrance from view. Once I had entered the densely wooded area behind, the air was damp and warm and I couldn't see much more than the shadows of the branches in front of me. As I pushed my way through, I couldn't help but remember the terrified screams of the drowning citizens and the shock I had felt the last time I had used this hidden path in the opposite direction. The fear almost paralysed me, and I made extremely slow progress to begin with. Around half way through I stopped, convinced that I could hear someone else breathing. Listening intently, and peering into the shadows brought me no comfort. I still couldn't be sure that someone or something was not lurking in the darkness of the trees beside me.

Hurrying onwards, I emerged into the gloom on the other side a little out of breath. Clearance looked no more pleasant than the last time I had visited. I glanced down to the harbour, where Shadow Patrol officers were unloading a catch of fish from the boats that I had previously witnessed carrying people to their deaths. I found it hard to stomach that the very vessels which brought food to sustain the citizens of The Beck

248

should also be employed to bring an end to so many of their lives. Shuddering, I forced myself to focus on the task ahead and made my way towards the Warehouse, where Clearance citizens worked to create the uniforms for the entire Beck. I was assuming that the backpacks I was transporting needed to be delivered there, so that they could be reused.

Head down, I set off along the path towards the centre of the compound. As I passed the sick pods, I noted that some of the entrances had been propped open to allow air inside. On my last visit, these pods had been crammed with people about to be drowned. This should have left them empty, but in the months that had passed they had clearly begun to refill. There was no shortage of sick and injured people in the Beck. Knowing that I couldn't help them, I averted my eyes and continued down the hill.

The Warehouse was as noisy and hot as ever, and I braced myself as I flung open the door. Inside, I was assaulted by the noise of the thunderous machinery. The space was crammed with large numbers of citizens who were working hard, despite the fact that many of them looked ill. I made my way to the two bored-looking Shadow Patrol officers in charge. Both wore headphones to protect their hearing from the incessant drone that Clearance citizens had to endure. Proffering the backpack, I stepped back and, taking a deep breath, looked around properly for the first time. I could not immediately recognise Harper among the crowd. My heart was thumping in my chest as I contemplated what could have happened to her since I last saw her. The thought that perhaps she was not here at all was one I tried desperately not to consider.

A tap on my shoulder alerted me to the Shadow Patrol

officer. He thrust the pack back at me, and pointed to a woman wearing a headscarf. She was standing apart from the machinery and seemed to have some kind of supervisory role. I wondered briefly if, even here in Clearance, some citizens managed to engineer better treatment than others. I made my way towards her.

She took the backpack and peered inside it, nodding and turning away to mime something to a woman standing close to the next machine, who took her place. The woman beckoned me to follow her and headed towards the door at the far end of the Warehouse. Before we could reach it, a figure appeared at her side, tapping her on the arm. She had her back to me, but I would have known her anywhere. Miming furiously to the first woman, she conveyed something to her which I couldn't understand.

The woman stepped back and handed the pack over to Harper, who nodded and continued towards the door. She hadn't looked at me yet, and didn't attempt to. I took the lead from her and simply followed her outside, as if we were total strangers. At the door, we passed through and crossed the small courtyard to the building behind. Once inside, Harper made her way to one of the tables and put the pack down. I waited cautiously while she wandered down to the front of the room and checked that there was no one in the small space which clearly served as a food preparation area. Then she opened a door at the side of the room and beckoned for me to bring the backpack to her, before disappearing.

Chapter Twenty Nine

The door led to a smaller room which was clearly used as storage by the Clearance staff. It was not large, but clean, and packed from floor to ceiling. Most of the shelves were neatly stacked with overalls of varying colours, all separated into the different Sectors that made up the Beck. The final wall held shelves piled with large spools of thread, boxes of scissors and other relevant equipment.

Harper moved behind me to close the door. A moment later she had flung her arms around my neck and we were both crying.

"Har," I managed to choke out eventually, "you're choking me!"

She backed away a little, still holding tightly to my neck. "Sorry. It's just…"

"I know."

Eventually I drew away and took a proper look at her. As I had been holding her she had felt solid, far sturdier than when I had last encountered her. She also had more colour in her cheeks.

"Har, you look…" I struggled for words.

"Good? I know! Can you believe it?"

"Honestly, no." I smiled, the news that Harper was not only here, alive, but also far healthier than the last time I had seen her, was extremely welcome. "What happened?"

She grinned broadly. "Well I'm not exactly sure. I think a number of different things." She hastened to the door again and listened outside, before returning to my side. "Look. We don't have long. We need to empty your pack and sort the materials into the various bins. It should only take a few minutes, and then I'll be missed, so I'll talk fast."

"There's another pack I need to collect and bring from the other side. Can you bring me through for a second time maybe – give us longer?"

She nodded thoughtfully, "Maybe. But let's focus on telling you as much as I can now just in case."

She emptied the contents of the bag on to the floor and knelt down, beginning to sort the different colours into piles. I joined her, following her lead, folding the sections of material and placing them in the heaps she had begun to make.

"Life over here is not so different really. Except, maybe, citizens are even more desperate to survive. I think the people sent here do one of two things. They give up. Or they find a way to rebel."

She paused for a moment and began to place the piles of clothes on the relevant shelves. Sadness clouded her features for a moment.

"Miller's dead, you know."

I nodded.

"One night they came and took some of the citizens away. Mostly those from the sick pods, but not all. They never came back."

I moved towards her in an attempt at comfort, but she shrugged my arm away.

"Sorry. Not much time left. Need to tell you the good stuff.

Anyway when I packed up in Agric and came over here I didn't exactly leave everything behind. I managed to bring some seeds with me. And I found somewhere to plant them." She smiled wickedly, her pleasure at her quiet rebellion evident and suddenly, I knew what she had done. "I can only work on them at night, but I've found a place where I can tend the seeds in secret."

"I've managed to produce a few vegetables, the fast-growing ones, just some beets, kale, and a few beans. It's meant that my rations here can be supplemented. Also, the work is hard, but there were a lot of us here when I first arrived and they had so many people that our shifts weren't that regular. So I rested. Slept every chance I got, made sure I drank lots of water. Began to eat better once I had managed to grow some food."

"Har, that's amazing." I smiled, realising I was crying, but happy that the tears were ones of joy for a change.

"And then there was Cameron."

I jolted at the name. "What?"

She smiled shyly. "The Super from the wall that night? He came and brought me some pills. Just a few nights after I got here. Not sure what they were, but I took them. All of them. One a day for a week. And then he brought me more. And I started to feel better."

"He did that for you?"

"Yes. He's a miracle. He's helped quite a few people over here actually. Not everyone. He has to be careful, but when he can… he does. I think he gets the pills from a scientist in Dev. She makes them for Governance. For the important citizens who 'matter'." She sighed, "Because we lowly citizens don't matter. Not to them anyway."

I hugged her again. Threw my arms tightly around her and held on to her for as long as I dared, marvelling at her newly developed muscles. She returned the embrace for a moment, then jerked back abruptly.

"Someone's coming."

"How d'you know?" I whispered.

"Experience." She hissed. "We meet secretly here sometimes. There's a loose floorboard near the entrance which creaks. Early warning system."

I could hear the approaching footsteps myself now. Hurriedly, we placed the last few overalls on the shelves and straightened up as they came closer.

"Come back and tell me about you. And Cass." Harper turned and opened the door as a Shadow Patrol officer reached it.

"Just coming," she murmured, her head down. All semblance of her earlier optimism was gone. I marvelled at her acting ability.

She hurried past the officer and out of the door. He turned to me.

"All done?"

"There's actually one more pack. I couldn't carry it. Left it back at the guard hut. I'll go and get it now."

He nodded and spun on his heel to leave. Following him out, I left by a different path and headed back up the hill again. It didn't take me long to reach the wooded passage out of the valley, and this time I found I could almost skip through, the news of Harper's survival buoying me up. When I reached Jackson she stared at me, a quizzical expression on her face.

"What happened? I could tell from two hundred metres away that you're happier."

"Well all the other issues still apply, but Jac, something wonderful... you won't believe it!"

"Go on!"

I ducked inside the hut again and we sat while I told her about Harper's improvement. When I had finished she was smiling too.

"Well I'll be damned. The way you described her... I was terrified she wouldn't be there, but..."

"She totally defied the odds. Isn't it brilliant?"

Jackson hugged me. "It is. Get back over there quickly. See if you can talk to her again, get any more out of her."

I prepared to set off through the tunnel for a second time, picking up a bread roll and apple to consume on the way. Tucking them inside the pocket of the backpack, I grinned at Jackson as I left.

"Don't be too long. There are groups of Patrol officers all over the woods. I'll feel better when I'm not standing here alone."

My thoughts turned back to Wade and I wondered where she was. Clearly she had managed to evade them so far, but I wondered how long she would be able to hide. I was making my way through the hidden passage for the third time when I heard a noise. Not the eerie breathing sounds I had imagined earlier, but a cough. I froze. No one should be up here but me. Any legitimate Shadow Patrol Officer would be striding through with confidence, not skulking in the shadows.

I had no weapon. The only thing I was carrying was the backpack and, the most I could do with that was use it to hit someone with. It wasn't heavy enough to do much damage and might even knock me off balance. I wasn't sure whether I should run or attempt to tackle the stranger lurking in the darkness of the foliage around me. After a few moments of panic, I realised that whoever it was had not attacked me yet. Perhaps they were not an enemy. Perhaps it was a Clearance citizen attempting escape. I decided to risk a different strategy.

"Hello?"

Nothing. Uselessly I swung the slim beam of the torch around me. The shadows only seemed to deepen and swirl as I imagined an assailant preparing for a vicious attack. I became aware of someone else breathing again, this time convinced it was not my imagination. This person had been hiding in the woods here before, twice, when I passed by. Their lack of communication with me suggested they were also afraid. I tried once more.

"Who's there? I'm not a threat. Maybe I can help you."

A hand grasped my arm from behind and ripped the torch from my grasp. I stifled a scream as the arm circled my neck and tightened against my windpipe. Terrified, I allowed myself to be pulled to the floor and imprisoned further by a second arm. The figure was much taller than me and definitely male. He had not bargained on the backpack though, so I was further from him than he had perhaps intended and he could not reach all the way round my body. I stayed very still, trying to work out what my next move might be, when he spoke.

"Who are you?"

His voice was deep and rich, and I could feel it resonating through his chest despite the bag that lay between us. I brought a hand up to the arm which encircled my neck and tapped on it to indicate that I couldn't speak. Immediately, it loosened.

"Quin. Patrol Sector. You?"

CHAPTER TWENTY NINE

"Never mind. Got any food?"

I nodded. He loosened his grip a little further.

"In the pack?"

He was already stripping it from my back.

"Don't turn around." The command was firm, but there was no malice in his tone.

I risked a reply, making sure I continued to face away from him. "Carefully please. I'm expected over in Clearance soon. I need to take the pack across. You're welcome to the food – it's in the outer pocket."

I could feel him delving through the contents, but he stopped at my instruction and located the outer pocket instead. Then all I could hear was the sound of him consuming the bread at an alarming rate.

"There's an apple too. You hungry?"

He grunted in reply. I wondered whether to run while he was occupied by the food, clearly his chief reason for attacking me.

"Do you have a weapon?"

I wondered at the question.

"No. Wouldn't I have used it by now if I did?"

He thought for a moment. "Maybe."

"Are you from Clearance?"

He snorted.

"Then where?"

"Never mind."

"Are you going to let me go?"

There was a silence, as if he was considering my words. Then a rustling sound, followed by the sound of him biting into the apple. Clearly food was of the most importance to him at the moment. I wondered again if he was one of our enemies from across the water, sent to steal from us. At first I was afraid, but then I thought of my original conviction that maybe those across the water were not so different. That we might find common ground, help one another.

"Did you come here by boat?"

He didn't reply, but the atmosphere changed slightly and I knew that I had struck a chord. I wondered if a correct guess would further anger him, but he still didn't make any other move towards me. We sat in silence, only the sounds of him crunching the apple disturbing the peace. Eventually, he tossed what was left of the core on the ground and turned his attention back to me.

"You said you're expected over there. How long before they miss you?"

"Not sure. Maybe fifteen, twenty minutes? Half an hour, if you're lucky."

"You said you were Patrol?"

"Yes."

"How long have you been Patrol? What were you before?"

"Three months. Agric." As I answered his questions, I wondered how he knew so much about our system. If he had come from over the water, did they have more knowledge of Beck workings than we realised?

"Who trained you?"

"In Patrol? Tyler. Barnes. Sometimes Cameron."

I felt him relax a little at the names. "Reed still in charge?"

"Yes."

Surely he had to be a Beck citizen. He knew too much not to be.

"How well d'you know Tyler and Cam?"

"Pretty well. For a newbie."

Silence again. I could feel the man thinking things through in his head. I took a chance. Perhaps sharing information with him might help me out of this.

"I had a shift with Tyler in Meds yesterday."

"Meds?"

"Yes."

I felt him pass the bag back to me and back away.

"You're letting me go?"

Silence again.

"I could try to bring more food. Will you be here when I come back through?"

I knew that he would not. He couldn't risk me bringing officers back with me to discover him.

"Where will you go?"

He didn't respond.

"Do you know Cameron? Tyler?"

He moved closer to me again and I held my breath. He felt down my arm until he had hold of my hand. Prising the fingers apart, he pushed the torch into my hand.

"Don't turn it on yet."

"Can I let them know you're here?"

There was a further silence as if he were weighing something up. Then, just as I thought he would not speak again, his rich voice echoed in my ear.

"Rogers."

"That's your name?"

But he had retreated again, back into the cover of the trees where he had come from. I knew I had to leave.

"Good luck." I called to him as I moved off, making sure that I didn't glance in his direction. I wondered if I would ever see what he looked like.

Coming out into the light on the other side of the woods, I blinked as my eyes adjusted. Shaking my head, I realised I had been far longer than I should've been, and Jackson would begin to worry about me if I didn't hurry. Sprinting down the hillside, I made it to the Warehouse in record time. This time, there was no sign of Harper. Instead the woman with the headscarf took me through to the storage room.

She didn't speak to me at all, simply took the overalls and sorted them as Harper had done. I helped her as best I could, and then collected the backpack and turned to go. As I put my hand on the door handle to leave, she stopped me.

"She was called to a different job. Said she was sorry."

I smiled my thanks, sad that I had not been able to exchange more information with my old friend, but grateful to be reassured that she wasn't in any trouble for her recent conversation with me. The woman spoke no more, but opened the door and let me out of the store room. She headed back to the Warehouse while I jogged back up the hill, feeling light and fit enough to almost sprint some of the way. My spirits had been lifted hugely by the good news about my friend, and I couldn't wait to tell Cassidy.

Chapter Thirty

I listened hard as I moved into the densely wooded section of the path for the final time, but could hear nothing. Clearly the man was gone. Where to, I had no idea. I hurried out of the other end and down towards Jackson, suddenly concerned that if he had headed her way she might have been in danger, but she was standing outside the Patrol hut staring into the forest.

"Ok?" she said as I approached, her face unconcerned.

"Yes, but you won't believe…"

At that moment, a crackling from the radio inside the hut prevented me from continuing. Jackson went to listen to the call.

"Extra units to the Hydro Plant please. Immediately."

The call was repeated twice and the radio went dead again. Jackson frowned. "Wonder if they've found Wade."

"Maybe. Something's going on."

For the first time, Jackson seemed to pick up on my altered mood. "What's up?

I filled her in on the man in the tunnel. Her face went pale as she listened.

"Who is he? Surely a Beck citizen, knowing Tyler and Cam."

"More than likely a Patrol citizen too, knowing Reed."

"Well he didn't pass me," she said, glancing nervously at the tunnel exit. "At least I'm pretty sure he didn't."

"Perhaps he went back into Clearance. The trees on the other side are quite thick – he could be hiding over there."

"You need to tell Tyler. Or Cam. They probably know who he is."

"I'll tell them when we get back."

She shuddered a little and came out of the hut to stand beside me. "I'm glad you're back. I don't much like being here alone with all these Shadow Patrol on the hunt. Too many weapons around. Easy to make a mistake."

I saw her point. It wouldn't take much for one of the extra patrols, primed to search for a young woman in Patrol uniform acting suspiciously somewhere in The Beck, to shoot before they were certain of their target. Governance would be set on catching Wade quickly, before she could do any further damage, using their precious guns to deal with what they obviously considered a serious situation. It would not do for innocent parties to get in the way.

We spent the rest of the shift nervously alert, watching the entrance to the Clearance tunnel closely, but there was no sign of the man. A few more messages came over the radio about extra patrols being directed here and there, but none seemed to have any pattern. There were certainly no definite reports of Wade being identified or caught. Jackson and I discussed the potential sanctions she could face, debating whether being sent to Clearance would send enough of a message to deter others from similar defiance. We both felt certain that Governance would take further action against her, but shuddered to think what the true consequences might be.

Our replacements arrived in the late afternoon. Clearly

Shadow Patrol were being diverted to the search for Wade still, as Anders and Dean, two ordinary Patrol officers, turned up to take over. I didn't know Dean well, but Anders had trained with me, though he had always been a much quieter, more private member of our group. A Dev transfer, he was an oddity really, as I had no knowledge of anyone else ever transferring from that Sector. Davis had, on more than one occasion, jokingly referred to him as a spy, but he kept his head down and did a decent job, and had in the three months we had been in Patrol become an effective officer.

He nodded on approach, acknowledging at least that he knew us. Jackson wasn't about to let him get away with that on such an important day.

"Hey, how are things down there? Have they caught the recruit yet?"

Unsurprisingly, Dean was the one to reply. "Nope. No sign as yet. She's giving them a run for their money!"

Anders didn't respond, ducking inside the hut instead to check the log.

Jackson continued to quiz Dean. "She? Have they announced it's a woman?"

"Nah. But rumour has it the recruit who's missing is female."

I passed them to retrieve my jacket from the hut, making no attempt to speak to Anders, as he rarely talked to anyone unless it concerned work. He surprised me by placing a hand on my arm as I turned to go.

"Tell your friend Cameron not to mess with Montgomery." His voice was barely a whisper.

I whirled to face him, intrigued. "What?"

He looked startled at my reaction, and a look of panic crossed his features for a fleeting moment before he quashed it. "Montgomery."

I lowered my own voice. "What about her?"

"She's a nasty piece of work. Cameron needs to watch himself where she's concerned."

"But how do you–?"

"I saw her coming out of the offices in the Jefferson Building earlier with Cameron. And… well let's just say I hear things from Dev from time to time."

I realised that he must have some way of communicating with his old Dev colleagues despite this being forbidden. I felt a new respect for him, and for the fact that he had trusted me enough to share the information.

"What did you hear?"

He looked back at the log and I wondered if he would answer at all, but just as I had given up, he began to speak. His voice was quiet and controlled, betraying no emotion.

"Now and again I manage to exchange information with a couple of friends from Dev. When I'm on shifts close by. Everyone knows Montgomery is dangerous. But Governance loves her. She's some kind of genius with chemicals."

I nodded, even though he wasn't looking at me. Dean and Jackson were still chatting happily outside. I realised that Anders had never spoken this many words to me in all the time I had known him.

"So she'd be difficult to get rid of. And life would be difficult if you got on the wrong side of her. She's not physically powerful, but Governance would do a lot to protect her, believe me. They think she's indispensable."

He turned a page in the log before continuing. "Last week she had some kind of project she was pretty excited about. Testing some new kind of chemical under what she referred to as 'unusual circumstances.' But something went wrong. I don't know what exactly, but there was some kind of break-in. Completely wrecked her experiment."

He paused, considering. "She's always so cool and calm, you know? But apparently she was furious. When they investigated, they figured out that the entry card used to access her lab belonged to one of the other Dev Supers, Randall. None of the ordinary citizens' cards would've granted access to somewhere so secure."

"What happened?"

Anders finally looked up at me again, his eyes heavy. "She had Randall out within the hour. Straight to Clearance. He said he didn't know anything about the break-in, but she wasn't listening. And like I said, Montgomery gets what she wants. Adams himself came down to check that she was happy with the consequence he was given."

"And was she?"

"I'm not sure that she was. My friend said she'd been overheard saying she should be allowed to use Randall in her next experiment, but that might just be hearsay. And I didn't much like Randall myself when I worked in Dev, but I don't think he was responsible. He always did everything by the book. I think it was someone else. And then I saw Cameron talking to Montgomery today, and..."

He trailed off, a worried expression crossing his features again. I managed a smile, trying to hide my own fear at this confirmation of Montgomery's power.

"Thanks Anders. I'll pass on the warning."

He gave a small nod before burying his attention in the log again. I waited another moment before realising that I had received all the information I was going to get for now.

"See you Anders."

He didn't respond as I headed out the door. Jackson was still deep in conversation with Dean, who seemed in no hurry to get rid of her. I grabbed her arm and tugged it, wanting to try and find Tyler or Cam before it got too late for them to act on my information if they needed to. Dean reluctantly said his goodbyes as we headed off into the woods. I felt like he wasn't relishing the idea of an entire night shift with Anders.

Jackson and I made our way back through the woods and headed for the canteen. There was no sign of either Tyler or Cam. Mason and Davis joined us for the meal, tired and cranky after a lengthy shift on the wall.

"Ok?" Jackson enquired, sensible enough not to discuss the unusual events of our day in front of them.

Mason grunted and began shovelling his food in, clearly in no mood to chat.

Davis was more forthcoming. "Tired is all. Cam was better today though. Seemed less stressed."

This was followed by another, louder grunt from Mason.

Davis continued. "Still had a ton of work to do though. Painting those barriers is hard work."

"And the length of time it takes to suit up for it!" Mason burst out, "We could have been done hours ago if it wasn't for Cam's insane obsession with safety."

"What do you mean?"

"Well the stuff we're painting on the barriers is a deterrent." Davis' explanation was again more patient. "Nasty stuff apparently. We've always had to wear gloves, but lately Cam's been insistent about us securing them in the outer sleeves of our overalls and he's really hot on checking every single one of us."

"Every. Single. One of us." Mason's scorn was apparent.

He was always more scathing when he was tired, and usually I didn't bother to argue. Thinking back to the state Lewis had been in when he was brought to us at the Hydro Plant though, I shuddered.

"Do you know what the result would be of the substance actually touching you?"

He looked surprised at my challenge. "No."

"Well shut up then. Believe me, Cam is trying to save your knuckle-headed life."

He stopped abruptly in his grumbling and continued with his meal.

After we had eaten I used my Rec time to circle the compound, trying to appear as though I was simply exercising, but in reality searching for either of the Supers I needed. Donnelly's pod was still cordoned off, as was the field set up for the recruits. There was no sign of anyone there, and I began to worry about Cass again. I had circled the whole of Patrol twice before I spotted Tyler returning from some kind of shift in the Lower Beck. She looked harassed and was heading for the canteen, when I caught up to her.

"You'll have to walk with me Quin, no time."

I fell in step beside her, managing with difficulty to keep up. "Need to speak to you."

"Shoot. I'm listening."

I looked around. The area around the Jefferson was empty now. Clearly Tyler was not going to stop, and the mood she was in was not very promising, so I wasted no more time.

"Does the name Rogers mean anything to you?"

She stopped dead.

"Tyler?"

Grasping hold of my arm, she steered me into the empty Jefferson Building and into one of the cubbies which was usually occupied by an office worker during the day. Shoving me into a chair, she knelt beside me, her face very close to my own.

"Talk."

"What?"

"You said Rogers. Where did you get that name from?"

"I think I… well, I think I met him."

Her eyes widened. "You met him? Where? No, scratch that, what did he look like?"

"I don't know."

She scowled. "Quin, stop playing games. This is important. What did he look like?"

"I don't know. It was dark. I only heard him speak. I couldn't actually see him."

She stared at me for a few seconds before speaking again. "Look Quin. Tell me what you know. Everything. And when you're finished I'll try to answer some of your questions."

Accepting this, I told her about my encounter with Rogers. It didn't take long, but she devoted her attention to me throughout. When I was finished, she sat back on her heels, a look of astonishment on her face. Then, without warning, she sprang to her feet. Flinging open drawers in the desk, she began pulling out various items, as though trying to locate something essential. Pulling out a radio, she switched it on, then looked back at me and thought better of it, fastening it to her belt instead.

Finally, she blurted out, "I have to go."

"But what about answering my questions?" I stammered, desperate to get some answers before she ran off.

"I need to find Cam."

"I can help you. Just tell me something please, Tyler. Who is he? Who is Rogers?"

She paused for a second. Turning to face me, she grinned inexplicably. "An old friend."

And then she was gone.

Giving up on any further information, I slowly followed her out of the Jefferson. By the time I reached the courtyard, she was almost at the edge of the woods. I could see her using the radio now, and wondered if she was calling Cam. Was she using some kind of code though? The radios were all on the same station and Governance heard everything. One thing was for sure, she hadn't wanted me to overhear.

I suddenly felt completely drained, and headed back to the pod, thinking I might get some extra rest by going to bed early. The extra hours in the luxurious Meds bed felt a million years ago. After a quick wash, I returned to the pod, assuming it would be empty and wondering if my racing mind would slow down sufficiently to allow me to sleep. I was desperately curious about Rogers, concerned about how Cass was coping with Carter's questioning and, at the back of my mind, still in turmoil about Cam's feelings for Montgomery.

As my eyes adjusted to the dim light inside the pod, I saw that I wasn't alone. Blythe lay on her bed, a blank expression on her face. Unsure whether to approach her or leave her alone, I undressed in my own space. Then, thinking back to my shift in Meds, to Riley and Perry, and Tyler's concern for her friend, I hauled myself up and went to perch on the cot next to her.

She heard me coming and managed a small smile that didn't reach her eyes. "Hey Quin."

"Hey yourself. How was your first proper shift?"

"Ah not bad. I managed."

"Good."

The silence stretched between us for a moment before she spoke again. "I was lucky. With one of my old Patrol colleagues. She was kind. I took it easy mostly."

"That's good." I cursed myself for repeating the same platitudes, but found I had no idea how to bring up the sensitive subject of her child. She surprised me by doing it for me.

"Ty said you went to Meds with her yesterday."

"Um, yes."

"And how did you find it?"

"Oh, wonderful! I mean – unimaginably good!"

"It is pretty great, isn't it?" She looked sad again. "I hear you met Perry."

My heart was pounding. The thought that I had seen this woman's child when she could not seemed so wrong. Unable to speak, I reached out and instinctively clasped her hand.

"Isn't she a beauty?"

Wordlessly I stared at her, unable to comprehend how she was holding it together.

"It's alright. I'm glad you got to meet her. I want her to see as many of my friends as possible, so I know she's surrounded by people who will look out for her."

I was flattered that she considered me a friend after such a short space of time. "But you seem–"

"Ok? I'm not. Not really. Cam gave me something. Takes the edge off the pain, if you know what I mean. I can remember how I was feeling, but it's kind of dulled, you know?"

I didn't really, so I continued to hold her hand, squeezing it gently. Cam certainly seemed to be the one with access to relevant medicines, and I was guessing that his close relationship with Montgomery was what made this possible. The drugs explained the glassy look in Blythe's eyes, and the strange calm which had overcome her.

"I'm so sorry. About the system. About Perry. It's not... not..."

"It's not fair. No." Again she sounded far too calm, dangerously so. I wondered what would happen when the drugs wore off. "But it's the way things are. I know she'll be well looked after. Babies in The Beck are valuable. They're only born when we have space for them and they cost a lot to rear, so we invest time and resources in making sure they're brought up well. At least I can count on that."

"Don't you want to have some say though, in her life? In how she is brought up?"

Her tone remained calm, but was slightly colder, "Of course I do. But this is how it is. I have no power to change anything."

I realised she had stopped making eye contact with me and her eyelids were flickering closed. Standing up, I backed away from her bed, finding myself completely unable to comfort her. The drugs she was on were not only sending her to sleep but also preventing her from experiencing feelings which, although negative, were natural. She should have been screaming from the rooftops. But what good would it do? I could see why Tyler and Cam had given her the pills.

I let go of her hand. "Sorry," she murmured quietly, "These pills. They make my head fuzzy." She waved a vague hand in my direction, unable to keep her eyes open at all now. I was about to leave when she whispered my name, "Quin, just pray you don't… pray you never…"

And she was gone. I knew what she had been trying to say though. No matter how calm she was on the surface, it was clear that her experience in Meds was one she wished she had never had. Thoroughly disheartened by the conversation, I climbed into my own bed, wondering how much more horror I could take before I too required drugging to remain sane.

Chapter Thirty One

When I woke it was dark, and Jackson was shaking me. It took me a few moments to come to, but her persistence told me something important was going on. I dressed quietly and we crept out together.

Once we were out of earshot of the pods, we began to run. I was so grateful that I had gone to sleep earlier than usual, and stored up a few extra hours that I would no doubt need.

"Meeting." Jackson hissed in my ear as we hugged the edges of the field which led to the forest.

We made our way quickly to the clearing, curious to hear the reason for the sudden gathering. It was too much of a coincidence for this not to be connected to Rogers, but I was still unsure as to what he meant for the Resistance. Part of me was hoping for some sign that we could begin to actually do something to fight against Governance at last. At the same time, I dreaded the severity of the actions we might have to take once the Resistance had begun its work in earnest.

Cam and Tyler were waiting in the usual space, a tall man who I didn't recognise was standing beside them. He was long limbed and more muscular than Cameron, but what drew my eyes to him was his hair. It was far longer than any I had ever seen, curling down below his ears, a thatch of jet black. I felt myself longing to touch it. No one in The Beck had hair that length. The strangest feature of all was the hair on his face. Beck men made daily use of the standard Governance-issue razors. Failure to do so resulted in punishment. But this man's face was covered in hair, all over his chin and underneath his nose. I found myself unable to stop staring at it, and when I managed to tear my eyes away, saw that others were having the same problem.

There seemed to be fewer citizens at this meeting, but I wondered if the sudden nature of the arrangement had prevented many people from getting here, or even knowing about it. I noticed Will, who smiled at me and, with a start, saw Barnes sitting off to one side, a sullen expression on his face. Harris, the Governance citizen, hurried in last, bustling to the front and whispering urgently to Cam. We had clearly been waiting for him, and as he sat down, Cam stepped forward.

"Thanks for coming. I know how much you risk. I also apologise for those who we haven't managed to contact about tonight. It was rather a hurried and unexpected arrangement."

He looked at Tyler, who stepped forwards. "We have some fairly exciting news. This," she gestured at the long-haired man at her side, "is Rogers. Many of you won't know him, but he was a citizen here in Patrol. One of those who attempted to travel away from The Beck by boat just over a year ago."

The gasp from some of the group was audible, although older members of the community who knew him had already made the connection, and were smiling broadly.

"So, as you see, this makes our discussion from the last meeting more significant. We now have proof that some of the citizens leaving by boat did survive, and it is in fact possible to escape from The Beck. I'll let him tell you a little."

Rogers stepped forwards, and many of the citizens around

us leaned towards him visibly, desperate to hear what he had to say.

"A year ago, I stole some provisions from the Patrol stores. Along with three others, I took a small boat from Clearance and we set off across the water to see if we could escape. We were fairly desperate. We knew the mission was a challenging one, but we all had our reasons for wanting to leave. It took us a few days. Our provisions ran low, but we were lucky with the weather and eventually we reached land."

A complete silence surrounded the group. We hung on Rogers' every word. There was no muttering of dissent or agreement as there often was when Tyler and Cam spoke. Rogers was a heroic figure to us, and was being treated as such.

"We found land and the ability to sustain ourselves. It wasn't easy, and our lives have been tough. We've encountered other people. Some friendly, some not." He paused, a broad grin spreading across his face. "But we take any decisions by a fair vote. We rule our own lives. We are free."

There was a lengthy silence after his speech. It was eventually broken by Mason, who thrust a hand into the air. Rogers nodded at him.

"Why did it take you so long to come back?"

"Our boat was wrecked. It was just a small fishing vessel. We only just made it safely to shore and several of us were injured. It took us time to recover, for those of us who did. We lost one of our party in the end. His injuries were just too severe. It devastated us." He stopped and took a breath.

"Look, for a long time we were only just getting by. We had to figure out how to survive in our new surroundings. We had nothing: no food, no shelter, no defences. Eventually we began to make some progress. And then we had to find another craft to get back here safely. I have to say we stole it. Or borrowed. I was hoping to return it. Sadly, it wasn't a much sturdier boat than the last one, and I decided to come alone. After Lee's death on the journey over… well the others weren't too keen to make it a second time. But I promised Cam I'd come back, so I had to try." He exchanged a smile with his old Patrol colleague before continuing.

"Anyway, I managed to get here, but again, the boat suffered. I had to come in without being spotted and I ran aground on some rocks trying to hide just outside the Clearance harbour. I left it there, but it's not going to be much use to anyone now. From there, I managed to swim to shore and I've been hiding in the woods ever since, looking for my chance to find someone I knew I could trust."

There was silence for a moment as we took in what Rogers was saying. And then questions erupted all around me.

"Where've you been living?"

"What's it like over there?"

"Where did you get the boat from?"

"Can more of us make it back over there?"

Cam held up a hand and eventually, the group settled down. "Look, I realise we all want to know more, but we're really pressed for time. Can I ask that you save your questions for now so we can continue? We have more we need to discuss tonight."

"Look," Rogers stepped forward again, "I guess I'm just here to say escape is possible. And, to take some of you away with me, if we can secure a better boat. But I also need to warn you that life elsewhere isn't easy, and that those of you who come need to be prepared to adapt. Equally, those of you who stay behind need to ensure that Governance never discovers that you had any inkling of the plot to leave."

Cam took over. "I can see you all agree that this is extremely interesting news. We need to discuss what action we'll take as a result of it. We haven't had a lot of time for discussion, but we think in the next few weeks, in the days running up to the next Assessments, we will look at sending a boat with selected citizens over the water, with Rogers as their guide."

Tyler placed a cautious hand on his arm and stepped forward to speak. "This will need careful thought, and those people leaving need to be aware of a number of things. First, it will be dangerous, and there may be no coming back. Second, that the plan is to return to The Beck in the future, and take more people across, but the more citizens that leave, the more Beck Governance will take action. That means a higher risk to those left here, as Governance will work hard to discover who was involved. There will also be heightened pressure on those remaining here, because there will still be the same amount of work to do, with fewer citizens. We have all experienced what it's like to have a heavier workload over the past few weeks since the new security measures began to kick in. Once people begin to leave, it will become more and more difficult for those left behind."

"In the future," Cam cut across her speech, which was beginning to have a negative effect, "we aim to rescue enough citizens to set up our own colony across the water and return to liberate all Beck citizens, but that will mean a battle. And we're not ready for that yet."

"So for now," Tyler finished, "decide whether you would like to be one of the citizens who leaves, potentially risking your life, for a chance at freedom and escape."

"Or," Cam chimed in, "whether you wish to remain here and continue to support those citizens living in The Beck with a view to being on the inside when the fight begins. We will try to consider your views before making the final decisions about who will be given a place on the boat."

The group around me was quiet, considering the potential consequences of leaving. I suspected citizens' opinions would be hugely divided. It struck me that either option required a great deal of faith.

"Like Rogers said, we feel it will be safer to leave on a larger, more sturdy boat than last time. He has made the journey twice in two smaller crafts, and both times experienced problems. We are contemplating ways that we might steal one of the large Clearance vessels, although this will immediately put Governance on the warpath. Like Tyler said, it all needs careful consideration and thought. In the meantime, there are other concerns, which Harris has come to share with us tonight." Cam beckoned him forwards.

He sprang to his feet nimbly and was beside Cam in seconds. With a grim expression, he took some papers from his pocket and stepped forwards.

"I came here tonight to share some information with you. I think we need to–"

But his words were interrupted by the sound of footsteps racing towards the clearing. People started clambering to their feet, ready for flight, when a young Patrol citizen, clearly a lookout, burst into the space breathlessly.

"They're coming! A group of Shadow Patrol. With Reed. They know something's going on. Need to leave. Now."

Panic spread through the group rapidly, and within seconds people were on their feet.

Tyler stood on a tree stump and raised a hand for attention. "We knew this was a possibility. They're approaching from the woods. The only option is the cliff. Climb people. And help one another. We don't have much time."

So we did. The cliff face was not wide, so only six or so people could climb abreast at one time. Those who were faster went first, which was inevitable but also seemed sensible, in my mind, because they wouldn't hold others up. Cam and Tyler remained at the base, speaking with urgency to Harris and Rogers. Jackson and I approached them cautiously.

"Anything we can do?"

Cam's face reflected his alarm as he noticed me. "Other than climb out of here? Nope."

Tyler placed a hand on his arm, nodding towards Harris. "Yes they could."

He looked like he was going to argue, but thought better of it. "Alright. Go with Harris. He isn't familiar with the Patrol compound. Take him round the Solar Fields and make sure you get him safely to the woods so he can find his way back to Governance without being seen. Ok?"

We nodded and took off towards the cliff face, which most people were at least halfway up now. Most of the fitter citizens were already at the top and had waited to assist those coming up behind them, pulling them the last couple of metres in pairs to make sure that everyone reached the top. It struck me as wonderful: citizens working together towards a common aim with no ulterior motive. Jackson and I attacked the rock face together. Harris, I noted gratefully, was also managing to ascend with some speed.

Tyler and the others brought up the rear. There was no sign of an enemy approaching the clearing as yet. I was so busy watching below that I didn't notice a tall figure approaching, climbing quickly and overtaking me easily. Rogers startled me by hanging back a moment.

"I hear you're the one responsible for my meal earlier today." He gave a relaxed grin. "Sorry if I scared you. I was starving. I'd been in that tunnel for a day waiting for my chance to escape to the woods."

"It's ok," I managed, continuing to climb.

"Though you didn't seem scared," he added as he began to clamber past me with ease.

And then he was gone. Jackson raised her eyebrows at me, but I ignored her and continued to climb. At the top I found several hands waiting to help me. Reaching out for the lowest one, I felt myself being hoisted up as though I weighed nothing at all. As I looked at the person responsible, I found myself staring again at Rogers, the broad smile still in place.

"Glad of the chance to return the favour," he said, before dropping my hand and going on to assist Tyler behind me.

We all reached the top without calamity. I noticed that Will had waited until last to see if she could help anyone. Barnes was heading into the distance with a small group, presumably trying to get people as far as possible from the cliff top before Reed arrived. Far more exposed here than we had been in the woods below, we set off at a rapid pace, trying to reach the cover of the trees as soon as possible.

As we ran, I wondered about the report Harris had brought from Governance, which he hadn't had the chance to share with us. For the first time, I seriously considered the reality of escaping from The Beck into the unknown. Now we had a true rebel, someone who had proved it was possible to get away from The Beck and survive elsewhere, things felt both hopeful and utterly terrifying.

Chapter Thirty Two

We made it to the Solar Fields without detection, the guards there seeming to be half asleep as we crept around the edges of the field. We had no idea whether or not the Shadow Patrol had followed us, having reached the clearing and found it empty. But we didn't dare risk stopping, and kept up a fair pace until we reached the edges of the Patrol Compound.

It was more difficult to manoeuvre through the camp itself, but most citizens were in bed and the place silent, aside from a couple of guards posted at the edges of the new recruits' area. They were more alert than those at the Solar Fields had been. When we arrived, it was difficult to see how we would get past them unnoticed. We had stayed together as a group due to the fact that we were all headed in the same direction, but there were too many of us. We gathered together under the last few trees in the woodlands, wondering what the best plan was.

Will gestured at Jackson and Mason. "You two– head out there together, as a couple. That'll divert them."

It was a brilliant idea. Mason and Jackson understood at once. Together they would look like they had a legitimate reason for being out of bed and distract the guards, giving the rest of us a chance to return to our pods. They would be unlikely to get into trouble for their actions, which might well save the rest of the group.

Grasping Jackson's hand, Mason pulled her up and they wandered into the compound, their arms wrapped around one another. The two guards made some suggestive remark to them as they passed by, and Mason acted up, winking and sending them a thumbs-up behind Jackson's back as they passed. Meanwhile, the rest of us shuffled around the edge of the field and scattered back to various pods as fast as possible. I guided Harris the rest of the way to the woods without issue. Within a minute the field was deserted other than the guards.

I turned to my companion, managing a tired smile. "Are you ok from here?"

Harris smiled. "Sure. I know where I am. Thanks for guiding me. That was a little close for comfort."

"Do you mind if I ask what was in the document you were going to share with us?" I hesitated, but wanted to grasp the chance while I had it. "I mean now that we're not going to get the chance to hear about it as a group?"

He grimaced. "I suppose. We were going to share the information anyway." He led me behind a clump of trees and fished the paper back out of his pocket. "Here. Take a look for yourself."

Following him, I took the papers and unfolded them. The first was a list of dates, and figures, with some kind of training schedule attached. The numbers appeared to relate to citizens being transferred from the Lower Beck in the coming months.

"This is a recruitment schedule, yes?"

He nodded, "You're quick. Yes—the list indicates how many Lower Beck citizens they need to train to ensure they're able to fully defend The Beck against the attack they're expecting."

I pointed at the two different columns of numbers on the

chart. "What do these mean?"

"From what I can tell, they show the projected number of troops needed, dependent on our losses."

"Losses?"

"The numbers of our soldiers who die defending The Beck during the invasion. If we sustain huge losses we'll obviously need more recruits trained and ready to take their place."

"And what are these names here?" I pointed to a list of citizens underneath the chart. My heart stopped as I noticed Cassidy's among them.

"They're the recruits assigned to be our first defence. Once their training is over, they'll be on the front line."

I shuddered inwardly, thinking of Cass being among the initial group of soldiers sent into combat. Would she be one of the first victims? I felt sick. Turning to the other papers, I tried to work out what new horrors they might convey. There was another list, this one simply containing names divided into different sections, with various symbols attached to each one. Scanning down the list, I was distressed to see Harper's name too. Fighting to control my tone, I continued to press Harris.

"This shows us who Governance wants to transfer where, right?"

He looked mildly surprised at my rapid comprehension of the information. "Pretty much. You know we have Assessments coming up in a couple of months? In the time running up to that, the Supers report on the progress of the different citizens in their charge. There are people in Governance who look over that information, at how well different citizens have performed in the half-year period between assessments. Then someone considers the different factors and makes decisions. Looks at the total number of useful Beck citizens. Considers how many we need to get rid of, and how many more will come up from Minors. How many we can afford to birth each time."

"It's a complex game of numbers, and Adams has overall charge. Don't let his speeches about 'the good of the many' fool you. He knows everything about the citizens here, and he'll do anything to make sure that Beck life continues as he wants it to and those in charge retain control."

My hands shaking, I thrust the paper in Harris' face, pointing to my friend's name.

"Am I right in thinking this symbol is the one for those citizens who Clearance want to drown next?"

He shrugged, "Yes. I'm sorry."

"But she's doing well! I saw her today." I bit back tears. "She's managed, despite everything, to get through it all and survive in Clearance. Why get rid of her now? Isn't she useful?"

"You didn't believe that citizens sent to Clearance could remain there indefinitely, did you? It's a death sentence. Your friend will be for it in the end, no matter how long it takes. No matter how well you think she's doing, in the end it all comes down to numbers." He paused and peered into my face, looking concerned as he realised the effect his words were having. "Governor Adams' words, not mine. Either way, they've never allowed anyone back from Clearance. Surely you know that?"

I felt sick. My two best friends. The two people I used to be able to tell anything. Now both essentially sentenced to death.

"Was Cam planning to act on this information?"

"Not sure. Think about it. Does knowing who will be

terminated change anything? Not really. I mean, they'd have been on the list whether you had access to it or not."

"But this time we know who they're targeting. We can do something!"

Grasping my hand in his own, slightly damp palm, he smiled sadly at me. "You don't have any kind of power against those in Governance. What could you do?"

In truth I had no idea. I just knew that I couldn't stand by and let more of my friends and colleagues die. I pulled my hand away from Harris'.

"You're right. I don't know. I just know that I can't… I can't just stand by and watch for a second time."

He frowned, worriedly. "I understand your feelings, but don't do anything drastic, will you? It wouldn't end well. Anyway," he cleared his throat awkwardly, "I'd better get back."

"Me too."

"Thanks again for the escort. I appreciate it."

"Any time."

I watched as he retreated through the woods, his grey suit standing out in the darkness. Hoping that he wouldn't get caught, I made my own way back to the compound. A waxy sun was beginning to streak the sky with light and the rain had finally stopped. It would soon be morning.

I knew I wouldn't be able to sleep until I had spoken to Cam, so I made my way to his pod. I had never been inside it. Generally citizens didn't go into one another's living spaces, but most people were asleep, and I thought I could rouse him without disturbing anyone else. The entire compound was silent and I was far enough away from the guards on the trainees' field to steal through undetected.

I stood outside Cam's pod, an agony of indecision paralysing me. If I was caught, if I woke anyone up, if they reported that I was skulking around so early a mere day after a Super had been murdered in his bed, I knew the consequences would be severe. But my need to see him overwhelmed me. I pulled aside the canvas and peered into the pod. There was no noise, except for the gentle sound of breathing. Not wanting the dim light of the dawn to wake anyone, I crept through the opening and let it fall closed behind me.

Waiting until my eyes adjusted, I looked around at the sleeping figures. Thankfully Cam's cot was closest to the door. I wondered if this was a strategy on his part, knowing the amount of times he left the pod in the middle of the night and didn't want others asking awkward questions. I bent over his sleeping form, nervous about waking him now. I didn't want him to be startled and cry out. Kneeling beside him, I touched his arm gently.

There was no reaction at first. His chest rose and fell smoothly and his face was calm. I realised I had never seen him look so relaxed. He looked younger, somehow. I fought the urge to brush a smudge of dirt from his cheek. Across the pod, another sleeper snored loudly, thrashing around in their sleep and startling me. Suddenly I regretted my risky behaviour. I had no business here. Deciding I would talk to Cam tomorrow, I began to back away. As I did so, he stirred and turned to face me.

I held my breath, pausing in my flight, and waited to see if he would settle back into a deeper sleep. His lids flickered open and he stared straight into my eyes. My heart jolted with fear and I found I was holding my breath. And then a beautiful smile spread across his face, as though waking up with me next to him was the most wonderful thing in the world. I felt my heart lurch again, this time for a different reason.

I watched as Cam's eyes refocused and he came to, taking in the amount of light in the pod, remembering where he was and beginning to wonder why I was here. It was agony, watching the stress and concern invade his features again. He became the Cam I knew, but I longed for the relaxed, happy man I had watched wake up a moment ago.

Eventually, he managed to speak. "Is something wrong?"

I shook my head and whispered, "No. I just wanted to talk to you. Bad idea, I'm sorry."

I turned to leave, but his hand shot out with surprising speed, considering he had been asleep only minutes ago.

"No. Stay. That is, I'll come out and speak to you."

I backed out of the pod and waited nervously.

Chapter Thirty Three

Within seconds he had joined me and motioned for me to follow him, threading his way between the pods and taking a circuitous route to the edge of the field. Once there, we wandered towards the woods and took refuge behind one of the trees.

"You ok?" His face was filled with concern. I hated how much he felt he had to worry about everyone.

"Yes. I just needed to talk to you. Selfish, I realise. You've too much on your mind already."

He managed a smile. "I'm glad you came."

I shot a quizzical look at him.

"I mean I'm flattered. That you felt you needed to see me." He looked embarrassed, "Quin, I fight the need to see you most days."

I glanced up at him, surprised at the sudden admission. "Why do you fight it?"

He sighed heavily. "I just don't think it's healthy to get too close to anyone here. I'm afraid you'll get hurt. Distract me. I'm too involved with the Resistance. There's too much at risk." He shrugged. "But I'm tired of pretending. I keep coming back to the fact that I want to see you. Every day."

"Is that why you helped Harper?" It was his turn to look surprised. "I was in Clearance today. She looks so much better."

"She's amazing. Mutiny of the quietest, most successful kind. Cultivating a vegetable garden in Clearance? Managing to grow stuff over there and provide extra rations for the citizens? She's done so well."

"She'd never have managed it without the drugs you gave her. They obviously took care of whatever was wrong with her... the sickness I mean. So she was able to plant the garden and grow the vegetables in the first place."

"Well, I–"

"Do you do that for all the Clearance citizens? Or just those you know I care about?" I smiled gently at him and took his hand.

He squeezed it back. "Well she isn't the only one I've helped, but yes, helping her probably had a lot to do with you."

It was the first time he had admitted any kind of feelings for me in a long while. I wanted to revel in the moment, but the sun was rising and I had more I needed to discuss with him.

"Look, I just spoke to Harris. He showed me the documents."

Cam frowned. "I wish we'd been able to share them with everyone."

"Do you realise that Harper is on that list? The Clearance one? After the next assessment they're going to drown her."

He hung his head. "I know. I'm so sorry. But with Rogers' return, there is some kind of hope. It's changed everything really. The thought that we can get people across the water in boats safely, well..."

"Do you intend to leave with Rogers, or stay?"

"Setting up in a new place will be a challenge, but Rogers seems to have that in hand. I think I have to stay here and fight, now that I've made so many useful connections in other Sectors." He hesitated, "You?"

"Not sure." I bit my lip. "When's the next–" I hesitated, hating the horror my next words brought flooding back, "*drowning* scheduled?"

"Couple of days after the Assessments. We should have around two months to put a plan into action." He took me by the shoulders. "Quin, I promise you I'll do my best to save Harper. And if you want to go with her, well…" He trailed off.

I believed him. He was so easy to trust. But that led me to my last concern.

"Can I ask you something else…?"

His earnest brown eyes continued their steady gaze.

"I overheard you and Montgomery talking earlier, in the Jefferson."

He looked a little shamefaced. "Yes, I saw you."

"Well, I just… I wondered – how well do you know her, exactly?"

He put a hand on my arm gently. "You thought… me and her… didn't you? I could tell by the look on your face."

I averted my gaze, ashamed that I cared so much.

"Look," he took hold of my chin and brought it up so I had to meet his gaze. "Honestly? I flirt a little with Montgomery. I take advantage of the fact that she likes me. But I do it to get access to the drugs that I use to help others. Like Harper."

I nodded.

"And I do not," he paused, smiling, "feel remotely the same way about Montgomery as I do about you. Not at all, I can promise you that. Look Quin, you have the right to choose whether you stay or go." He stopped for a moment, as though he wasn't sure whether he should continue. With a deep breath, he ploughed on, "But when I think about you leaving, it hurts."

My sharp intake of breath was audible. I wondered what had made him decide to lay his feelings so bare, after so many weeks of deliberately avoiding contact with me. Registering my shock, he smiled again, sadly this time.

"I think it's because you didn't judge me for what happened with Lewis. And having Rogers back gives me new hope. Finally, we have a chance to actually make a difference, and I wanted you to know how I felt. Because your jealousy over Montgomery suggests you might just feel the same…"

I felt like he had read my mind. As he let his words trail off, he looked more vulnerable than I'd ever seen him. His face was full of expectation as he waited for my response.

After a moment's consideration, I returned his hopeful smile. "Cam," I murmured, "If we can get Harper and Cass out together, so they can look out for each other, I'll stay."

My grin broadened as I watched the relief spreading across his face. Hesitantly, he leaned forwards, encircling me gently with his arms. I stepped closer, lining my body up with his, and returned the embrace. With my head resting on his chest, I revelled in being this close to him, secure in the knowledge that we both felt the same way. When he pulled away slightly I was disappointed, until I saw the intensity in his eyes and understood his intentions. His lips lingered a little distance from my own for a brief second and I could feel the warmth of his breath mingling with my own.

Then he was crushing my mouth firmly against his own, the pressure betraying weeks of denial. This was not like our first kiss, which had been gentle and tentative, nor was it the desperate, angry experience linked to Lewis' death. The movement of his lips across mine only cemented my feelings for him and reminded me how I was completely swept away every time he was this close to me. This was what Jackson had been talking about. One of his hands crept up to hold the back of my neck, gently pushing me closer to him, stroking it gently, sending tingles down my spine.

I responded instantly, echoing the movement of his lips at first, but then becoming bolder, applying a lighter pressure, drawing away and then returning to match the fervour of his own kisses. I heard him groan softly and marvelled at the effect I had on him. Shifting slightly, I tightened the grip my arms had around his back and pulled him even nearer, feeling as though I could never be as close as I wanted to him. He felt solid and strong, the muscles in his shoulders knotting as my fingers explored them. I could feel our heart rates accelerating in time with one another.

A shrill alarm pierced the silence around us.

The alarm was not a regular occurrence in Patrol. It symbolised that something serious was wrong, and meant that we had to gather in the top field as soon as humanly possible. We shifted apart, startled. Cam peered between the trees at the citizens who were beginning to stumble out of their pods and wander blearily towards their destination. My heart, which had been pounding already, hammered against my chest as I assessed the potential of us being caught out of bed like this.

"What do we do?" I forced my voice to remain calm.

"What do you mean?"

"People will notice that we're out of bed. Know that we were out at night."

"And? They'll just think we were together. Like Mason and

Jackson." He paused, taking my hand between his. "There are plenty of others who sneak out at night to meet someone secretly in the woods."

I thought for a moment. "It's just... well it's never been me before. What if someone from the Resistance sees us together? You're their leader. People look up to you."

"And does that mean I'm not allowed to spend time with someone I like?"

"Well, no, I suppose not. But I'm not sure that people will approve... of me, I mean."

"Why on earth not?"

"Because I'm so new to Patrol. You're older. Important. You've been here longer."

He took my hand. "I'm not that much older. You'd be surprised. Perhaps you're right though. If people know it might cause problems." Looking towards the compound again, he frowned. "We should go though. They'll notice if we're late."

We hurried together out of the trees, aiming to slip in amongst the throngs of people all heading in the same direction. No one appeared to be looking our way, everyone either focused on the Jefferson Building or still half asleep. But within a few paces we met a familiar figure: Tyler. She smiled in greeting at Cam before her gaze slid to me, then to the direction we had come from and his hand holding mine. She froze.

I remembered witnessing an embrace between Tyler and Cameron when I had just arrived in Patrol. One which I had come across quite by accident, a quiet moment where they had believed they were alone. Tyler had kissed Cam and he had backed away as gently as possible. He had since told me that, although she had those kinds of feelings for him, he didn't return them. I believed him, but had never discussed the matter with Tyler, who mostly kept her own feelings very guarded. The expression on her face now told me two things. Firstly, that she still had those feelings, and secondly, that she understood exactly what had been going on between Cam and myself.

The shock branded her face for a fleeting moment before she crushed it, her face becoming a mask of cold, hard focus. But I didn't think I'd ever forget her hurt expression. She was close to Cam as a friend and had clearly helped me out because he had asked her to, without having any idea about his true feelings for me. Or perhaps she had suspected, but chosen not to believe it. Either way, I was concerned about what it meant for the future of the Resistance. If our two leaders were divided, where did that leave us?

She began to jog with the rest of the citizens, speeding up as she got further and further away from us. I went to run after her, but Cam put a hand on my arm.

"Leave her."

"But she's–"

"It's my fault. I should've told her. But let it go for now."

We had reached the outskirts of the crowd forming in the top field. Cam squeezed my hand and moved away to line up with his own pod while I slipped in next to Jackson, who gave me a quizzical look.

"Later." I whispered, as Reed appeared at the front of the crowd and stepped up on to the outdoor podium which was usually set up for Patrol Pledge Ceremonies.

The crowd fell silent instantly. Citizens were too curious about the unusual wake up call to make him wait. Towards the front I noticed an additional line of the new recruits, who were clearly being given a close-up view of what was about to happen. They were too far away for me to tell if Cass was among them. I silently prayed that she was.

"Tonight I call you here to witness something." His voice boomed out across the silent, nervous crowd. "To witness the consequences for the perpetrator of the terrible crime which was committed here last night."

I squeezed Jackson's hand. They had found Wade.

"We are all aware that the circumstances we live in are difficult. That we owe it to one another to follow the rules and support each other to keep our community going. Well there have to be sanctions for those who disregard those rules. Those who put the rest of The Beck in danger must suffer the appropriate consequences."

"Making an example of her." Jackson hissed in my ear. I couldn't help but agree. Never in my years in The Beck had anyone gone as far as to kill another citizen, aside from Governance themselves of course. They were never going to let Wade escape with an ordinary punishment.

"Last night, a recruit who was only recently promoted to Patrol, took the life of a respected Super, Donnelly. She viciously stabbed him to death in his pod. We have no idea how many more citizens she was planning on killing. Donnelly was an experienced, effective citizen, a Super who did his job diligently and with pride."

I exchanged glances with Jackson. This was not our experience of Donnelly at all. While I had not wished him dead, I had never had a dealing with him that had filled me with anything other than revulsion. They were turning him into a martyr to excuse the horrendous sanction they were about to dole out to Wade. I didn't want to watch, but I knew there was no other option. They had called all of Patrol here to witness, in the same way we had been made to watch Mason's whipping back in the days of our training. This way, they made sure that anyone else thinking of resisting could see the terrible consequences suffered by those daring to defy Beck rule. I thought of our tentative plans to rebel, fuelled by Rogers' return, and wondered how many citizens would still support us when this night was over.

Reed carried on, from his position on the podium. "And I know all of you will join with me in realising that there is only one appropriate sanction for this girl's crime."

I heard a few of the citizens around me murmur in agreement. Reed's speech was actually working. Never mind that most of this crowd had seen Donnelly in action, had watched him abuse and threaten others. They were buying into Reed's lies and would therefore embrace Wade's punishment. It was terrifying.

Reed's face twisted with pleasure. I remembered the expression from Mason's whipping, and hoped that my friend was managing to keep a lid on his sometimes volatile feelings. Before continuing with his speech, Reed beckoned to two Shadow Patrol officers who stood at the foot of the steps to the platform. From behind the stage they brought a figure. Dressed in filthy, blood-stained Patrol overalls, she had a sack over her head and tied around her neck. She could barely walk—which made me think her capture had not been gentle—and had to be almost carried up the steps.

Wade was dragged to the centre of the stage. I wondered why she wasn't making any noise. She wasn't the type to go down without a fight, and I wondered if she had already been so badly injured that she was unable to speak. They removed the sack from her head and I understood why. A gag was fastened tightly across her mouth, rendering her voiceless. Her face told a different story though, the look of fury telling me that she had not given up yet. Her hair stood up around her head in spikes, the sweat soaking her. She swayed a little and blinked as the light hit her, but remained upright, a defiant look in her eyes.

Reed stepped forward again. "This is Wade. She came from Sustenance. Selected specially as one of our new recruits because she showed such promise. Given the responsibility of undertaking special weapons training. But she let us down. She caused problems from the moment she got here, displaying defiance and unpredictable behaviour. Despite numerous warnings and chances to amend her behaviour, she continued to display signs of rebellion. Eventually, she stole a knife, which she concealed until she could use it to viciously attack Donnelly as he slept."

"She has betrayed the very foundations of our society and deserves a harsh punishment. Let this stand as a message to anyone," he paused for dramatic effect, "anyone, who might be thinking of any similar kind of resistance. She will not be sent to Clearance. There is no point in us wasting any more precious Beck resources feeding and clothing her, when she has done nothing but spit in the face of this society. She used a knife to take another citizen's life. She shall meet her end in the same way."

He stood back and allowed this to sink in. Reed held the knife above his head, and I recognised it as the one Wade had stolen in the first place. A retribution of significance, where the weapon used to punish was the weapon used in the original crime. Jackson was holding on to my hand so tightly, her fingernails almost cut into my skin. They were going to stab Wade in the chest. Right in front of us. There could be no clearer message. Rebels were not allowed to win.

But we didn't have to watch. Looking around, I noted that there was no sign of Adams or Carter. There were only a handful of Shadow Patrol citizens, and they were gathered around the podium. We were close enough to the rear that we would go unnoticed. I glanced at Jackson. We nodded in agreement. There would be no loud, noticeable objection. It would only lead to our own elimination. But we would not bear witness to the horrible death of this girl, misguided though she had been, for attempting to fight against some of the injustice in our world.

Reed motioned to the officers either side of Wade, who held her hands behind her back. A third removed her gag. She stood, silent for a moment, working her mouth as though she was trying to speak, although the material had been in her mouth for so long she didn't seem able to. She attempted desperately to form words, to call to us. But though her mouth moved, no sound came out. Reed stood to one side of her, the knife in his grasp, making sure his audience had a clear view of what was about to happen. Tightening my hold on Jackson's hand, I closed my eyes.

I didn't see what followed. But I could not block my ears without attracting attention to myself, so nothing could prevent me from hearing the noises that followed: the grunt as Reed drove the knife into flesh. The gasp of the crowd around me who were watching obediently. And, finally, the howl of agony: the only sound that Wade was capable of in her final moments.

Chapter Thirty Four

Once the horrendous scream had died away, a heavy silence hung over the crowd. To avoid suspicion, I forced myself to open my eyes, keeping them fixed on the ground to begin with. As the sounds of lifting and shuffling receded into the distance, I moved my gaze slowly upwards. The stage was now empty, aside from the solitary figure of Reed. He stood, staring purposefully at the crowd, his voice cutting through the air once more.

"I apologise for pulling you all out here so early. We felt it was essential to reassure citizens that this criminal had been dealt with. Rest assured, you can now sleep safely in your beds. Please return to your pods. This morning's meal will be served an hour later, to provide you with an extra hour's rest, hopefully making up for your disturbed night."

With that, he stepped down from the podium and walked away, leaving citizens to return to their pods in stunned silence. Jackson averted her eyes as we passed the stage, but I was unable to tear mine away. The wooden platform was empty now, except for a single Shadow Patrol officer, who was kneeling down, scrubbing at a large scarlet stain.

The return journey to our pod and the fitful hour's sleep which followed passed in a blur. The canteen was buzzing with speculation at breakfast, as most citizens seemed to have overcome their shock. The majority of the conversations seemed to focus on how citizens felt safer knowing that 'the rebel' was dead. It made me sick how easily Governance tactics worked on such narrow-minded individuals. Our own table focused on a very different discussion, voices lowered to avoid being overheard.

"He's clever. Reed I mean." Mason, never a fan of the Patrol Leader, was furious. "Making out Wade was a danger to everyone. Most citizens feel safer for that spectacle today. They're actually thankful!"

For once Jackson was in total agreement with him. "Too right. Hardly anyone seems to realise she was only a danger to those in charge. Those who'd hurt the people close to her."

Davis, always cautious, sent them both a dark look. "Keep it to yourselves. They'll be listening especially closely for conversations like that today." His voice dropped even lower. "Not that I don't agree with you. But she was a real loose cannon. She'd never have been useful to the Resistance."

Jackson turned her attention to me. "How do you think her death will affect Cass? Might she learn to be more cautious now?"

I didn't answer. At that moment, the remaining recruits were being brought in to eat. I searched the group anxiously, sighing with relief when I spotted Cassidy, looking sullen and red eyed, but alive. As she made her way from the serving hatch, I noticed she was moving slowly, almost shuffling. Her expression was pained and she was biting her lip, although there were no obvious signs of an injury.

As she passed our table with her tray, she met my gaze and nodded slightly, as if to reassure me. She was hurt, but would survive. I imagined that her conversation with Carter was the cause of her current state. Perhaps a whipping similar to the one suffered by Mason during our training period. Feeling sick at the thought, I attempted a supportive smile in return. I wondered whether or not she had given Wade away. There was no opportunity to speak to her, and I had to put away my concerns and continue as normal for now.

After the meal was over I checked on my work schedule and headed up to the Solar Fields. I wasn't certain whether I would appreciate the peace of the remote assignment, or whether I would rather be assigned somewhere more populated, where I might see Cam or hear some more about Rogers. Reaching the Plant, I relieved the officers on duty and waited for Will, who I had been glad to discover was working with me today. She arrived soon afterwards with a smile of greeting.

"Hey."

"Hey yourself. How are things?"

I grimaced, "After last night, not good."

She shook her head, "Agreed. It was horrible. Want to talk about it?"

"No thanks, if you don't mind."

"Not at all. Shall we focus on getting on with a peaceful shift then?"

It sounded good. We quickly completed the daily tasks of cleaning the panels and checking that the grass around their edges had not grown high enough to obscure them. After that, we took turns to jog the perimeter and said very little to one another, both content to be lost in our own worlds for the time being. Before long, we had reached the mid-point of our shift and settled together to eat our oatcakes in companionable silence.

The fields were flanked by woodlands, and as we ate I had

a growing sense that we were being watched. I craned my neck, peering into the trees intently, but could see nothing. I sat back to finish my food, and was startled by a voice hissing from the undergrowth.

"Hey!"

The two of us spun round. A pair of eyes was staring at us from behind a clump of bushes. My first instinct was to panic, but Will relaxed beside me and turned back to look over the fields again.

"Hey yourself. Do you always skulk around in bushes, Rogers?"

"Nope. But if I'm caught there'll be all sorts of trouble and you know it."

I followed Will's lead and looked away from the woods to disguise the fact that we were conversing with a fugitive. To anyone watching from a distance, it would seem like Will and I were chatting normally to one another.

"Do you two know each other?" I asked, curious as how relaxed Will seemed to be around Rogers, who so far I found fairly alarming.

She smiled. "We do. Rogers transferred the same time as I did. We trained together."

"Miss me Will?"

She rolled her eyes, still not looking at him. "Like a hole in the head."

"Ever the charmer I see."

"Did you meet Quin?"

"I did. She saved me from starvation yesterday."

"You mean that was you, on the Clearance shift?" Will nodded with respect, "I heard he ambushed someone but I didn't know who."

I shifted uncomfortably, unsure of how to respond. Rogers saved me the trouble by changing the subject.

"Not sure how long I can stay here, Will. Cam and Tyler want to wait and form a plan, but the longer I'm here, the more I'm at risk. And if I'm caught, they'll figure out that we survived and go after the others. Can't have that."

"What's their plan?"

"Not sure. Think they want to plan it carefully, try and avoid some of the mistakes we made last time. But once they've sent one boat load, they'll have to consider what happens next. When citizens realise there is a way out, there'll be a lot more wanting to leave. People are getting desperate."

I butted in. "Not to mention all those who don't understand how badly they're being taken advantage of."

"True Quin, but you'll have a job saving them all at once." Rogers sounded vaguely amused, as though I was naïve. "Start with those who want out, at least for now."

"Are you hungry?" This was Will.

"Cam managed to sneak me some breakfast before he left for his shift but it wasn't a lot. So yes, I could do with something if you have any to spare."

Will tossed him the other half of her oatcake. I regretted having consumed my own so rapidly.

"Thanks."

We were silent as he ate.

"You're in a lot of danger though, aren't you?" Will sounded concerned. "Until you get out of here."

"I am. But there's not much I can do about it for now."

"You could shave off that monstrosity of a beard. It makes you stand out a mile. And we can get you some Patrol overalls. Then at least from a distance you won't look out of place."

"Maybe. I kind of like the beard though. Took me a long time to cultivate. Marks me as a proud escapee of The Beck."

"Well don't be stupid about it." Will sounded angry at his stubbornness. "You can grow another beard. You can't grow another heart, if they decide to stab you in it."

I shuddered, thinking of Wade again. There was further rustling in the woods. At first, I thought that Rogers was leaving, but as Will stiffened beside me I realised that there was another presence. Praying that it was an animal of some kind, I pushed myself up to a standing position, trying to work out what I could do if the new arrival was unfriendly. Despite our conversation of the last few minutes, it hit me that, without Rogers' guidance, we might never escape The Beck.

Rogers himself had shrunk down into the brush and was silent. Several moments went by with no further noise. And then a voice came from the trees beyond where Rogers was hiding.

"Rogers? You here?"

I sighed with relief. It was Tyler. And while I didn't relish facing her after she had seen me with Cam the previous night, she was a far preferable option to Shadow Patrol.

"Sure am Ty. How's it going?"

She appeared between the trees and shuffled forwards until she was level with him. Glancing over at Will and myself, she nodded a hello, though her eyes never really met mine. She tutted irritably.

"How are you always so insanely cheerful Rogers?"

"It's the only way to be."

"Well you'll be even happier when I tell you."

He was instantly alert. "Tell me what?"

"We've had new information from Harris. It's been kept under close wraps, the full extent of the plans for the new recruits, but he's overheard several conversations lately which made him curious. This morning when he got back to Governance, Adams and Carter weren't there. He took the opportunity to search through more of the records, the ones that he doesn't often get access to."

We were all listening now, Will and I working hard to appear as though we were nonchalantly observing the empty fields in front of us. Rogers' earlier relaxed attitude had disappeared completely.

"He found information detailing Governance's aims for the recruits. And it turns out that they're in for more than just the usual training."

"What do you mean?"

"There's a Dev Super called Montgomery. She's a whiz with chemicals, and has been working on some drugs which can be administered to the recruits who'll be defending us against our attackers from over the water. They're supposed to make soldiers stronger, fitter, better in combat. But they have side effects. Not sure what they are as yet. It seems they're mostly untested. The upshot of it all is that they're beginning a programme tomorrow which has a small test group of the recruits taking some of these drugs, in different strengths and doses, so they can see how well they work."

Instantly I thought of Lewis. "You mean they're going to experiment on them? To try the drugs out?"

Tyler had still not looked at me, and even now she avoided my gaze. "Essentially, yes. Gov has selected the citizens from a particular pod to be tested, based on the Supers' observance of their performance so far." She hesitated a moment, before forcing herself to meet my gaze. "Your friend Cassidy is among them."

My heart jolted painfully in my chest. "But it could kill her—all of them!"

"That's hideous. They're getting worse." Rogers seemed shocked, as though Governance had not always been so brutal.

"Well it means you get your wish Rogers. To leave soon. The first group is going to be moved to Dev tomorrow to start the testing. They've been preparing them already. Putting them on a specific diet, weighing them, taking measurements. But they haven't administered any drugs as yet. Cam and I feel that we can't have them used as guinea pigs without attempting to do something."

Rogers straightened up as best he could in the foliage. "So when?"

"Tonight. Give us a chance to put some plans into place. Decide who we need to get out of The Beck with the most urgency. And then, get on with it and damn the consequences."

Chapter Thirty Five

That night I crouched next to Mason and Davis in the bushes on the outskirts of Clearance, my head spinning. The rest of the day had gone by in a whirlwind of whispered communications: decisions being made rapidly, instructions given to relevant people, messages passed along via other members of the Resistance to those who could not be reached directly. Now here I was, in charge of my own part of a very complex plan to get the relevant citizens to the Clearance harbour at the right time. So many elements had to come together at the same time for the escape to be a success. And in a plan that involved so many different people, I wasn't naïve enough to believe that nothing would go wrong.

Mason stared at me, a determined look on his face. I tried to display confidence, knowing he was still angry that Cam hadn't allowed him to go with Jackson to assist with her role in the mission. I thought Cam was sensible, not pairing people with those they cared about most. We would be more likely to do what we had to do if we weren't directly concerned with the survival of those we were closest to. Mason and Davis had a vital task: preparing one of the Clearance boats for its voyage, which meant immobilising the Shadow Patrol officers currently guarding the harbour. It was definitely a two-man job.

Shaking my head, I tried to refocus. All I had to do was carry out my own task successfully. If I managed that, if everyone managed that, we might just get away with it. But we all knew that we were risking our lives. If we were caught, it would be the end of everything. I was terrified, but determined not to be the one to let everyone down.

As we lay waiting for our time to act, Jackson was headed for the Patrol Compound where she would tell Cass' pod the truth about the horrors that Governance had planned for them, and see how many were prepared to come with her to the boat. The entire pod meant twelve citizens, including Cass, who we hoped would attest to Jackson's honesty and help convince people to trust her. We weren't sure if they would all be prepared to leave, but knowing that they were a group chosen specifically by Governance for their potential strength and speed, they seemed a good cohort to bring to a new community across the water. Rogers had calculated the space available on the boat, and there were places for them all if necessary.

Cam was making his way to Governance to meet with Harris, who would then take him to Rep to find a friend of his. Harris had risked so much secreting all the private Governance documents to us. He didn't want to escape himself, feeling he could still be useful to the Resistance in the future, but his friend in Rep was sick and headed for Clearance during the next Assessment period. Despite his remarks about Clearance being a death sentence we had to accept, Harris had clearly found it difficult to follow his own advice. His only stipulation to helping us further was that we get his friend out of The Beck on the escape boat.

Barnes was currently trying to persuade Blythe to accompany him to the boat. He and Tyler were extremely worried that she wouldn't survive for much longer in The Beck. A fresh start in a new place, it was hoped, would help. Tyler was on some kind of secret mission which neither she nor Cam would reveal to anyone. I wondered if Cam had sent her into the Dev compound to grab some of Montgomery's supplies. Remembering Anders' warning, I hoped not. We had been told that she stood only a slim chance of success, and they didn't want more people than necessary aware of Tyler's task. I suspected this was in case we were captured. Shivering, I thought of Cass' treatment at the hands of Carter. If any of us were caught, Governance would act swiftly and was not afraid to resort to torture. Secrecy was a sensible measure to take. We couldn't reveal what we didn't know, no matter what kind of duress we were put under.

The boat would carry these people across the water, where Rogers would introduce them to the rest of his group and show them how things worked over there. With more citizens available to complete tasks, his small community would be capable of so much more. So with a potential crew of twenty people, the boat would depart for its new home, and hopefully be available for a return journey at some point in the future.

Honouring my earlier words to Cam, I had made a difficult decision. I knew that he wanted to remain in The Beck, and now he had made his feelings towards me clear, I wanted to stay with him. Tyler had chosen to leave, and I suspected that this had a lot to do with Cam. She still hadn't spoken to me since the previous night, and Cam had confided that her conversations with him had been brief and perfunctory. I comforted myself with the thought that we could go across the water at a later date, when things were more settled. Perhaps

Tyler would have calmed down by then. I also felt better that Cass and Harper would be travelling together, so they could support each other. For the first time in a long while, I felt a little hopeful. But we had to get all the relevant people to the boat first.

The trick was the timing. Since people were travelling here from all over The Beck it was no use us commandeering the boat too early. As soon as the right people were on board, they needed to get going. Those of us staying needed to get out of sight and back to our pods quickly. That way, when the disappearance was noted, we were a good distance from the scene. Cam had drawn up a rough timeline, and we were in position waiting to act when the time was right. We didn't dare to use radios for fear of being overheard by the wrong people, so here we were, waiting and watching. It was agony.

Mason and Davis were silent. They both carried a baton and a knife, and Mason also had a cattle prod. There were two guards on duty down in the harbour, and they would both need to be taken out of action before anyone could board a boat. Neither of my friends wanted to kill anyone, and they had been assured by Cam that it should not be necessary. A sneak attack where they knocked out or tied up the guards in the storage huts at the side of the beach would be sufficient. But it couldn't happen too early.

I had the trickier task of locating Harper and getting her down to the beach. Harper had no idea I was coming, and although I knew she would be thrilled at the thought of escape, I did not want to alert those around her. An attempt to take all the Clearance citizens at once would only swamp the boat, rendering it useless.

"Five more minutes." Davis estimated.

I shifted awkwardly. "You both ready?"

"Ready as we'll ever be." Mason grunted, grumpy as usual. "Wish Jac would hurry up and get here though."

He was clearly worried about her. Davis shot a quick smile in my direction and reached out to squeeze my hand. I had not told them that I was staying. Jackson knew, and while she was upset, understood my reasons. I saw no need to complicate things further by telling the two men lying next to me now. While I didn't think Mason would have an issue, Davis liked me more than he cared to admit, and would find it difficult starting a whole new life without me. I was hoping that, once he got away from here he would have time to adjust, and by the time I made it over the water he would be completely over me.

Detaching his fingers gently, I began to move away. Mason turned towards me, a questioning look on his face.

"I'm going to look for her. I'll edge down there now and start to work out which pod might be hers. I won't grab her straight away."

Mason frowned. "It's not time yet."

"I can't sit here any longer ok? I'll go mad." I shuffled forwards until I was close enough to see the path on the hillside. It was clear.

"Be careful alright?" Was Mason's parting shot. "We'll be gone ourselves in the next few minutes. We won't be able to come and rescue you if something goes wrong."

"See you in the harbour," whispered Davis.

I nodded absently as I slid out of the bushes and headed down the hill, hugging the edges of the path as I went. I had only been to Clearance a handful of times, and although I knew that Harper would not be in the sick pods, there were a lot of other places she could be sleeping.

At the edge of the clearing where the pods were situated, I paused and listened. There was complete silence. All I could hear was the distant sound of the occasional wave lapping on the shore. Clearance was completely deserted, most citizens probably passed out from exhaustion. Moving closer to the first pod on the left of the path, I pulled open the flap across the entrance. The sound of heavy breathing told me the pod was filled with sleepers, so I took a chance and slipped inside.

It was crammed full of people. In Clearance, citizens slept on the floor, so there was no real limit to how many of them could be packed in together. There was a vague path left through the centre, and I made my way along it, tiptoeing cautiously. Most of the citizens in this tent were male, it seemed, and I saw no sign of Harper anywhere. Ducking back outside, I took a deep breath. The night air was cold and fresh after the stuffy atmosphere of the pod.

The pod on the other side of the path was easier to slide into, as the flap which acted as a doorway was torn, leaving a hole which was easy to slip through. This one looked more promising, being filled mostly with female citizens, and I only had to go half way down the row before I spotted her. She was sleeping soundly, and looked so peaceful that I almost didn't want to wake her. Filling my head with images of Harper living happily on the other side of the water, I moved forwards and bent down by her side.

She was pressed close to the woman next to her, the two of them sleeping with hands entwined, as though they had been comforting one another. She had always been a light sleeper though, which was what I was counting on. Jackson would have a more difficult task with Cass, who slept like the dead. Tapping her leg, the only part of her that I could easily reach, I called out her name softly, hoping against hope that my voice wouldn't wake anyone else.

She stirred, her eyelids fluttering slightly as she came to. Looking up at me, she smiled, and then a puzzled look crossed her face. A moment later she sat bolt upright, jolting the woman next to her as she let go of her hand.

"Quin!"

"Sshh!"

She looked around, as if realising the danger for the first time. We held our breath as the woman beside her shifted and settled again. Across the other side of the pod, someone snored loudly, startling us. Harper dragged her eyes back towards me.

"Is something wrong?"

"No. Well not exactly." I stood up and beckoned for her to follow me, hoping against hope she would still trust me enough to obey.

Chapter Thirty Six

Harper grasped her blanket and inched the edge of it from underneath the woman sleeping next to her. This time, she didn't stir. Wrapping it around herself, Harper shuffled forwards and I helped her to her feet. Together we crept though the darkened space to the pod entrance, where I checked that the coast was clear. Once we were through, Harper pulled me behind the pod and we knelt on the ground to ensure we remained out of sight.

Her eyes were large and pale in the darkness, and she looked frightened. I had considered all the different ways I might deliver the news to her, and still couldn't decide which would upset her the least. I began cautiously, hoping she would still trust me.

"Look Har, there's a ton of stuff going on which you don't know about. And I haven't time to tell you right now. But I need you to trust me."

She stared at me, completely awake now. "I trust you Quin."

"I'm getting you out of here. Tonight." Her eyes widened in shock. "I need you to come with me. Now. We're going to the harbour, and you're going to get on a boat. It will take you to a place across the water where you'll be safe. You won't have to live here in Clearance anymore." I hesitated, not wanting to lie to her. "It might not be easy, but it will mean that you're free. It will mean you will have another chance to live."

So far she had listened patiently, but suddenly words began tumbling out of her mouth rapidly, as though she had no control over them. "Leave? On a boat? But why? Where to?"

"To a place where you can start again."

"That's not an answer!" Her voice was still hushed, but carried a firm tone. This Harper was not the quiet, sensitive girl I had known. Clearance had changed her, as Patrol had changed me. Somehow, she had managed to find a way to survive here, and I could see it had made her harder, tougher.

"It's for your own good, I promise. I couldn't do anything to save you when you were sent here in the first place. I'll never forgive myself for not trying to do more. But I can help you now. There's a group, a kind of Resistance, and we're working to help people. Like Cam helped you." I paused, seeing that her face still looked set against the idea, and tried to make my tone gentler. "I promise you that you need to go."

"But why? I'm settled here now, and I'm surviving, despite this place being hellish, and without you and Cass." She raised her chin stubbornly. "Are you surprised I've managed without you?"

I stared at her, struggling to comprehend this fierce creature in front of me. I wanted to stop and admire the woman she had become, but knew there wasn't time. I was wondering desperately how I could persuade her when she continued, as if this was something she had been wanting to say for a long time.

"I have friends here. And we try our hardest to support each other. It's not easy, but we have our little ways. Like we had back in Agric. And I'm doing ok. I stay under the radar, do enough to pass at work, but not so much that I'm noticed. I'm ok."

I hadn't wanted to tell her the whole truth right here and now, but I didn't see I had any more options left. And this woman who sat beside me was different from the girl I had known back in Agric. She deserved respect. She deserved the truth.

"If you don't leave tonight on that boat, Governance has you scheduled for termination. That means they'll kill you, get rid of you, like some kind of pest. And not only that," I added, wanting to share the entire truth before I got cold feet. "Cass has to leave, or she'll suffer too. She's already injured, and has been selected for a process which might hurt her further. Might kill her, and will definitely change her forever."

She waited until I had finished and took a deep breath. "And you really think that getting on a boat to who knows where is the answer?"

"Well I can't guarantee it, but at least you'd have a shot at escape. If you stay here you will die. If they catch me here, I will die. Please Har," my voice dropped as low as I could manage, "I'm begging you. Come with me?"

She looked at me for a long time, and I had no idea what she was going to say. Her face was tormented, torn. I had blindly assumed that she would be ready and willing to drop everything and leave with me, but here she was considering whether or not she should go. How could I have assumed that she wouldn't have forged some kind of life here, no matter how difficult the conditions were? Like me with Jackson and Cass with Wade, she had selected new friends who could support her when I could not. I couldn't blame her for that.

Eventually she took a breath. "I'll come with you. Because I trust you, and because I believe you."

I sighed with relief and began to stand, "Thank goodness!"
I took hold of her hand, but there was still some resistance.
Looking down at her, a feeling of dread came over me as she
began to speak her next words.

"I will come. But there are conditions Quin."

I knelt down again. "Conditions?"

"I'm not coming alone. How many do you have room for?"

"What?"

"On the boat. How many can you take?"

"We can't rescue all of–"

"I'm not that naïve. I'm not asking you to save the whole of
Clearance, much as I'd like to. But could we take a few others
with us? Where's the boat? How large is it?"

I pointed towards the harbour. "We're taking one of the
boats in the harbour."

Her eyes widened. "What? How?"

"I have the support of quite a few others. Two of my friends
are down there right now, disabling the Shadow Patrol. There
are others arriving from various points around The Beck,
bringing a few of our friends who desperately need to be
rescued."

"Cass?"

"Yes, among others. You won't be alone."

"So those boats are quite large. How many could we take
alongside me?"

I had begun to sweat, the strain of attempting to persuade
Harper to come was taking its toll. I had anticipated sneaking
out of the Clearance pods with Harper to be stressful because
of the threat from Shadow Patrol, or other citizens waking up.
I had not thought that the actual task of getting her to come
with me would be so difficult. We were running out of time.

Every minute we delayed was costing other people who were attacking guards, stealing boats, collecting other citizens from the various places around The Beck and sneaking through the tunnel into Clearance. They wouldn't wait forever.

"A couple, maybe. I daren't risk any more. Harper, if we're caught... it'll all be over."

"I know." Her tone was matter of fact. "How about three?"

"Three?"

"Yes. There are two women in my pod I'd really rather not abandon, and one more citizen in that pod over there." She pointed at the first pod I'd searched.

"There's not a lot of time now Har," I tried desperately to sway her, "and if anyone wakes up..." But I could see the determination in her eyes, and knew there was no way she was coming without them. Relenting, I took a deep breath. "Ok. But you have to get them now. And quietly."

"Thank you!" And suddenly there was a flash of the old, happy Harper, who was my friend and incapable of bargaining with anyone. I smiled, despite myself.

"Go and get them then. Tell them to bring something warm. And for goodness sake, hurry."

I crouched at the side of the pod and waited, trying to slow my breathing sufficiently to calm my racing heart rate. Harper disappeared inside, reappearing a moment later with something in her hand. She thrust it at me, and disappeared again. It was a sack, and its contents made it fairly heavy. Pulling open the string holding it closed, I peered inside, my heart leaping when I saw its contents. Some vegetables, presumably grown in Harper's secret garden, wherever it was located in Clearance.

And seeds. Always seeds. Surely these would be of massive

use if we were attempting to set up in a new place. I marvelled at my intelligent and resourceful friend, wondering if an unsuspecting Shadow Patrol member would one day discover her Clearance vegetable patch, overgrown and weed-filled, and wonder about it.

It was not long before she emerged with two others, the woman who she had been sleeping next to and another I didn't recognise. Both looked frightened, but seemed happy to follow Harper. Whatever she had said had clearly had more impact than my own words to her, as it had taken her mere seconds to fetch them. I considered the possibility that she was providing them with extra rations from her garden. If she was responsible for feeding these people, keeping them alive, no wonder they were willing to follow her anywhere.

We dodged across the central path to the other pod. Harper motioned for me to take the first two citizens with me and wait on the edge of the woods, so we retreated and watched as she disappeared inside. There was silence, and I wondered whether Mason and Davis had made it to the harbour as yet, and whether they had been able to deal successfully with the guards. I was struck by a sudden fear: a red-hot flash consuming my body for a moment while my senses were assaulted by a vision of Davis or Mason lying motionless, a pool of red spreading out around them. I dismissed the thought quickly. No good would come of thinking like that.

I forced my mind back to the task at hand. There was no sign of anyone emerging from the pod as yet, and the two women crouching beside me were beginning to show signs of terror which I was afraid might give us away. I gave them what I hoped was an encouraging smile, and looked back at the pod. I could hear whispered voices now, coming from inside. Clearly Harper was not having the same success as she had had with the two other citizens. My heart sank.

The voices grew in volume until I could almost make out the individual words. Then there was a rustling, and Harper appeared with another shadowy figure behind her. They still appeared to be having some kind of dispute. As the second citizen emerged, I saw with some surprise that it was a man.

"–has to be now. Tonight!"

"But we can't just–"

"Yes. Yes we can."

"All these others though, we said we would try–"

"I know what we said." She stopped and pulled his hand into her own. "I know. But this is our best chance, for now at least."

I stepped forward. "Hey, I'm Quin. We need to go now."

He glared mutinously at Harper. "I don't want this. It's not what we discussed."

"No it's not. But maybe…" she hesitated, "maybe we come back. In the future. When we're more able to help. To make a difference." To my surprise, she placed the palm of her hand against his cheek before continuing. "How are we going to do that if we're both dead?"

He capitulated, his shoulders shrugging hopelessly. He didn't look happy, but would probably come along quietly now. I wondered what he meant to Harper, and if I would ever find out about their plans once they set off across the water together and I remained here.

We huddled together and I motioned down the hill through the trees, which was the least conspicuous path to the harbour and would hopefully shield us from view. As we were about to leave, the woman next to me grabbed hold of my hand and squeezed it tightly, pointing with the other one at the pod Harper had just exited. Her warning gesture was unnecessary. We had all heard it.

Voices. Coming from inside the pod. As though there were other citizens awake. And who knew whether or not they would return to sleep or come out to investigate. Knowing we could waste no more time and furious for allowing myself to be delayed, I beckoned hastily to the others to follow me. The five of us began racing down the hillside, desperate to get as far away from the pod as possible, and to arrive at the harbour before it was too late.

Chapter Thirty Seven

We made it halfway down the hill before I stopped and turned to look back over my shoulder. Although we were too far away now to hear the whispers, I couldn't rid myself of the terror which washed over me in continual waves. I was sweating, and had begun to feel sick. My heart was pounding faster than I had ever thought possible. No one had emerged from the pods above, for now at least, and I tried to tell myself that the owners of the voices would settle back to sleep without taking further action. I couldn't contemplate the idea that I would be the one responsible for our plan going awry.

We made steady progress towards the bay and I held up a hand for the group to stop as we reached the trees which bordered the beach. Once we left the cover of the woods, we would be in plain sight, and I didn't want to risk that until I absolutely had to. So far the area seemed deserted. The night was cold and a drizzle had begun to fall again. I sighed, knowing this would make it more difficult to see when navigating the water. I comforted myself that it might actually aid our escape, the rain masking any sounds we might make.

Our group settled down between two thick clusters of bushes and seemed willing to wait, for now. Peering into the darkness, I thought I could make out a shape on board the boat which was furthest away from the shore. There were no Shadow Patrol officers in sight, at least, and I fervently hoped that Mason and Davis had been able to secure them somewhere safely. We had agreed to wait in the trees closest to the beach until we could be certain that everyone was here, and then board the boats together at the last minute. That way, only Mason and Davis were at risk and vulnerable until the very last moment.

A rustling in the trees behind startled us all, but when I spun round it was only Rogers. He squeezed my shoulder and grinned at me broadly.

"Make you jump?"

"A little, yes." I glared at him. Despite his near-constant cheeriness, he was impossible to dislike. He was extremely tactile, which I found a little disconcerting, but he didn't make me uncomfortable the way Donnelly had always done.

"Some of us are here already. I'm with Barnes and Blythe just over there in those bushes. We won't come any closer, it's better to wait in smaller groups. Less chance of being spotted. Just waiting on a few more. Cam's not here yet, and we don't have Jackson and the recruits either." He clearly noticed my horrified expression and put his arm further around me. "Don't worry. They'll make it."

I tried to smile back. Looking towards the jetty, I could clearly see two figures on board the boat now, moving around and presumably preparing the boat to sail. So far, there seemed to be no hitches in the plan. The problem was going to be once the boat engine started, as the noise would carry, undoubtedly alerting other Shadow Patrol officers to our presence. But if all the relevant people were on board by then, and those remaining behind had enough time to retreat into the woods, we hoped the boat would make it. And once it had moved away from the shore, there was very little that the Shadow Patrol would be able to do to stop it. At this thought, excitement coursed through me. For the first time, our end goal actually seemed achievable.

"By the way, don't you have a few more than you were supposed to have?" He nudged me and gestured towards the four citizens sitting a few feet away from me.

"Tell me about it. She wouldn't come without them. Will there be space?"

"For three extra? Yes." He winked at Harper and chuckled. "Plenty of room, don't you worry."

Rogers slid off into the darkness, back to his own group, or perhaps investigating whether or not any more of us had arrived. I felt another presence at my side and glanced down to see Harper had approached me. She looked nervous, but determined.

"Are we ok?"

"Think so. We just need to sit tight while a few more people arrive, then we can get on our way."

She nodded, looking a little more confident now, and reaching down to squeeze my hand. "We'll be alright, won't we?" she whispered, then, lowering her voice even further, "Sorry about earlier. You took me a little by surprise that's all. And I couldn't leave them behind."

I smiled down at her. "It's fine. I understand."

Returning the smile, she moved backwards and began conversing with the others around her, presumably filling them in on the plan. I looked back up the hillside, hoping to spot some sign of Jackson or Cam heading this way. I couldn't see anyone on the path yet, but some of it was hidden from view by trees, and I knew that as soon as they entered the valley they would head under cover anyway. If I had missed them exiting the tunnel, chances were that they were already on their way down.

Running my gaze along the path and following it down towards the Warehouse, I saw something which made my blood run cold. There were lights, presumably from lanterns, close to some of the pods. Those we had come from only a few minutes ago. People were clearly awake. Picking up a small pebble, I shot it at Harper, hitting her squarely on the shoulder. She glanced up, annoyed, but followed my pointing finger to the area around the pods where there was now light and movement. Whoever we had woken up had clearly alerted Shadow Patrol to the fact that there were citizens out of bed. A look of horror spilled across Harper's face.

In the next few seconds, a number of things happened. Rogers appeared back by my side, his grin gone and a serious expression on his face.

"Time to move out." His voice was commanding, brooking no refusal. He motioned at the boat, then at the other group's position in the woods, then he set off towards them.

In the distance I heard the boat engine sputter to life. Clearly Mason and Davis had not been blind to the lights either, and the engine was the signal to go. Terror paralysed me as I realised that we had to act soon, or no one would make it out. But we were still missing several key members of our party.

As we stood paralysed, sudden noise erupted from the area above us. The sound of running feet in large boots, a great clamour of voices shouting. I could see Shadow Patrol officers arriving at the pods and beginning to search them. Glancing back up at the path from the tunnel anxiously, I made out some figures racing into the woods at the top of the hill. Feeling a hand on my arm, I looked down at Harper, whose expression, I was certain, reflected the same fear as mine. Reaching down, I squeezed her hand and stood up.

"Let's go."

The four Clearance citizens followed me with no qualms. I was reminded of an earlier experience where the most vulnerable citizens from this compound had been loaded on to boats. But not this time. I strode out on to the beach, my hand clenched around the only weapon I had, a small knife. As I did, I saw others heading in the same direction, presumably Rogers, Barnes, and Blythe. I could only hope that the people heading down from the tunnel made it in time.

We reached the boats first, and Davis was waiting on the gangway to help bring people on board. He smiled with relief when he saw me, but the pleasure didn't last long.

"Quickly," he gasped, "We need to leave soon, or we're all done for."

I pointed to a space towards the centre of the boat, away from the ship's wheel and the gangway where others would need to enter with speed. Harper and her Clearance friends hurried on board and followed my direction, crouching towards the edges of the vessel out of sight and protected by the boat's sturdy wooden frame. Joining Mason at the helm, I reached out and squeezed his hand gently.

"You ok?"

"To drive this thing? No. But Rogers is here now so I won't have to." His expression was fixed and to most observers he would have looked quite calm, but I knew better. I forced him to meet my gaze and kept it as steady as I could, thinking of Jackson and Cassidy racing down from the top of the hill.

"She'll make it. They'll make it."

He managed a grimace in my direction before bending to untie one of the ropes securing the vessel to the dock. "Well they'd better hurry. We can't wait much longer."

I raced back to the gangway to find Barnes, Rogers, and Blythe climbing on board. She looked shaky and pale, so I settled her next to the Clearance citizens, hastily asking Harper to keep an eye on her. Barnes was staring at her, his haunted expression demonstrating both relief and anguish. But at least they had made it. There were more figures running across the beach, too far away to identify. In the distance, I could hear the disturbance in the Clearance pods growing in volume.

It would not be long before several Shadow Petrol officers arrived at the beach, discovered their colleagues bound and gagged, and a gang of rebels trying to steal a boat. I watched Rogers force open a locker at the side of the boat and empty out its contents. Guns. Presumably kept on the boats for use by Shadow Patrol during the drownings, to control those who attempted to resist. I shuddered, glad we had weapons, but afraid I might have to use one myself. Rogers handed one to Barnes and Mason, who accepted them with varying degrees of enthusiasm, before bringing one across to me. He held it out but I found I couldn't take it.

"I've never used one."

"Neither have most people here. I'm afraid you may all have to learn pretty quickly. It's not hard." He bent to show me how, turning me around to face the shore, demonstrating how to brace the gun against my shoulder.

"Keep low. And make sure you know who you're shooting at before you pull the trigger." He stopped and patted my arm. "Hopefully you won't have to use it."

Moments later footsteps thundered down the jetty and Tyler flung herself through the gangway. She looked odd, larger than usual, and then I realised that she had something bulky strapped around her somehow, hidden underneath her overalls. Rogers attempted to hand her a gun, but she refused it. I had assumed she would embrace the necessity for the deadly weapon far more quickly than I had. For a moment I was surprised, until I realised the reason for her hesitation.

Crossing the deck to where Blythe was seated, she knelt down beside her. Unbuttoning the front of her overalls, she lifted something from underneath them. I couldn't see at first what it was. And then I heard the yowling sound I associated with Meds and realised she had succeeded in her mission. The expression on Blythe's face confirmed it as she handed the bundle over. It was Perry. Tyler had perhaps risked the most, by sneaking into the heavily guarded Meds compound to retrieve her friend's child. But the tears streaming down Blythe's face and Tyler's brief smile showed that she didn't regret it.

I had to agree with Cam's earlier assumption that Tyler had been very likely to fail in her task: Meds was one of the most difficult Sectors to access. Presumably, she had gained access by exploiting the fact that the Meds Supers knew her. Gov would be incensed by the theft of a baby: one of the most precious of the Beck's resources. Its reaction would be far beyond anything I had previously witnessed. I shuddered at the thought.

Once she had handed the baby over, Tyler shed the large pack she had been carrying on her back and thrust it at Barnes, who looked startled.

"Supplies." She barked shortly, pointing at Perry, who had

quieted once she was settled in Blythe's arms.

Clearly relieved to be rid of the huge responsibility she had born, she spun straight back to Rogers. Taking hold of the gun without hesitation as I had first expected, she went on to recount what she had seen on her way down into Clearance.

"Someone must have woken up. Shadow Patrol is definitely on the move. Currently they're in the upper camp, but with the noise of the engine down here, it won't be long before they realise what's happening. We need to be prepared to fight. Or leave. Or both."

"There are several people still missing."

She glanced around the deck, doing a rapid headcount. Her face fell.

"I was hoping I was one of the last." She closed her eyes and wiped a hand across her forehead. "Ok. We arm ourselves and wait as long as we possibly can."

She strode to the rear of the boat and bent over, weighing the gun in her hands before leaning over to line it up with the shore. She seemed to have no concerns about using it.

I made my own mental headcount of the missing. Cam was yet to arrive with Harris' friend. Jackson was not here, which meant no Cass. And the rescue of the recruits was the main reason we had brought the mission forward to tonight. If we went without them, who knew what kind of agonies they would undergo tomorrow under Montgomery's hand?

Once one boat was gone, there was little chance of us returning to collect others until we had worked on a proper strategy to do this on a larger scale. Governance would investigate, put extra security measures in place, torture anyone they thought might know anything about the escape. Right now they were ignorant of our plans. Another time, they would make sure they were ready. It would be that much harder. I had resigned myself to this idea, but with Cassidy's name on that list, her need was far more urgent.

I made my way over to Rogers, who had taken over from Mason at the wheel.

"I'm not supposed to be on the boat. I'm going back with Cam and Harris. Staying behind."

"Well you'd better get off. Get into the forest now, or you won't have that option. As soon as Shadow Patrol gets near enough to see you, you won't be able to stay."

I hesitated, aware that I had only agreed to stay on the proviso that Harper and Cass would be able to support each other. If Cass wasn't here, who would fulfil that role? Remembering Harper's new stubbornness and the three Clearance citizens she had insisted on bringing with her, I realised that she would be fine. She had made friends on her own and proved herself a survivor against all the odds. If Cass didn't make it to the boat and was left behind, I wanted to be here for her. She would be the one who needed me. My decision made, I turned to Harper, intending to explain my decision and say goodbye.

I never reached her.

"Look out!" The shout had come from Tyler, stationed at the rear of the boat. "They're coming!"

At first it was not clear who she meant, but then I saw them. From the higher levels of Clearance, a group of at least six Shadow Patrol officers were sprinting down the path towards the harbour. The heavy guns strapped to their backs were unmistakable. Clearly this situation constituted an emergency.

"Are you ready Rogers?" she commanded.

"Ready, willing, and able!" he called back.

"Look!" This time the shout came from Barnes, who had collected a gun for himself and stationed himself on the other side of the boat. "Here they are."

My eyes were drawn to the group who I had seen on the path at the top of the hill a few moments ago. Somehow, they had scrambled down through the undergrowth in record time and were now out on the beach, in plain view, racing towards the boat. It was some of the other recruits, six of them at least. I strained my eyes, attempting to pick out two familiar figures. After a moment I found Cass, towards the rear of the group, still moving stiffly. The injuries inflicted by Carter had clearly not healed yet. But she was here. I searched again. For a moment I couldn't see Jackson, and then she emerged from the woods. She seemed to be limping a little, and was lagging far behind the others. She had barely cleared the trees as the recruit at the front of the group made it to the end of the jetty.

The first shot rang out as their feet began pounding along the wooden pier. The Shadow Patrol had made it on to the beach and were clearly determined to prevent us from leaving at all costs. The recruits on the jetty hit the ground instinctively and began to crawl towards us from a safer position. Barnes, Tyler, and Mason began returning fire rapidly, the rest of the citizens on board the boat ducking low in an effort to avoid the flying bullets.

Davis held on to the mooring rope close to the gangway entrance, crouching behind the wooden boat side and looking terrified. I secured my own gun on the lip of the boat and attempted to aim at the Shadow Patrol. My hands shook and the tears in my eyes made it almost impossible to see the direction I should be firing. I longed to support my fellow citizens, but with so many of our own on the beach, I didn't dare fire in case my shot went wide of the mark.

A shout echoed across the deck as Cass and several other recruits arrived. Most of them hastily gathered a weapon, as instructed by Rogers, lining up around the perimeter of the vessel so we were better defended. I looked back towards the edges of the beach, where I had last seen Jackson. I spotted her, still on her feet, determinedly limping a few paces at a time. A sudden piercing alarm ripped across the beach, startling her. As I watched, she stumbled, her sturdy frame crashing to the sand.

My heart was in my mouth. There were Shadow Patrol on the beach now, and while most of them were focused on the boat, it would not be long before they worked out where the passengers getting on the boat were coming from. I silently willed Jackson to get up and run. Mason appeared by my side, his gun hanging uselessly at his side. Tears were streaming down his face. I tried to take his hand but he shrugged me off, staggering to the edge of the boat, his eyes fixed on her.

A movement further away caught my eye and I jerked my gaze to the far end of the beach, where more figures had emerged from the woods. One was extremely familiar. Cam had made it at last, but he was too late. I watched as he assessed the situation and made the best of it, racing over to Jackson. Scooping her up, he carried her to the relative safety of the trees. The Shadow Patrol officers seemed not to have noticed the citizens at the other end of the beach, and were advancing on the jetty rapidly now. A few of their shots had hit the boat, making small holes but so far not hitting anyone or rendering it unusable. But the danger was too close. We had to go.

I heard the engine throb beneath us, primed to charge out into the bay and escape the enemy which came nearer with every passing moment. I saw the figures of Cam and Jackson melting away into the trees. Shuddering, I watched the advancing Shadow Patrol, every step they took bringing us closer to disaster. I clutched Mason's hand, which he had finally allowed me to hold on to, and glanced across the deck at those citizens we had managed to save. I nodded at Rogers, tall and steady at the wheel, ready to take us away.

Finally, I watched as Davis stepped on to the jetty to unhook the final rope from the mooring peg it was anchored to. His hands were shaking as he unwound it, desperately racing to beat the advancing soldiers and their guns. He pulled the rope free and straightened up to step back on to the boat. As he made the move and the boat began to power away from the shore, his body jerked strangely and he lost his balance. Mason let go of my hand and leapt across the deck, hauling him safely on board before he could fall. Once on the deck, he lay ominously still.

The Shadow Patrol reached us as the gangplank slid away, tumbling into the murky waters below. One of the officers attempted to leap across the gap onto the boat but was hit, mid-flight by a direct shot from Barnes and followed the length of wood with a loud splash. The boat cleared the jetty. Rogers gunned the engine and we roared away, leaving the remaining Shadow Patrol firing into the night behind us.

I slumped against the side of the boat, overcome by a wave of exhaustion. It was several minutes before I managed to take stock of what had happened. The successes and the failures of our operation. We had done it. Managed an escape from The Beck. Taken several Clearance citizens with us.

Rescued a mother at the brink of desperation and reunited her with her child. Protected several recruits from the horrors of experimentation. Left on a boat which was sturdy enough to make the journey safely and ensure we had a way to return.

But we had left people behind: Jackson, and Harris' friend. And I was on the boat when I should have been on shore, celebrating the success of the mission and planning the next phase of the Resistance with Cam at my side. And, worst of all, the body of my friend lay under a thin blanket on the far side of the deck. Davis, hit by a single bullet as he loosened the rope which was our final tether to The Beck. In setting us free, he had lost his life.

The passengers around me were silent, all lost in their own thoughts. I stared out into the endless water, the tears streaming down my face, as we sailed into the darkness beyond.

Author's Note

Thank you for reading Break. I hope that you enjoyed getting lost in the world of The Beck again. I love building relationships with my readers. Quin and her friends will return in Book Three of the Flow series, but if you enjoyed Break, and would like to get additional free books, please sign up for my mailing list below:

http://bit.ly/freebies-break

If you sign up, I'll send you occasional newsletters with details of my new releases, as well as other special offers and exciting freebies.

About the Author

Clare Littlemore was born in Durham in the UK. Her parents were both teachers, and she grew up in a world surrounded by books. She has worked for most of her life as a teacher of English at various high schools in England, where she has shared her passion for books with hundreds of teenagers. In 2013, she began writing her own fiction. She lives in Warrington in the North West of England with her husband and two children.

You can connect with Clare:
- on Twitter at twitter.com/Clarelittlemore
- on Facebook at facebook.com/clarelittlemoreauthor

or send her an email at **clare@clarelittlemore.com**

Reviews

Liked this book? You can make a big difference. Reviews are really powerful. Being a self-published author, getting my books noticed can be difficult. If you enjoyed reading Break, please consider spending five minutes leaving an **honest review** (it can be as brief as you like) on the book's Amazon page. I would be very grateful. Thank you very much.

Acknowledgements

After writing Flow, the first novel in my series, I naively believed that creating the second would be easier. I was wrong. There are many people who deserve a huge thank you for supporting me with Break.

Firstly, to my editor, Beth Dorward, who has truly gone above and beyond with the process, making sure that Break not only makes sense but also (pardon the pun) flows on well from the first in the series. Writing the book wasn't so hard, but editing it has taken considerable time and care in terms of making sure that elements of the story work alongside the first book, as well as future plotlines. Beth and I have gone back and forth many times, discussing a range of points in the manuscript, and her commitment to ensuring that Break is the best story it can be must be given appropriate credit. I massively appreciate her hard work, patience and dedication.

Similarly, my cover designer, Jessica Bell, deserves accolades for creating Break's arresting cover. She worked closely with me again, making several changes to the artwork until the cover had strong enough links to Flow to ensure the series was effectively tied together. She also made sure that the Break cover had its own distinctive feel and represented plot elements of the second book well. Her creativity, as well as her practicality in advising me against certain less-than-sensible requests on my part, has been hugely helpful for a second time.

My ever-faithful band of pre-readers continue to assist me with noticing typos, pointing out any continuity errors, giving me feedback on the developing plot and, of course, encouraging me to carry on, even when I get completely frustrated with my writing...

So to my Mum: thank you (again!) for your proofreading abilities and for always showing an interest in how my books are progressing. To my Dad: thank you for your consistent support and your belief in what I'm trying to achieve. To Linda, my mother in law: thank you for always being the first and fastest to respond to a request to read and comment on anything I've written. Particular thanks to Lucy B, who has fast become my second (unofficial!) port of call in terms of editing and cover-design decisions, as I know she will always give me her honest opinion. And lastly to Ria, Rachael, Allison and Alison, thank you for all your supportive, helpful feedback along the way. I hope you will continue to assist me with the next book in the Flow series. Yes, there's more to come...

I'd also like to show my appreciation for the lovely people on my mailing list, who responded to my calls for support during the Flow launch. I was totally overwhelmed by the generosity of readers who helped me in so many ways. They shared information about my book with others, introducing it to many new readers, and many of them bought a copy of Flow, despite being given a free copy prior to the launch. For this I will be eternally grateful. Special thanks to Clare G and Harriet, who are both far better at marketing than I am, and who were a huge help in promoting Flow, getting me noticed by the press and enabling me to liaise with the local library service about my books.

As always, a massive thank you to my hero and husband Marc, for all he does. Aside from his expertise with technology, and his constant belief in my writing, he is usually the one providing our family with nutritious sustenance while I tap away obsessively at my laptop. My children's health lies in his hands... left to me they'd probably exist on toast and jam! But seriously, thank you Marc. For everything.

And finally, thank YOU, for reading this book. Without readers, a writer is nothing, and I'd like to say how much I appreciate you reading the second book in the Flow series. I hope you will stay with me for the third, and beyond...